"What does it take to get rid of you?"

Ben's voice was raw. He sat on the end of the wooden bunk, his shoulders slumped.

"You don't have what it takes."

Without giving herself time to think, she crossed the room and took him in her arms, cradling his head against her breasts. It was like the first time she'd reached out to him. Then, he'd been a stranger and she'd wanted to give him simple human comfort. Now, it was so very much more.

"Ben, don't shut me out. Not now."

For a heart-stopping moment there was no reply. Then she sensed the change in him, sensed his need almost as quickly as he was aware of it himself. When his lips found the edge of her cheek, she turned her head and their mouths melded as they had once before. Once, they had kissed and broken away. This time, there was silent acknowledgment there would be no breaking away.

ABOUT THE AUTHOR

Ruth Glick chose her birthplace of Lexington, Kentucky, as the setting for her second Superromance novel. A prolific author, she is also one half of the Rebecca York writing team, creators of the ongoing 43 Light Street series in Harlequin Intrigue. Ruth Glick is married, has two children and two cats, and lives in Maryland.

Books by Ruth Glick

HARLEQUIN SUPERROMANCE
382–THE CLOSER WE GET

Make Me A Miracle

RUTH GLICK

Harlequin Books

TORONTO • NEW YORK • LONDON
AMSTERDAM • PARIS • SYDNEY • HAMBURG
STOCKHOLM • ATHENS • TOKYO • MILAN
MADRID • WARSAW • BUDAPEST • AUCKLAND

Published May 1992

ISBN 0-373-70499-2

MAKE ME A MIRACLE

To John and Kerstin Warner
for all the help they gave me
researching the Kentucky locale
of this book

CHAPTER ONE

ELIZABETH SALVATORE gave it one more desperate try. With an arm that was numb from cold, she stretched upward toward the gnarled tree limb jutting over her prison. Tantalizingly, her fingertips grazed the pine bark. But even though she tried with every ounce of waning strength, she couldn't curl her fingers around the broken branch. Her slender body shook with the effort. Exhausted, she slumped back against hard gray rock—the ancient limestone of the mountains.

It would probably be her tomb.

Far above, a canopy of stars twinkled in the velvet darkness, and the currents of wind that stirred the pines sang of freedom. But not hers.

The hours of imprisonment were too painful to endure. Her mind leaped to escape and landed in quicksand.

"Dr. Salvatore, do something."

"I'm doing everything I can, Mrs. Pierson. Everything. But Billy just doesn't have enough strength to fight anymore."

"He's going to die, isn't he?"

"I'm sorry."

"You don't know how it feels."

But she did.

She'd been trying to outrun the sorrow of Billy's death when she'd left her car in one of the parking areas in the Daniel Boone National Forest and trekked off into the eastern Kentucky back country. Billy Pierson. God, what a bright, articulate little boy, and what a gentle sense of humor. Well, there was nothing more she could do for Billy.

Or for herself, it appeared. She stared at the boulder that held her right leg fast. She might be here for days before anyone found her. If anyone ever did.

"Dr. Salvatore, I have to know what to expect. I mean—how long does Ellen have?"

"It's hard to say. Cystic fibrosis is so unpredictable. She could have five or ten good years. Or she could do much better than that. Partly it depends on her will to live—if she keeps fighting the disease."

"I was so scared when we brought her in. She couldn't breathe. What you've done for her is a miracle."

"The antibiotics have the infection under control."

"Oh, Doctor, I don't know what we'd do if you weren't here to take care of her."

"I'll be here."

Would she be? Elizabeth wondered. Wrapping her arms around her shoulders, she rubbed her arms with brisk strokes. She couldn't really warm them, although the energetic activity seemed to do a little bit of good. At least it was late May. Otherwise she'd be even colder in this hole in the ground.

After easing into a prone position, she closed her eyes and wished there were some way to get comfortable on the pile of loose rocks at the bottom of the crevasse. Her thoughts scattered and coalesced like bits of glass in a kaleidoscope. Uninvited, another episode from her recent past leaped out at her.

"Elizabeth, could you stop by my office for a moment, please?"

"Of course, Perry."

"I'd like you to take a look at the new grant proposal we're submitting to the Morgan Foundation. So much is riding on additional funding for the new programs."

"I know."

"Perhaps we could discuss it over dinner sometime later in the week."

"I'll be glad to take a look at the proposal. But I'm afraid..."

"Don't turn me down again, Elizabeth."

"Perry, if there were anyone I'd want to get involved with, it would be you. But I'm just not ready."

"Think it over. We'd be good together."

Oh God, Perry Weston. If she was thinking about the chief of staff at Children's Hospital, maybe she was starting to hallucinate. She laughed. It was a hollow sound in the darkness.

How much power was left in her flashlight batteries? she wondered; she slid her hand down beside her left hip and retrieved the metal cylinder. The barrel was scratched and pitted, although not from the fall. She'd tried to use it as a lever to free her leg. The shaft just wasn't long enough.

Switching on the light, she played it over the rock walls above her, hoping against hope to see something different. Nothing had changed.

Perhaps in response to a noise she heard in the darkness, another scene began to play through Elizabeth's mind. This time it was a rescue fantasy.

"Hey—you with the light. Who's down there?"

It took several heartbeats to realize that the deep male voice was real. The human contact was so unexpected that she jumped.

"Somebody down there?" the man called again.

Her answer was a hoarse croak. "I am. Elizabeth Salvatore."

As a dark shape loomed over the edge of the crevasse, she turned on the light again and swung it around to get a better look at the stranger whose voice had suddenly become a lifeline. All she caught was a quick impression of wheat-colored hair and a rugged face before a denim-clad arm came up to block her view. "Tryin' to blind me?"

"Sorry. I wasn't thinking."

He acknowledged the apology with a grunt. "You hurt?"

"My leg's trapped. A big piece of rock came tumbling down after me."

His flashlight snapped on. "Close your eyes. I'm going to have a look."

Elizabeth squeezed her eyes shut and heard the stranger whistle through his teeth.

"You're in a fix all right, darlin'."

He swung a long leg over the side of the opening, and loose stones rattled down the side of the crevasse. He swore. "Okay, it looks like I'm going to have to take this nice and easy."

Elizabeth leaned her head against the cold rock, aware that she'd been holding herself together with little more than baling wire and chewing gum. The man set the flashlight down on the rim of stone above her. With the light behind him, she couldn't see more than a silhouette. However, she could follow the progress of his large form as he inched downward, his back against one limestone wall, his hiking boots braced against the other. It looked like a pretty uncomfortable way to travel. Yet he moved with the agility of a man who knew what his body could do and was comfortable with the assessment.

Ben Rittenhouse gave the woman below him an appraising look. Wide-set brown eyes under a mop of curly dark hair regarded him with a mixture of apprehension and relief.

Despite his caution, his toe dislodged another shower of rubble. He heard her involuntary little gasp and decided he'd better stop and evaluate his options.

"It's okay." Even as he murmured the reassurance, he was cursing his luck. As soon as he'd seen the beam of light knife up from this hole in the ground, then flick off again, he'd known he had to investigate.

He was close enough to see her better now. Her skin was pale, her nose just slightly upturned. Elfin. A wood spirit. Except that wood spirits didn't get themselves into this kind of trouble. Her delicate features were streaked with dirt. No—dried blood. She'd scraped her face on the way down. What other damage had she done?

His gaze swept over the petite figure half sprawled, half upright on the hard ground, and he couldn't repress a purely male assessment. Small, but nice proportions. Then he remembered he was supposed to be looking for possible injuries. He couldn't tell much

through the heavy plaid shirt. On the other hand, there
was a rip in the thigh of her jeans. Well, no use speculating what was underneath the torn fabric until he
could do something about it.

The big, brown eyes with their fringe of dark lashes
pulled his attention back to her face. They were beautiful—by far her best feature. She was watching him
watch her.

He wasn't a man who'd ever enjoyed idle chatter.
Now he found he needed to fill the silence.

"How long you been down here?"

"Since about two in the morning."

"You were tramping around in the middle of the
night?"

Elizabeth felt her face heat. It was bad enough to be
stuck like this. "I had to get out of my sleeping bag—
you know."

"Oh."

"I guess I'm lucky you happened along. What's
your name?"

"Ben Rittenhouse." He had almost reached her.
"You're not from around here."

"I guess the Yankee accent gives me away."

"Yeah."

Too bad they'd ended up on the same patch of
mountain. As soon as he finished this little rescue op-
eration, he was out of here. He'd headed for the wilderness because he'd felt like a powder keg about to
explode. The last thing he needed was to get tangled up
with some dumb female who didn't watch where she
was going in the middle of the night.

He hesitated, his body wedged against the rocks just
above her. It was apparent that there wasn't going to

be much room for a large man in the confined space at the bottom of the crevasse.

"Open your legs."

The gruff order got her attention. "What?"

"I've got to put my feet somewhere."

The only leg Elizabeth could move was the right one. After she'd shifted it to the side, he planted his feet between her knees. They were big feet—even bigger because of the sturdy hiking boots.

She hadn't been prepared for the physical impact of his very masculine body in this confined space. All at once, the forced togetherness was awkward—intimate. Elizabeth looked up through a screen of lashes as he hunkered down between her legs. It had been a long time since she'd stared at a man from this perspective.

"You're sure you're all right?" he asked in a low voice.

"I don't think anything's broken."

A couple of fingers grazed the dried blood on her face. The touch was surprisingly gentle for such a leathery hand. "We'll get you cleaned up in a little while. But first things first."

Elizabeth searched his features, curious about the man who'd rescued her. His face was square, the proportions very rugged and masculine. The nose was aggressive, the chin cleft. Even in her present condition, she found the effect sexy. Especially since the bold features were set off by a shock of wheat-gold hair and a pair of eyes as blue as a cloudless sky in June. The easy smoothness of his voice, like honey dripping down the side of a spoon, didn't detract from the image, either.

"If this were a scene in a TV comedy, the audience would be in stitches," he observed wryly.

"It's a heck of a way to audition."

"Sure is. Let's see if we can cut the scene short. When I give you the signal, haul that leg out of there like sixty."

"Right."

Turning, he grasped the boulder that held her trapped. She heard him grunt, watched the well-developed muscles of his back and shoulders strain through the fabric of his denim jacket.

"Now!"

Elizabeth yanked her leg out so fast that she tumbled backward onto the hard ground. For the first time in hours she was free.

He let the rock fall back into place with a thunk that made the ground vibrate. Then he was kneeling beside her, inspecting her leg. She winced.

"You're hurtin' worse than you're letting on."

"It's not all that bad. I don't think it's broken." She flexed her muscles and rolled her shoulders.

"Good. Because I didn't know how the hell I was going to boost you out of here if there was any serious damage."

"What do you mean?"

"I mean, I don't have a rope with me. I can't tie a safety line around your waist and haul you up."

"I don't think I can climb up there by myself."

"You don't have to. I'm going to lower a pole. You can grab the end of that."

"All right."

"Sit tight. I'll be right back."

"Do I have a choice?"

He laughed. "Guess not."

She smiled back. There'd been a moment when she'd almost been afraid of him. But only a moment. What came through strongest about this man was bedrock solidity—like the mountains.

When he held out his hand, she let him pull her to her feet. The unaccustomed movement made her light-headed.

"Easy."

His arms came to support her as she slumped against his hard frame. Her face was buried in the rough fabric of his shirt. She caught the musky, male scent of his body, felt the power of the arms holding her upright. It was such a long time since she'd been this close to a man, she thought again.

With this particular man, it was oddly exhilarating. And his strength—not simply the physical force it had taken to move the rock—was reassuring.

Usually she was the one who issued orders and doled out reassurances. Now, surrendering responsibility was strangely appealing. It was wonderful not to have to be Dr. Elizabeth Salvatore, the tower of strength, for a change. Her hands hooked themselves over the broad shelf of his shoulders. She didn't have the will to fight the urge to cling.

For a moment his fingers smoothed across her back, and he murmured something low and comforting that she couldn't quite catch. Then, as if he'd suddenly become conscious of what he was doing, the moving hand stopped abruptly. "Are you going to be all right?" he asked in a voice that had grown a bit huskier.

Her own hands loosened themselves from his shoulders. "Yes."

If there had been room to maneuver, they both might have stepped away.

"I'm going back up. You lean against the rock and get used to being vertical again. I'll be ready for you in a minute."

The sun had burst over the edge of the gully, bathing the pale rock in a welcoming red glow. Ben climbed up with as much agility as he'd demonstrated coming down. In fact, in the morning light, he made faster progress. He was dressed for the wilderness, Elizabeth noted. Faded jeans, denim jacket and hiking boots. Did he come out here often? Or was this where he lived?

A surge of panic swooped over her when he disappeared beyond the limited scope of her vision, and she wanted to call out to him. Instead she clamped her lips together and waited. After what seemed like an eternity he reappeared.

"How you doing?"

"Fair to middling."

"You've only got a little ways to go."

Leaning over the crevasse, he lowered a long pole— apparently a sapling he'd cut.

Elizabeth looked at the makeshift lifeline, feeling unaccountably weak. She wanted to tell him it wasn't going to help—except that she couldn't let him down. Not when he'd done most of the work.

"When you start to climb, I'll pull."

Dutifully she grasped the sapling, but her hands slipped off the end.

"It's okay. Brace your back and feet against the rock the way you saw me do. I think you can do it that way."

"All right."

Elizabeth began to inch upward. She hadn't realized the pressure of her leg against the rock was going to make her thigh throb. A few feet above the bottom of the gully, she stopped.

"We don't have to do it all at once."

She dragged air into her lungs, willing her body to stop trembling. "I'll be all right in a minute."

"It's your leg, isn't it?"

Instead of answering, she started to climb again. But she had to stop once more, halfway to her goal. Sweat broke out on her forehead. She felt the strength ebbing from her hands.

With anyone else she would have said she couldn't go on, but the intensity of Ben's blue gaze simply wouldn't let her utter the words. He clearly wasn't a quitter, but then, neither was she. Clamping her jaw in concentration, she began to work her way upward again. However, she knew that if she didn't make it to the top soon, she never would.

"Just a little more, darlin'. You're doing great."

Sure, she thought. Her muscles had turned to marshmallow salad. Vaguely she wondered if some magic force kept her braced between the rock walls.

When she was almost at the top, Ben reached out and clamped a hand around her wrist. His strong fingers closed around her flesh was one of the most welcome sensations she'd ever felt. Then he was clasping her under the arms and pulling her to safety.

He let go of the sapling, which bounced to the bottom of the pit, and she clung to him with relief. She felt as breathless as a trout flopping in the bottom of a canoe.

For long moments he held her close, it was as if he'd just regained something of immense value. Or had he just gotten caught up in her fear?

"You did that real well."

Elizabeth was too winded to answer, so he lifted her into his strong arms and carried her to her sleeping bag. With a corner of her mind she registered the information that he'd pulled the bag out of the sun and under the shelter of a little grove of poplars. After the sharp limestone rocks at the bottom of the gully, the air mattress was as soft as a feather bed.

"Catch your breath."

He was back in a moment with his canteen. Propping her up, he offered her a drink. The water was sweeter than a draft from a cool mountain stream.

When he eased her down again, she closed her eyes. "I think I could sleep for a week."

"In a little while. Can you get your jeans off by yourself, or do you need help?"

Her eyes fluttered open.

"I've got to do something about that leg of yours, if you don't want to end up with an infection."

"Oh, right." She fumbled for the snap at her waistband, then realized she'd reached the end of her strength.

"It's okay." He didn't ask for permission. He simply reached out and unsnapped her pants.

They were both silent as he eased down the zipper.

"Lift your hips."

She was in no position to protest. But in the next moment she caught her breath as his warm fingers brushed her underpants and then her bare legs.

He was looking down, away from her face.

She heard him suck in air through his teeth and had a pretty good idea what had caused his reaction. The puckered white line on her leg wasn't exactly pretty.

"It's an old scar. From an auto accident." She didn't elaborate.

"I was more impressed with your new bruises and abrasions. Let's get the scrapes cleaned up and hope they don't give you any more problems."

Dr. Salvatore wanted to tell him that she could take care of her own leg. Elizabeth didn't have the energy to get the words out. In fact, as Ben washed the injury with water from his canteen, she realized it was surprisingly comforting to let someone else take charge.

She watched him work, pretty sure the cloth he was using was a strip torn from an undershirt. Then he opened a first-aid kit and got out antiseptic.

"Where'd you learn first aid?" she heard herself asking.

"The Marines."

Elizabeth studied his face again. He didn't have that hard-bitten look. "Were you in for long?"

"No. I was just a kid running away from home. I did a couple of hitches." Ben gave the cap of the bottle of antiseptic a sharp twist. Then he was brushing some of the strong-smelling liquid onto her thigh.

"Ouch!"

"Sorry." He was more gentle when he applied a sterile dressing. Next he peered at the scrape on her face. "Looks like you were pretty lucky."

"Yes."

After washing off the blood, he wiped on disinfectant. This time, his touch was almost delicate. When he had finished, he helped her into the sleeping bag.

"You get some rest."

Elizabeth nodded and closed her eyes.

Ben leaned back against the trunk of a tree, bent his legs, and clasped his hands around his knees. Now that he had the leisure, he studied Elizabeth's face, wishing that he didn't find her so damned appealing.

It took only a few moments for her breathing to settle into the rhythm of sleep. In repose she was the essence of femininity. Her lips were sensuous—the kind a man would love to kiss awake. Yet he was pretty sure the short haircut was the recourse of a woman who rarely spent time fussing with her appearance. Why? he wondered. Didn't she have anyone who cared?

He canceled the last thought. It wasn't any of his business. He didn't really know anything about Elizabeth Salvatore except her name. And the best thing would be to keep it at that.

All the same, he couldn't stop mulling over what he'd learned in the past hour or so. She had guts. She wasn't afraid of physical pain. She wasn't a whiner. And she had an inner strength that had kept her from going to pieces in a damned frightening situation. Right now he could tell, by the way she was sleeping so peacefully, that she'd put her complete trust in him.

It was exhilarating, that trust. Or maybe it was the unexpected feeling of being needed. But she hadn't made any demands. She'd just accepted the help he'd offered without trying to impose any of her own conditions, the way most women did.

He sighed. A lot of people depended on him. But it wasn't anything personal. In fact, it had been a long time since he'd allowed himself to feel close to anyone. No permanent attachments, he'd told himself. No one he'd hate to let down when it came to the crunch. But he wasn't a hermit by nature, and knew there'd been something vitally important missing from his life for a long time.

Maybe that was why Elizabeth Salvatore had sparked his interest. Hell, maybe that was why he'd been thinking he'd enjoy spending a little bit of time with her. But he recognized the danger of the impulse. He didn't have the right to get involved with anyone—especially someone he might really be able to care about.

CHAPTER TWO

ELIZABETH SLEPT. Unbidden, her unconscious mind served up another scene. She was back at the hospital again. Fantasy General.

"Please, Dr. Salvatore, I just got out of the hospital a couple of weeks ago. I hate this place. I don't want you to put me in here again."

"Ellen, honey, I've got good news. Your lungs are in much better shape. See, look at this X ray."

"They are? Really?"

"Yes!"

"Then I can go to the career fair at school tomorrow. All my friends are going to be there. And I promised Mrs. Patchen I'd help in the afternoon."

"Sure. Go ahead and have a good time. We'll want to check you over again in six months. But right now everything looks fine."

Images shifted. Another face. Jim. He didn't belong there.

"You've made her so happy."

"I know. I wish I could make all of them happy. I wish I could have made you happy."

"You did, honey."

"No. I killed you."

Elizabeth woke on a shuddering little sigh with a sense of disorientation. She took in the canopy of blue sky scattered with puffy white clouds and the poplar boughs above her head. She'd been dreaming about Ellen Jackson. And about Jim.

You could solve some problems in your dreams. Not others.

"You all right?"

Her eyes focused on Ben Rittenhouse. He was on his haunches beside her. Behind him was a crackling fire. A coffee mug sat on a flat rock near the edge.

"Are you okay?" he repeated.

"I was dreaming."

"I was about to wake you up. First you were smiling. Then your face scrunched up like you were in pain. How's that leg doing?"

She stretched the injured limb. It was stiff and a little sore. "Not too bad." The movement reminded her that she was still half-undressed. But she couldn't stay here much longer, she thought as she squirmed inside the sleeping bag. "I've got a problem, though."

He raised a questioning eyebrow.

"I have to get up. But I think it's going to hurt too much to pull on my jeans."

"You'd rather I go back to tendin' the fire?"

"Uh-huh."

He got up and returned to what he'd been doing, and she gingerly wiggled out of the bag.

He'd let her make an assumption, but Ben was fully aware that he hadn't really promised he wouldn't peek. This morning, male interest got the better of chivalry.

He waited until her back was turned before he gave her a direct look. Her bikini panties were just as sexy as he remembered. Mauve silk and lace. Not the kind of thing most women would have picked for a camping trip. He'd already decided, however, that she wasn't like most women.

The pants weren't any sexier than the rounded swell of her bottom and the nicely proportioned legs. Too bad about the scar that slashed across the front of the right one. Was that why she didn't get out in the sun much? And what about the car accident? But when you didn't want to talk much about yourself, you didn't ask a lot of questions.

She was limping slightly, but not too much. Which meant she'd be able to walk down the mountain under her own power in a little while. He'd fully intended to turn her over to a forest ranger as soon as she woke up. Then he'd got to thinking that she would probably be hungry after her late-night ordeal. He had plenty of food and he'd missed breakfast himself. What was the harm in fixing her something to eat before she left?

Elizabeth came back a few minutes later to find Ben setting several flapjacks on a plate beside the fire. The sight made her realize she was ravenous. Dinner had been a quick sandwich. Her mouth was watering as she slipped into the sleeping bag again.

"Ahem."

"I heard you comin'."

"I guess I wouldn't make much of an Indian guide."

"Do you have anything else in your pack you could wear?"

"Just some more jeans."

He considered the problem. "Tell you what, those pants you had on are ruined, anyway. I could cut off the legs. That way the denim wouldn't hit your scrape and bruise.''

"That's a good idea.''

He pulled a leather sheath from his own pack, extracted a wicked-looking knife, and picked up the jeans that lay folded on the ground.

Elizabeth watched him begin to cut through the fabric. Most men would have hacked a jagged line. He worked neatly but quickly with what must be a very sharp knife.

Competent. Efficient. In control. Those were the words that came to mind.

While she pulled on the newly fashioned cutoffs, he poured more batter into the pan. When she came over to the fire, he handed her the plate.

"What about you?"

"I already had some.''

She added syrup, picked up the fork and began to eat. The flapjacks were delicious.

"Want some coffee?"

"Please.''

He poured a cup from a battered pot that made her think of cowboys and trail drives. She reached for the mug and their hands collided. His skin was warm and dry and brought back the vivid memory of his arms around her.

"Oh, sorry.'' She heard the softness in her voice and wondered why her emotions were so close to the surface—and why she was so aware of him. She and Ben had touched before, far more intimately than the simple brushing of one hand against another.

He withdrew with a jerky motion, the first less than graceful thing she'd seen him do.

"Don't tell me you carry all this stuff around in your pack." She spoke the first words that leaped into her mind.

He had turned back to the pancakes in the skillet. "I have a little cabin not too far from here. I brought the supplies up the hill while you were sleeping."

"You live out here?"

"I just come out when I get the chance."

"I didn't know you could have a private cabin in the national forest."

"There are a few."

"Mmm."

After handing her another flapjack, he took the last one for himself. As they ate, she could sense his withdrawal. She wasn't sure why, but the silence was like pressure building in her chest. She tried to fill it with a question.

"How'd you get so good at outdoor cooking?"

"My dad used to take me on camping trips."

"Does he still come up here with you?"

"He's not well enough."

The tone of voice warned her not to pry. "Oh." She searched for a change of subject. "We lived in the city. Baltimore. My parents weren't the outdoor type. A picnic in Patterson Park was about as close as we got to nature."

"Sounds confining." His answer sounded automatic, as if his mind were somewhere else.

"It's all in what you're used to."

Elizabeth helped him wash the dishes in the kettle of water he'd set at the other side of the fire. They worked well together, quietly and quickly.

Yet she felt an undercurrent building between them.
A couple of times she caught Ben staring at her with a
doubtful expression on his face. When their eyes met,
he looked down at the dishes in his hands. It occurred
to her he hadn't called her darlin' in hours. Apparently the endearment was reserved for rescuees.

"We'd better be getting back," he finally said.

"Yes."

Ben handed her a walking stick he must have cut
while she was asleep. "It's about half a mile to where
my Jeep is parked. I'll carry your stuff."

"You have all the cooking things. Let me take my
backpack, at least."

"Okay."

Last night, when she'd charged into the woods,
she'd hardly looked at her surroundings. Now she
might have stopped to admire the scenery. Redbud and
dogwood were in bloom, adding delicate accents to the
new green of the forest.

She might have stopped to rest her leg. Now that she
was pushing herself, it had begun to throb.

But her guide was clearly in a hurry, although she
guessed his strides were probably shorter than usual as
they made their way down the mountain.

She was about ten paces behind him when she spotted a cabin nestled in a stand of pines on the far side
of a little meadow. The walls were of logs fitted together and chinked with mud. The door was fashioned of rough boards.

"I'll just be a minute. Got to stow my stuff." Ben
turned toward her for the first time; now he had to
notice how heavily she was leaning on the stick and
how badly she was limping.

"I'm sorry. I didn't realize . . ."

"I just need to rest my leg."

"There's a chair inside."

"Thanks."

He pushed open the door of the cabin and stepped aside for her to enter. "It's pretty rough," he apologized as he followed her in. She saw him look around. He seemed to be trying to judge the surroundings through a stranger's eyes. Taking the chimney from the kerosene lamp on the table, he lighted the wick.

"I like it." The structure might be primitive, but everything was as tidy as a military camp. There was a wide bunk against one wall, covered with an extra large sleeping bag. A table, two chairs, shelves and a cabinet rounded out the furnishings. A massive fireplace made of the same limestone that had trapped her dominated another wall.

Elizabeth dropped gratefully into one of the chairs. Even these rough surroundings represented civilization. All at once she was vividly reminded of just how much danger she'd been in, stuck in that crevasse in the rock.

"I'm just realizing how lucky I am you found me," she said.

"Don't turn me into some kind of hero or anything."

Enough people had tried to do that to her. She'd never liked the feeling, either. Yet his gruff tone seemed harsher than necessary.

"I'm not into hero worship. That doesn't mean I'm not grateful," she murmured.

He didn't answer. Instead he turned his back on her and started putting away the gear he'd brought inside.

"Can I help?"

"Sit tight. You came in here to rest your leg."

Outside the brisk walk had warmed her up. Now, with the forced inactivity, she found herself starting to shiver.

Although he didn't seem to be paying her any attention, he must have noticed. When he finished straightening up, he squatted in front of the fireplace and started arranging kindling. Next he added logs.

Elizabeth watched the set of his shoulders as he fussed with the wood. He was putting his full concentration into the job, trying to pretend he was the only person in the cabin. Finally he struck a match and waited for the twigs to begin to burn.

She drew her brows together. In the space of a few minutes, something fundamental had changed between them, something she didn't much like.

"You don't have visitors here very often," she finally ventured.

"I never have visitors."

"Isn't that kind of lonely?"

"I need a place for myself."

"I hope I'm not in the way."

He stood up and brushed off his hands. Then he folded his arms in front of his chest. "That's just the kind of thing a woman would say."

"What should I say?"

He ignored the question.

"At least be honest with me." She tried standing up so she'd feel on a more equal footing with him. "Tell me what's bothering you.'' The direct approach usually worked, at least with patients and hospital personnel. ''Have I done something to offend you?''

''Not really.''

''But . . . ?''

''All right. I guess I've decided that I made a damn fool mistake not turning you over to a forest ranger first thing in the morning. Now I'm stuck with you.''

The words stung. ''Are you trying to tell me I have bad breath or something?''

''Don't be ridiculous.'' The honey-tinged drawl had hardened to stone.

She felt confused, hurt. Her first thought was to get out of this man's way.

Glancing quickly toward the window, she was flabbergasted to see rain streaking down the glass. Sometime during their confrontation, one of the sudden mountain storms so characteristic of the area had blown in without her having noticed. It might pour for a couple of minutes or a couple of hours. But if she went out into the deluge, she'd get as wet as a drowned rat.

''Believe me, Mr. Rittenhouse, just as soon as I can vacate your cabin without getting soaked to the skin, I will.''

He sighed and shifted his weight from one foot to the other. At least he had the grace to be embarrassed by his lack of hospitality.

''I guess you think I'm acting like a bastard. That's what happens when folks start pushin' me,'' he muttered.

She might have leaped to her own defense. She certainly hadn't been trying to push him. However, something in the tone of his voice made her eyes lift to his. She had expected anger. She wasn't prepared for pain. Under the circumstances she shouldn't care. But she did.

"Something's eating at you." Although the statement carried conviction, her voice was barely above a whisper.

"Nothing you can fix."

"Try me."

"Listen..." He ran a hand through his hair. "I was enjoying this morning."

"So was I."

"That's the problem. Like I said, it shouldn't have happened. There are things in my life that mean...that make it impossible for me to get involved with anyone."

"Eating breakfast isn't getting involved."

"Are you trying to kid me or yourself? When I handed you that mug and my hand brushed against yours, you reacted like a woman who wanted to get involved."

That hadn't been her interpretation, although she had been aware of an emotional reaction. "I don't usually attack."

The ghost of a grin flickered on his lips.

"Yeah. The problem is, the reaction wasn't exactly one-sided. Frankly, after we came inside here and closed the door, I started feeling claustrophobic."

She swallowed.

"Maybe it's you," he said. "Or maybe it's because it's been a hell of a long time since I've had a woman."

"You sure know how to dish out the compliments."

"I'm just trying to keep my distance—for your sake."

"What are you, some kind of CIA or FBI agent vacationing between life-or-death assignments?"

He laughed. "Hardly."

"You have a crazy wife in an institution, and you've vowed to be faithful to her." She felt her chest tighten, and waited for his answer.

"No wife."

"Your dad."

His whole body stiffened, and she knew her arrow had hit the target.

"You're worried about your father. You're the one responsible for taking care of him."

"And just how did you make that brilliant deduction, darlin'?"

She ignored the question. "Is he—? I mean . . ."

"He's dying—inch by inch."

"I'm sorry."

"There's nothing you can do."

"You've gotten a second opinion, I assume."

He snorted. "We've been the whole damn route and then some." His expression grew savage. "Do you know anything about the state of modern medicine?"

"Something."

"Doctors act like they're God. But they know just enough to put you in the hospital and do a bunch of tests that are more painful than the disease you've got. Then after you've sweated blood waiting for the results, they tell you they're sorry, but they can't do a thing. The system chews you up and spits you out like raw meat." He flung the words across the space between them like spears.

Elizabeth winced. The blows had hit too close to home. No wonder he was bitter and angry. Modern medicine couldn't save someone he loved. He was stuck with the anguish, and with paying the gigantic bills.

"It must be pretty rough." She understood the pain and frustration better than he might imagine. She'd taken an oath to do battle with disease. Too often she was the one who ordered tests and then had to tell the parents of sick children that she couldn't do anything more than hold off the inevitable for a while.

"So what's your, solution, Dr. Salvatore?"

Elizabeth blanched. Then she realized he hadn't guessed her profession. He was just using the title as a sardonic gibe.

"Ben, if I could do something..."

"You can't." He sighed. "I shouldn't have dumped that on you."

She wanted to cross the room, fold him into her arms and make the hurt go away. Instead she settled for gentle words. "If getting that off your chest helped, I'm glad you did."

"I don't want your pity." Ben had sent powerful men scurrying for cover with the tone of voice he'd just used on Elizabeth Salvatore. The tiny woman on the other side of the cabin didn't flinch.

When she spoke again, her tone was still calm and quiet. "Is that what you think I'm offering? Pity?"

The silence in the little cabin was as thick and sharp as acrid smoke from a forest fire.

All at once, the frustration of not being able to intimidate Elizabeth Salvatore got the better of him. In a couple of long strides he crossed the few yards that

separated them and stood looking down at her before
he opened his mouth.

"Darlin', you're awfully stupid or awfully reck-
less." The laser intensity of his gaze burned into her
flesh.

Probably he was right. She didn't stop to think
about the consequences. She simply did what she'd
been wanting to do since she'd first sensed his pain.
Reaching out slender arms, she circled his broad torso.
As her fingers wove together behind his back, she
flattened her face against his chest.

She felt the surprise in his indrawn breath, noted the
way his body stiffened.

"No."

He was a brawny man. She knew he should have
been able to break free. Somehow her woman's grasp
held him captive. He was a stranger. Yet she wanted
to give him comfort, the way a mother comforts an
injured child. She ached to lend him some of her
strength—if he was willing to accept it.

"You don't have to do it all by yourself," she whispered.

"Yes, I do."

But she'd sensed his tactical surrender. Sure now
that he wasn't going to push her away, she unclasped
her hands and kneaded them across his back and
shoulders.

Ben felt the tautness seep out of his body. Somehow he found his cheek resting on the top of Elizabeth's head. It felt damn good. Maybe better than
anything else he could remember in a long, long time.

For years he'd lived with the knowledge that he
couldn't have a normal life. So he'd gotten into the

habit of thinking of women in sexual terms. Creatures who could satisfy the needs that built up inside a man. Right from the first he'd sensed that it would be better to keep his hands off this one. After he took what he wanted, he'd be left with the feeling that she'd deserved more than he was able to give.

There was, however, nothing overtly sexual about her embrace. It was simply generous and giving in a very basic way. All at once he was powerless to turn down what she was offering.

His own arms came up to clasp her tightly, aware he was drawing something from her fragile form that no one else had ever offered him. Perhaps it was because he'd never dared to ask.

He closed his eyes.

The moment seemed to exist out of time. An instant in the cosmic scheme of the universe. Or maybe it lasted for hours.

Ben was the one who finally broke the contact; the texture of the embrace was going to change unless he put some distance between them. He still didn't completely understand what had happened when she'd taken him into her arms, but didn't want to spoil the feeling by turning it into something more sensual. When he lifted his head and opened his eyes, he was surprised to see the sun shining in the blue of the sky like a newly minted gold coin....

He saw Elizabeth search his face. "I feel better."

"You?"

"That was nice."

He had thought he was taking, not giving.

"It's been a long time since I've hugged anybody like that."

He stared down at her.

"Maybe you'd like to know something about me."

Earlier he would have shaken his head. Now he admitted his curiosity. "Yes, I would."

She had surprised herself by making the offer. Stalling for time, she took a deep breath. "Since I moved to Lexington, there have been plenty of men who've—" she searched for the right words "—wanted something I just didn't think I could give."

The look in his eyes made her insides quiver.

"What didn't you think you could give?"

"Intimacy. I don't mean specifically sex. I mean I couldn't think in terms of sharing anything personal."

"Why not?"

"My husband—"

"You're married!"

"Not anymore." She couldn't meet his eyes now. "I'm not sure exactly what I'm trying to tell you, or why. In the real world, I guess you and I never would have met each other."

"I guess not."

"Maybe that makes it different." She continued in a rush of words. "I came out here because I was feeling rotten and wanted to be by myself. I don't feel that way now. It's because of you."

He stood very still.

She swallowed around the lump in her throat that was making it difficult to breathe. "I don't know. Maybe it happened while you were taking care of my leg. Or maybe it was while you were fixing flapjacks. Or while we were washing the dishes."

He didn't reply, which made her embarrassment worse. What had she expected? That he'd ask for her phone number or something? What would she do if he did? When he found out she hadn't told him she *was* Dr. Salvatore, he was going to be angry.

Wondering what to do now, she glanced toward the window. "I guess I can leave."

"I guess so."

"I'm not sure I can find my car."

"Where did you leave it?"

She described the turnoff to the parking area.

"That's not so far from here."

Elizabeth stepped around him and picked up her pack. Outside, the sun glittered off droplets of water clinging to the grass and leaves, the only remaining evidence of the sudden storm.

"I'll drive you."

"You don't have to. Just tell me—"

"Better to give that leg a rest."

"All right."

Outside she waited while he locked the door and stuck the key under a rock near the corner of the cabin. His battered Jeep was parked behind a screen of pines where she hadn't noticed it.

It was a short ride to one of the two-lane highways that wound through the park. In ten minutes, Ben pulled into the parking lot.

"It's the Acura Integra over there." She pointed. There were other cars in the lot. Across the way, a man and two boys were unloading picnic supplies and discussing the chances of another shower. Another man was removing a canoe from the top of his minivan.

Ben pulled in next to the silver sedan.

Elizabeth got out. "Well, thanks for everything. Especially the rescue."

"No problem."

Unwilling to prolong the goodbye, especially in front of an audience, Elizabeth opened her door and scrambled out. She was inserting her key into the lock when she realized Ben had gotten out and was standing beside her. Hearing his boots scrape the gravel, she tipped up her head to look at him, seeing indecision on his chiseled features.

All at once it was difficult to draw a full breath. The silence stretched taut. Then he cleared his throat.

"Listen—I'm, uh, comin' back here next weekend."

Elizabeth's hand froze on the key.

"Maybe, if you wanted, you could..."

He didn't finish the sentence, and at that moment her emotions were so raw that she was glad he'd stopped.

"I'll think about it," she murmured.

Ben watched Elizabeth Salvatore back her car out of the parking space and head toward the exit. Why in the hell hadn't he just left well enough alone? Because he'd been seized with a terrible feeling of loss when he'd thought about not seeing her again. She'd told him she'd been married. Had the guy walked out on her? Was that why she was afraid to try again? Or had it been so good that she couldn't imagine ever building a relationship like that with anyone else?

The thought suddenly made him jealous, and he shook his head, amazed that someone he hardly knew could tear that kind of response from him.

All at once he wished he could call back the almighty dumb impulse that had made him admit he wanted to see her again. She was too damned perceptive with her guess about her father. But Dad was only part of the picture. And he sure as hell wasn't going to fill her in on the rest. No way was he going to talk to Elizabeth Salvatore about what was really tearing him apart.

Muttering a curse, he kicked one foot against the ground, sending up a shower of gravel. Then he looked around self-consciously to see if anyone was watching. Luckily no one was.

He strode back to his Jeep, vaulted over the door and started the engine. A few minutes later he was on his way back to the solitude of the cabin.

For months he'd felt as if he were in suspended animation. The worst part was that he had to go on dealing with all the nagging little details of life. Well, one day the waiting would be over. Then he could make some new decisions—one way or the other.

For now, though, he still had to go it alone. Which meant he should have run the other way as fast as a scalded cat, instead of issuing invitations to a woman he'd found trapped at the bottom of a hole in the ground.

He laughed harshly as another thought struck him. Here he was, agonizing over what might happen. Maybe she wasn't even going to take him up on the

offer. She hadn't made any kind of commitment when
she left.

But if she was jug-headed enough to come back here
to meet a guy she didn't know a damn thing about, the
damage control was going to be easy. All he had to do
was stay home next weekend.

CHAPTER THREE

THE PHONE WAS RINGING when Elizabeth stepped through the front door of her apartment, which occupied half the top floor of a restored Greek Revival mansion off North Broadway. Dumping her pack and sleeping bag in the hall, she sprinted for the kitchen as fast as her injured leg would allow.

"Hello?"

"Dr. Salvatore. I've been leaving messages for you since this morning."

Elizabeth glanced at the answering machine. The light was blinking, all right.

"Did I catch you at a bad time?" It was Mrs. Bateman, the head nurse on the adolescent ward at Children's Hospital. Elizabeth had come to think of her as a cross between a staff sergeant and Mother Goose.

"No. But I'm not on call this weekend."

"I know that. And I'm sorry. But we had an emergency admission on Ellen Jackson. She was very upset when we told her you weren't available."

"Another infection?" Elizabeth thought back. Ellen's last admission had been three months ago.

"No. This time she hemorrhaged."

Elizabeth reacted with an indrawn breath. "That hasn't happened to her before."

"Dr. Gorelic came to start an IV, but she threw a hissy fit. She said she wanted someone who wasn't going to turn her into a pincushion."

"Controlling little things is one of the ways sick kids hang on to the illusion that they have some control over their illnesses," Elizabeth reminded the nurse.

"I know. But sometimes it's frustrating dealing with them."

Elizabeth had been looking forward to getting cleaned up, crawling into bed, and sleeping for the rest of the weekend. Now she glanced down at her dirty shirt and cutoff jeans. "Just let me get presentable, and I'll be over."

"Doctor, I hate to lay this on you—"

"It's okay."

Five minutes later, she was standing under a spray of hot water in the shower, washing off the effects of her disastrous thirty-six hours in the woods. She'd thought about Ben Rittenhouse the whole way home from the national forest, playing and replaying the scenes between the two of them as though she were rewinding a videotape in her mind.

Now it was almost a relief to turn her attention to someone else's problem, even though she was worried about Ellen.

When she'd been a pediatric resident, Elizabeth had been especially struck by the plight of kids with cystic fibrosis. Young patients were born with the disease. First they experienced digestive disorders. Then the lungs began to fill up with sticky secretions very different from the mucus that cleansed normal lungs. Therapy centered on trying to keep the airways clear, but they became increasingly clogged and susceptible to infection. When the infection eroded a major vein or artery, the lungs hemorrhaged.

More than once she'd been asked why she'd chosen to work with kids who had the odds stacked against them so heavily. A few lived into their thirties. Others didn't even make it into their late teens.

There were days when she wondered why, herself. Usually that was when she lost a patient, the way she had on Friday. But more often her answer reflected a basic determination not to give up.

An hour after she'd dumped her camping gear in the hall, Elizabeth pulled up at the red-brick Children's Hospital building. On the outside it could have been a luxury country club. Inside was a well-equipped hospital facility with everything from CAT scanners and laser treatment units to a state-of-the-art intensive care wing. In the adolescent ward, dove-gray carpeting and walls were accented with bright squares of red, green, blue and yellow. Elizabeth stopped beside a giant rubber frog perched on the counter of the nurses' station and read Ellen's chart.

"What happened to the other fellow?" Mrs. Bateman peered at Elizabeth's scratches.

"The other fellow was a rock. I wasn't watching where I was going."

"Now I'm really sorry I dragged you down here. You should be resting."

"I'm fine." Elizabeth bent to the chart, cutting off further conversation about her health. Ellen was on strong cough suppressants. The hemorrhaging had stopped. But the attending physician recommended a massive dose of antibiotics administered by IV.

Elizabeth sighed and made her way down the hall. Television sets suspended from the ceilings or radios were on in most rooms. In some, youngsters were talking on the phone, playing cards, or practicing tricky wheelchair moves. One bed was occupied only by a large stuffed panda. Across the hall, a boy was laying up basketball shots with a foam rubber ball and a portable hoop. She suppressed a grin, wondering how Mrs. Bateman was going to react when she saw that. Actually, she was usually a pretty good sport, unless fun and games got out of hand or interfered with treatment.

Ellen was sharing a semiprivate room with another teenager who also had CF. The girls were watching *Music Television*—MTV, as it was universally known. Ellen had the back of her bed cranked up almost vertically probably because it was easier to breathe in that position.

Neither roommate looked up when Elizabeth stepped into the doorway. *Ignore the hospital staff and they'll go away,* she thought wryly.

"Hi."

Her patient's face registered surprise. "Dr. Salvatore! I'm glad you... What are you doing here? How did you hurt yourself?"

For the second time that day, Elizabeth wished she'd put on more makeup. "I'm fine. But I wanted to see how you were doing."

The other girl drew the curtain to give them some privacy.

"How are you doing?" Elizabeth repeated.

Ellen was the kind of youngster who hid the details of her illness from her friends. The more normal she could be, the better. But Elizabeth had gotten her to agree to be honest with her doctor. "I was scared."

"I'll bet."

"I felt this funny fluttering in my chest—like something strange was happening. Then I started coughing. A real weird cough. Different."

Elizabeth sat down in the chair beside the bed. She'd heard other kids describing the sensations Ellen had experienced. "Where were you when it happened?"

"Drum majorette tryouts. I'm not stupid enough to think I can go out for the squad, but a couple of my friends are trying out. I came along to watch." The girl hurried on. "Penny drove me home. And my mom brought me to the emergency room."

"I see from your chart that you haven't had any more bleeding. That's a good sign."

"Yeah." Ellen played with the plastic hospital identification bracelet that circled her right wrist.

"Do you have any questions?"

Ellen shifted her body carefully so that she was facing the doctor. She moved as if she thought she might break. Elizabeth understood that, too. Ellen was afraid a sudden motion would start another hemorrhage.

"Am I going to bleed like that again?" the girl asked in a low voice.

"I hope not. But we don't have any way of knowing. That's one of the reasons you're in the hospital, so we can keep an eye on you. The other is so you can rest. That's the best treatment."

Ellen's face took on a tense look. "Could I bleed to death?"

"Anything *could* happen. But it's not very likely."

Some of the anxiety eased out of the teenager's expression. "At least I get out of thumps for a couple of days."

The most important part of CF treatment was vigorous pounding of the chest and back several times a day to loosen secretions. It was called "thumping." Elizabeth had never encountered a patient who liked the process, but a lung hemorrhage was the only reason the routine was stopped. It was a fine line to walk. Without the thumping, the lungs could get congested, which could lead to erosion of another artery. However, thumping itself could trigger another episode of bleeding. Dr. Salvatore was also aware of walking a fine line in what she could say to Ellen. Although she didn't want to frighten her patient, it would be a mistake to minimize the seriousness of her condition so much that the girl would ignore instructions—or refuse treatment.

"That's right, you get out of thumping for a couple of days," Elizabeth agreed. "But I would like to talk to you about that IV the staff physician ordered," she added, keeping her tone conversational.

"Have you ever had Dr. Gorelic stick a needle in the back of your hand?"

Elizabeth shook her head.

"He's got about as much finesse as Freddy Kruger. Maybe he ought to audition for *Nightmare on Elm Street,* Part Umpty-ump."

Elizabeth laughed. "That bad?"

"Yeah."

"I'd like to get those antibiotics into you. What about if I do the IV?"

"You don't mind? I mean, this is your day off and all."

"I don't mind." Elizabeth stood up. "I'll be back in a couple of minutes."

Mrs. Bateman looked up inquiringly as Elizabeth approached the desk. "I'm going to start the IV."

"Good." The nurse inclined her head toward the lounge at the end of the hall. "Mrs. Jackson came in a few minutes ago. I told her you might want to talk to her alone. So she's waiting before she goes down to Ellen's room."

"Thanks." Elizabeth knew Mrs. Bateman had more in mind than wanting to give Ellen's mother a few minutes alone with the doctor. Suggesting that Mrs. Jackson wait in the lounge had also given Elizabeth a chance for a private conversation with her patient. That was often better than trying to talk in front of a frightened mother.

When Elizabeth stuck her head into the doorway, Mrs. Jackson jumped up from the modular sofa where she'd been sitting. "Oh, Dr. Salvatore."

"Ellen's doing much better."

"But the IV—"

"I'm going to take care of that."

"I was so frightened. The worst part was holding myself together so Ellen wouldn't panic."

"But you did it."

"When I went out to the car, she had a wad of bloody tissues in her hand. I thought—"

"A lot of blood can be scary. But it always looks like more than it really is," Elizabeth murmured.

"If she'd just take it easy. Not push herself. But she always wants to do things with her friends. Be like everybody else. Except that she's not. She's fragile."

Elizabeth thrust her hands into the pockets of her white coat. "Watching her friends try out for drum majorette didn't cause the hemorrhage. It could have happened anywhere."

"I..."

"Besides, Ellen's getting too old for you to forbid her to do things because you think they're bad for her health. She knows when she's pushing her body too hard. We have to rely on her good judgment."

"I know you're right. It's just so difficult."

"She's a levelheaded young lady. More than most kids her age."

Mrs. Jackson nodded. Then she cleared her throat. "Is this going to happen again?"

Elizabeth's answer was a little different from the one she'd given Ellen. "The fact that she's stopped bleeding is a good sign. So I think she's going to pull out of this episode very well. But yes, I'm afraid this could happen again."

"Is there anything we can do?"

"Only what you've been doing. When she gets home, keep her on her regime."

They talked for a few more minutes until Elizabeth excused herself to go take care of Ellen's medication. While she waited for a nurse to bring the plastic bottle of saline solution that would carry the antibiotics, she thought about what it must be like, trying to cope with your child's slowly deteriorating condition. When Ellen had been a little girl she'd been hospitalized once or twice a year. Now it was every three or four months.

Was that how it was for Ben Rittenhouse with his father? she wondered. Was that why he was bitter and frustrated? Had he spent years watching his father go downhill? Or had a formerly vigorous man been hit by a sudden, catastrophic illness?

ELIZABETH WAITED until Friday right after lunch to slip into Dr. Perry Weston's office with her notes on the Morgan Foundation grant proposal. His secretary apparently had instructions not to let her simply leave the material.

"I'm sure he'd like to talk to you about it," the woman told Elizabeth. She was already buzzing Dr. Weston on the intercom. A moment later he came bounding into the reception area like a hound on the scent of pheasant.

"Elizabeth, so good of you to stop by."

She tried not to flinch at the feel of his smooth hand on her arm. Instead she remained polite—but cool.

"Come on into my office and sit down. I want to hear all about your suggestions."

"They're in my written report."

"Of course. But I'd like the executive summary. What do you think about the plans for expanding the genetic counseling department?"

"It would certainly benefit a lot of people thinking about parenthood. Help them evaluate the risks of having a child with CF or Tay-Sachs."

"Yes, and it would give us the edge over some of the other hospitals in the area. Once we got a full-fledged program going, we could probably get support from other sources, too."

"Mmm-hmm." She'd suspected Perry might be out to build an empire. She hadn't known how far his thinking had gone. Still, the programs he had in mind would benefit the hospital and the community.

It took Elizabeth forty-five minutes to pry herself away. After that, she had some work to finish up in her office. But while she was looking over the results of various patient tests that had come back from the lab, she was thinking about Ben Rittenhouse and how much more appealing she found him than Perry Weston!

On the surface there was nothing wrong with Perry, if you liked a man who was slick as an eel, to use a country expression. He was a fine, upstanding member of the community, a power, not only in the hospital but also in the state—due as much to his family connections as to his abilities, Elizabeth reminded herself.

What she liked least was his fondness for subtle manipulations. Lately she'd come to realize that his most important goal was advancing his own position. He was probably going places. He'd let her know she could go there with him. Declining without turning him into an enemy was her chief problem. Why was it that every institution was riddled with internal politics and factions? Why couldn't you just do the best job you could with your patients? Or was that asking too much? Her thoughts returned to Ben Rittenhouse. Was hospital politics one of his frustrations? She knew so little about the man. Everything was inference and deduction. His lazy way of talking certainly didn't sound as if he came from high society. On the other hand, she realized the easy speech patterns and laid-back manner were what he wanted people to see. Maybe they were even a sort of camouflage. Under the unadorned exterior, she knew he was a complicated man.

Unlike Perry Weston, he hadn't demanded anything from her. However, she instinctively sensed he made demands on himself. Perhaps that was part of what made him appealing. Or maybe it was the need to understand the pain that he made such efforts to hide.

One thing she did know. If she didn't want another complication in her life, she'd better stay away from the man.

All week she'd been telling herself, "You're not going to meet Ben Rittenhouse on Friday. You're not going. You're not going to do it."

Once she arrived home, however, she headed for the bedroom and started laying out T-shirts and jeans, without allowing herself to analyze what she was doing. It took only a few minutes to throw the clothes into a duffel bag and pack the picnic supplies she'd ended up buying earlier in the week.

It was absurd to feel so lighthearted, Elizabeth scolded herself as she headed for Route 64. The carefree mood lasted only as far as the Mountain Parkway. Parts of the road had been cut through bedrock, exposing high limestone cliffs. They reminded her of the walls of the crevasse where she'd been trapped. Too bad they were all over the state.

The closer she got to the national forest, the more she wondered what she was doing. As she slowed for the turnoff that led to Ben's cabin, her stomach began to knot. The worst part was that she wasn't sure what she was most afraid of. That Ben wouldn't be there. Or that he would.

The knot in Elizabeth's stomach tied itself double when she rounded the last corner before the cabin. Her eyes probed the shadows under the trees, but she didn't spot the battered Jeep. So he wasn't here, after all.

What had she expected, anyway? she asked herself, slumping back in her seat; she felt disappointment wash over her.

Then she sat up straighter. She was here and certainly didn't need Ben Rittenhouse to go camping up on the mountain. Only this time she'd be more careful if she had to get up in the middle of the night.

After parking under a sycamore tree, she opened the trunk and stared ruefully at the cooler. Practical Dr. Salvatore hadn't really packed herself a very well-rounded diet. She had a few staples like bread, cheese, fruit and granola, but she was going to feel ridiculous sitting alone by a campfire, munching on marinated artichoke hearts.

With her duffel, sleeping bag and picnic cooler, it was going to take her two trips up to the campsite. She was just shouldering her sleeping bag for the trek up the hill when she heard the sound of a car engine. A minute later, the Jeep rounded the curve and pulled off the road beside her car.

Elizabeth wasn't sure what to do. Turn around and face Ben? Pick up her gear? Sit down? She settled for leaning against a tree. The stance was casual, but her heart had started to thump inside her chest.

He turned the corner of the cabin with the easy stride she remembered. A sleeping bag was tucked under one arm, a tote bag dangled from the other hand. Somehow when Elizabeth had thought about him over the past week, she hadn't let herself dwell on the physical impact of the man—or on the sexiness of the blue eyes that regarded her with a speculative glint. All at once she wondered exactly what he was expecting from the weekend.

"I wasn't going to come," she blurted out.

"Neither was I, darlin'."

Even as Ben voiced the denial, his lips flirted with a grin. His face almost lost the battle to remain solemn. She was pretty sure he was glad to see her, even if he wasn't going to admit it.

"Maybe we should start over again," she suggested. "Hi."

"Hi."

There was another long silence.

"How's your leg?" he asked.

"Much better, thanks."

"Good. I see your face is better, too."

"Yes. Mmm, how was your week?"

"Hectic. Exhausting. Frustrating. How was yours?"

"Some of that. But there were a few good parts."

When he didn't ask what they might be, she swallowed. "What do you do?"

"Construction, mostly," he said in a clipped tone, letting her know he didn't want to get into an extended conversation about his real life.

She'd been prepared to have him ask her the same question. In fact, she'd hoped he would. Then she could tell him the answer and wouldn't be hiding behind the anonymity she'd adopted last week. Instead he retrieved the key to the cabin from its hiding place and opened the door.

Elizabeth followed him to the door and peeked in. The room was just as small and intimate as she remembered. And there was still only one bunk. She closed her eyes for a moment. She'd been a perfect fool to think this was going to work.

CHAPTER FOUR

BEN TURNED TO FACE HER, his expression reflecting his own uncertainty. "I was thinkin'. There's a nice peaceful place down by the creek. We could set up camp down there."

"Yes. Great!"

"And if it rains, we can always come back and hole up here like a couple of groundhogs in a nice, warm burrow," he added with a teasing note that told her he knew exactly what she had been worrying about.

Elizabeth grinned. Ben laughed. Suddenly the ice was broken.

"I brought some food. Stuff we don't have to cook," she said, pointing to the cooler.

"That thing's going to be awkward to carry."

"I—"

"Not to worry. We can drive part of the way in the Jeep."

Elizabeth helped Ben transfer cooking equipment from the cabin and the things they'd brought to the battered vehicle. Then they set off down the gravel road in the opposite direction from which they'd come. It led into a hardwood forest and quickly narrowed to a dirt track.

The air was moist and rich with the scent of loam. Birds warbled in the trees above them. Elizabeth thought of cathedral windows as she watched the rays of sunlight slant through the branches and dance on the new, still furled leaves.

The track narrowed still more and led down into a valley. Below them, Elizabeth could hear the gurgle of water over rocks. She stole a sidelong glance at Ben. His face was serene, his body relaxed. He drove with one large hand on the steering wheel and the other resting on the window frame.

A couple of hundred yards further on, they ran out of road. Ben pulled the Jeep to a halt and got out. Elizabeth followed and started to reach for some of the gear.

"We'll get that stuff later."

Ben took her down a rocky path, deeper into the wilderness. As they descended, reality seemed to melt away like mist in early-morning sunlight. When they reached the bank of a fast-rushing little river, Elizabeth looked around in wonder at the dark water, the massive boulders and the lush ferns that clung to the bank. Tiny white flowers as delicate as an infant's breath carpeted the ground to their right.

Silent moments passed. Finally Ben whispered, "What do you think?" as if he hated to intrude on nature's solitude. Or on its perfection.

"This place is magic," she murmured, wondering why she had picked that particular description.

He turned and smiled at her.

"It's like...taking a trip to another world," she elaborated.

"That's why I come here."

Ben started toward a place where a series of stepping-stones jutted from the fast-moving water. "The campsite's on the other side."

"My legs aren't as long as yours. I'm not sure I can make it."

"Sure you can. I've been doing it since I was a little tad."

He came back and offered his hand. For just a heartbeat, as his large fingers closed over hers, neither of them moved. Then he was starting across from rock to rock, waiting while she found her footing before going on. In the middle of the water, when she had to take a particularly large step, she wavered, and they both teetered on the brink of disaster. His grip tightened.

"Okay?" he finally asked.

"I will be when I'm back on dry ground."

When they finally reached the opposite bank, he dropped her hand and pointed toward a ledge of rock above them.

"There's a natural shelter up there."

It was an easy climb. Soon they reached a wide overhang, where Elizabeth could see the evidence of Ben's habitation. The area had been swept clean of debris. A fire circle was black with the remains of charred logs. He came here often. Alone. But he'd brought her. Somehow the realization made her chest tighten with unexpected gladness.

"Why don't you fetch some wood while I bring the stuff from the Jeep? That way you don't have to cross again until we leave."

"The chicken way out."

"You said it. I didn't."

Elizabeth smiled as she watched him lope off. There was an almost joyful spring in his step. Maybe for him this place really was a magic kingdom. Suppose he was a prince under a curse, and he could only be himself two days a week, here in the woods?

She was bemused by her own fancy. Instead of dreaming up fairy stories, she should be earning her keep. Slowly at first and then with more determination, Elizabeth began to pick up fallen sticks. By the time Ben returned with a large portion of the gear, she'd collected a tidy pile.

On his second trip he brought the cooler. "What do you have in here, rocks?"

"Munchies."

While he made the fire, she spread a picnic cloth on the ground and brought out some of her goodies. As they progressed from her cheese and crackers to his marinated cubes of Kentucky lamb cooked over the open flames, a feeling of contentment stole over her. It was accompanied by an unaccustomed sense of freedom. No duties. No demands. No one desperate for her help.

She caught Ben watching her and smiled shyly. "The food's good."

"Yes."

The company's good, too, she thought.

An hour later, Elizabeth leaned back against a rock and licked her fingers. "I don't think I've eaten that much in years."

Ben finished off the last piece of lamb. "The fresh air gives you an appetite." He rummaged in his sack of supplies. "I hope you left room for dessert."

"What is it?"

"Ever roasted apples?"

She shook her head.

"It's a little like roasting marshmallows. You try to get the inside cooked without burning the outside."

"I don't have much experience with marshmallows, either."

"One of the pleasures you missed, growing up in the city?"

She looked at him in surprise. "I thought you weren't listening when I told you that."

"I was listening." He stopped abruptly. "Let's get on with the apple-roasting lesson. The trick is not getting it too close to the fire." He produced two large green apples from his pack.

"Granny Smith?"

"Mmm-hmm."

"Well, we have the same taste in apples—tart."

He nodded and carefully cut slits in the fruit to insert whole cloves and pieces of cinnamon. Then he skewered the apples on smooth sticks. Elizabeth watched to see how far he held his from the fire and did the same.

"It takes about ten minutes."

She wanted to ask him questions about his childhood camping trips. She was pretty sure he'd rather she didn't. So they cooked their dessert in silence, and Elizabeth contemplated the puzzle of Ben Rittenhouse. He knew how to find immense enjoyment in such simple things as watching a rushing river or roasting an apple over an open fire. It was as if he lived each moment more fully than other people she'd met.

Yet every once in a while he'd bring himself up short, as if...as if he'd suddenly stepped outside the scene and become an observer.

Ben looked up once and caught her gazing. Anyone else would have asked what she was thinking. He simply turned his attention back to the task at hand.

Finally he removed his apple from over the fire and tested it with his finger. "Done."

Elizabeth retrieved hers and brought it to her mouth.

"Let it cool a little so you don't burn yourself," he warned.

When he bit into his, she cautiously followed suit. The fruit was juicy and delicious.

"Yum."

He was contemplating her with a playful expression on his face.

"What is it?"

"It's hard to imagine someone with as formal a name as Elizabeth sitting cross-legged in front of a fire, eating a mushy apple on a stick. I think we'll have to rename you."

"Oh, come on."

"No. I mean it. There are dozens of nicknames for Elizabeth." He grinned. "Let's see. There's Bessie, Betsy, Else, Elissa. Or how about Lizzy?"

"Don't you dare."

"Libby."

She shook her head. "How long have you been thinking about this?"

He shrugged. "I like Lisbeth."

"Oh, you do." Even as she voiced the observation she wondered how he'd arrived at the preference.

"You're going to be Lisbeth. At least out here in the woods."

Elizabeth cocked her head. "And what if I decide to call you Wendell?"

"You wouldn't dare."

He was over six feet tall and probably two hundred pounds. He was right. She wouldn't dare.

The matter settled, he stood. "We'd better clean up while it's still light."

They washed the dishes in water he'd fetched from the stream and then tidied up the camp.

As she watched him inflate their air mattresses, she wrapped her arms around her shoulders. She'd never quite pinned down her own motives for coming back. Now she still couldn't help worrying that he might have the wrong idea about why she'd come here this weekend.

His expression told her he understood. "Don't look so nervous. I don't have any ulterior motives."

"I just—"

"You're just not sure about the etiquette of spending the night alone with a man in the woods."

She nodded.

"I'm not up on the etiquette, either. I've never brought anyone here before."

She'd supposed as much. "Why did you bring me?"

"The idea of spending the weekend with you was appealing."

"Yes."

"No strings attached."

She couldn't help wondering about the implications of his words. What would happen, for example, if he ran into her in the real world? Suppose they both ended up standing in front of the meat counter at her local grocery store? Would he pretend he didn't know her? She didn't want to ask.

"So I'll take the left side of the fire and you take the right."

"Okay."

He gave her an amused look. "We could sit around the campfire and tell ghost stories, if you don't want to go to bed this early."

"No, thanks."

Elizabeth had brought sweat clothes to sleep in. Now that it was almost dark, she'd probably feel comfortable slipping behind a rock and changing. But she didn't want to go through the hassle of getting dressed again in the morning. So she decided to sleep in the things she'd worn all day.

That made getting ready for bed a relatively simple matter. Fifteen minutes later she was lying in her sleeping bag with her pack propped under her head for a pillow.

As the night darkened, the incredible isolation of the forest seemed to settle around her. Beyond the circle of firelight, the trees were shadowy and indistinct, an impression that seemed to magnify the sounds of the night. Crickets chirping. Leaves rustling in the wind. The river gurgling over the rocks below them.

Since it wasn't really chilly, Elizabeth had folded back the edge of her unzipped sleeping bag. Now she stifled the impulse to pull the covers up to her chin like a kid afraid of the dark.

Ben, who was stoking the fire, glanced in her direction. "Comfortable?"

"Yes. Thanks."

"Well, good night, Lisbeth."

"Good night."

Instead of climbing into his own sleeping bag, Ben stood staring in the direction of the river. After a few minutes, he turned back toward the campsite and sat down, his back against a boulder.

"Aren't you going to sleep?"

"I'm going to sit up for a while." He clasped his hands around his knees and made himself comfortable.

Elizabeth watched the firelight flickering on the planes of his face. His expression had an intensity that made her want to share his thoughts. By now she knew better than to ask.

Of all the things she'd done in her life, coming on this camping trip with Ben Rittenhouse was one of the least characteristic. Yet somehow she hadn't been able to help herself. Which meant she was an idiot—or a fool—if she hoped that this man was going to fill a gap in her life that she hadn't been able to fill in the two years since she'd come to Kentucky.

However, there was no use trying to figure it out now, she told herself. It had been a long week, both physically and emotionally tiring, and she needed some rest. Without many more thoughts drifting through her mind, she made the transition from wakefulness to sleep.

But anxieties didn't simply turn themselves off. They were transmuted into another form. During the darkest part of the night, a dream stole up on her like a hawk swooping to stop a mouse in its tracks.

"Dr. Salvatore, do something!" Mrs. Jackson shouted, pointing to the bright blood soaking in the sheets of Ellen's bed.

Elizabeth shouldered aside a crowd of doctors and nurses and reached toward Ellen. But she knew there was nothing she could do. There was too much blood and no way to stop this hemorrhage.

She looked around in despair, searching the circle of faces that had begun to draw even closer. Perry Weston shook his head. One by one the others did, too.

Tears in her eyes, she turned back to Ellen. But the girl wasn't there anymore. It was Jim. In the car. Now blood was all over the place.

"Jim! Oh, God, Jim! He's bleeding to death! Somebody help me! Help!"

Then suddenly Perry was gone. Strong hands were on her shoulders.

"Lisbeth. Lisbeth. It's all right, darlin'."

"No-o-o. He's bleeding to death. Please—he's—you've got to save him."

The hands shook her gently.

"Wake up, darlin'. It's just a dream."

Elizabeth's eyes blinked open. In the light from the dying fire, she could just make out a dark form leaning over her.

"Oh..."

"It's me. Ben. You were whimpering in your sleep. And thrashing around. You did that before. After I pulled you out of that hole."

"I did?"

"Does it happen a lot?"

"Sometimes."

"Want to tell me about it?"

"I..." She swallowed. "I dream about the accident."

He waited for her to continue.

"My husband was killed."

There was a long silence. "What happened?" Ben finally asked.

She closed her eyes for a moment, trying to will away the memories. The pressure of the images was more than she could cope with. "I—I—wanted him to pull over on the shoulder so I could take a picture of a church I thought looked interesting," she began in a low voice. "I had just unbuckled my seat belt and opened the door when the truck came careening around the corner and slammed into our car. I was thrown out, into a ditch."

Clutching at Ben's arm, Elizabeth continued. "My leg was hurt. I tried to crawl to the car. It was smashed. Twisted. Jim was trapped inside. By the time I got there, the whole front seat...the blood...Jim..." The story ended on a sob.

Ben hesitated for a moment. Then he slipped into the unzipped bag beside her and drew her close, rocking her gently, stroking her hair.

For long moments she cried quietly against his broad chest. Finally she wiped her eyes with the back of her hand, amazed she'd shared this much with a man she barely knew.

"How long ago was it?" he asked.

"Two and a half years."

"That's how you got the scar on your leg?"

"Yes."

His voice was very low. "It must have hurt a lot."

"It wasn't so bad."

"I mean losing someone you loved."

"In a way I lost myself."

She felt his body tense.

"What do you mean?" he asked, his voice urgent.

"My sense of self, I guess. Who I was."

"But you got it back."

"I'm different now."

She felt him nod. "But you have to let go of the pain. The mental pain."

"I keep thinking I have. Then I dream it all over again and the loss is back."

He stroked her shoulders and hair and murmured soft, sympathetic, soothing words. Once again she had the wonderful sensation of feeling safe in his arms. With it came a new burst of freedom, a new lightness to her soul.

"How did you do that?"

"Do what?"

"Make me feel so much better."

"I just let you talk it out."

She looked up, wishing she could read his expression in the dark. And wishing she could give him back some of the peace of mind he'd given her. "What about you?"

"What about me?" he asked.

"Are you going to tell me what's bothering you? Besides your father, I mean."

"Lisbeth—"

"Ben, please."

"I can't talk about myself."

"Why can't you follow your own advice? Let go of the pain, whatever is it?"

"Darlin', if I could I would."

"Ben—"

"It's something I can't do yet. Maybe I never will."

Moments passed and neither spoke. There was no point in pushing Ben. Like the mountain bedrock, he wasn't going to budge for anything less than a major earthquake. Elizabeth closed her eyes. Common sense told her to draw away from him. Not just physically. Emotionally. She ignored the inner voice. Uttering a little sigh, she let herself snuggle closer to Ben. All at once she was aware how emotionally drained she was. "So tired."

"Mmm."

She hadn't been held like this in the middle of the night for such a long time. She'd forgotten how good it felt.

He'd forgotten how good it felt to hold a woman in the darkest part of the night, when the goblins came. Too damn good. He should get up and go back to his own sleeping bag. But he didn't want to move away from her. Maybe he couldn't.

He felt her body relax, heard her breathing change to the rhythm of sleep. She trusted him. What would she do if he flew into a rage and started tossing knives around the campsite?

He'd been a terrified ten-year-old, sitting at the kitchen table with a bowl of cereal, when his father had done that. There'd been harsh words and broken crockery before. The knives had been something new.

Dad had stomped out of the house, and Mom had bided her time. A few days later she'd packed two suitcases and taken him to live halfway across the country. In northern Florida, because that was as far as the bus ticket had taken them. Too bad they hadn't known a soul in town, or that once she'd arrived, Mom hadn't seemed to have the energy to find another haven. It had taken his uncle eight years to find them. Mom hadn't wanted to hear anything he'd had to say. Ben hadn't been able to turn away. Afterward he'd wished he had. No. That wasn't exactly true.

Long-forgotten memories chased each other through his mind like bands of warrior savages. He squeezed his eyes shut—then found himself pressing his face against the tender place where Lisbeth's neck met her jaw. God, she smelled good! Holding her had an almost healing effect on him.

Despite his reassuring little speech earlier in the evening, he'd wanted to touch her—to reach out and gather in more of that generosity and warmth he'd felt when she'd hugged him in the cabin.

Like truants, his fingers began to play with the dark, springy curls at the back of her head. His lips found the top of her forehead. Her hair was so soft, rich and alive.

He had to stop this. He was going to stop. In a minute.

Instead he carefully tipped her head back and followed the line of her jaw with his lips, ending with his nose buried in her sweet-smelling hair. Another wayward thought took possession of his mind. Even as he acknowledged that he was trespassing, he reached up to gently cup one soft breast through the soft fabric of her flannel shirt. It nestled like a dove in the palm of his hand, warm and quivering and vulnerable. He had to stop this. But before he could pull his hand away, Elizabeth murmured something in her sleep and shifted against him, pressing his fingers more firmly into her yielding flesh.

He heard her breathing quicken. At the same time, her legs began to move restlessly, and he felt them rub against his jeans. Uttering a curse under his breath, he moved his fingers greedily against her breast, feeling the nipple bead and swell.

The first gray light of dawn had chased away some of the darkness, and his gaze roved over her face. Her eyes were closed. But her skin was flushed and her lips were parted, as if inviting his kiss. He touched the lower one gently with his tongue.

She smiled.

"Lisbeth?"

She didn't answer. She was still asleep.

With infinite gentleness, his finger traced a path from her hairline to the tip of her nose. No other woman had ambushed him with such innocent finesse. Now he yearned to push her onto her back and cover the supple length of her body with his own.

But he couldn't do something like that to her. Sure, she was aroused. But she was responding to another dream—or to whatever he had started when she hadn't had a choice in the matter.

Regretting his own chivalry, Ben slid his hand off the sleeping woman's breast and tried to ease away from her. He was stopped by her arms, which had come up to clasp him around the shoulders.

"Darlin'?"

He found himself staring into the dark pools of her eyes. They were large and round. Passion warred with confusion.

"Wh-what are you doing?"

The accusation in her tone brought an answer to his lips that he hadn't intended. "Darlin', it didn't look like I needed to do much."

Her cheeks flamed, and her arms unclasped themselves from his shoulders. In the next second she rolled onto her other side, her back to him. It was several moments before she spoke. "I'm sorry." Her words were barely audible.

"Yeah."

He hadn't planned for anything like this to happen. He hadn't planned to get this close to her. Now his body was on fire, and his lips started to move before his brain could catch up.

"Were you dreaming about me—or your husband?"

She dredged air from the bottom of her lungs. "Not my husband."

He stared at her, wanting more answers. Wanting more than answers. But she kept her face averted.

Finally he eased out of the sleeping bag. "I'm goin' down to the river. Unless you're interested in some nice, brisk skinny-dippin', I suggest you stay up here."

Elizabeth didn't answer. For long moments after his footsteps had faded into the gray dawn, she lay on her side, her knees pulled up toward her chin.

The dream still burned in her memory. In it she hadn't let herself see the face of the man who was making her body hot with need. She'd kept her own face buried in the crinkly hair of his chest. But he had called her darlin', and she had responded to the exquisite touch of his hands and lips on her skin.

The thought was a vivid reminder of how it had been, and a wave of sensual tension swept over her again, making her suddenly feel as if her skin were too tight for her body. It had been so long since anyone had stirred that kind of passion in her that she was confused, utterly undone.

Had she been responding to Ben, or would some other man have done as well? She didn't think so. But that didn't solve her basic problem. The thought of eating breakfast with Ben Rittenhouse when he came back from his cold bath made her throat tighten.

She began to gather up her things. When he came back, she was simply going to fade out of the picture.

She had just rolled up her sleeping bag when she saw him coming slowly up the path from the water. Unwilling to meet his gaze, she pretended to busy herself with tightening the laces.

He stopped a few yards from her.

"Lisbeth."

She didn't look up.

"Some damn fool threw a rusty—"

The tone of his voice made her raise her head. It wasn't his words so much as his appearance that made her gasp.

"—wire thing in the water."

Ben was wearing only a pair of untied tennis shoes and wet jeans—the right side of which were marked with bloody palm prints. Then she saw the blood dripping from his right hand.

CHAPTER FIVE

BEN WAS STANDING with one leg rigid, the other slightly bent. As she watched, he sank onto one of the logs in front of the fire. His face was gray, his speech barely above a whisper now. "Can you believe anything so stupid? I cut myself on a damn piece of wire."

She believed it. Before he finished the sentence, Elizabeth was at his side. There was a deep, jagged cut across the palm. It must be painful. Yet he hadn't even winced when she took his hand. She sucked in her breath.

"Don't faint on me, darlin'."

"I wasn't going to."

As they spoke, she was fumbling in her pack for one of the new T-shirts she'd brought. Quickly she wound it around the jagged-looking cut and pressed. Then she glanced at his blood-soaked jeans. "You didn't have to pull your pants on for me."

"I couldn't exactly picture myself walking buck nekkid into a hospital emergency room."

"Where *is* the closest hospital?"

"Don't know."

"You're going to need stitches."

"Yeah."

"And a tetanus shot."

Elizabeth inspected the T-shirt she'd pressed into service as a bandage. Blood had soaked into the fabric. However, the red stain wasn't getting any bigger. Pressure seemed to have stopped the bleeding.

Ben hoisted himself to his feet with his good hand. "Let's get out of here. We'll come back for our stuff later." Then he eyed Elizabeth's rolled-up sleeping bag. "You were on your way home."

She nodded tightly.

"Why?"

"I was embarrassed."

"You shouldn't have been. I wasn't exactly being honest with you. It was as much my fault as it was yours."

He turned away and started down the path. When his foot slipped on one of the rocks, Elizabeth reached out to steady his elbow. "Hang on to me."

Ben ignored the suggestion until they got to the stepping stones across the rushing water. Then his left hand clamped around her right. There was no finesse in the way they crossed on the rocks. By the time they reached the other side, they were both sloshing in their shoes and their pants legs were sopping.

Sweat had broken out on Ben's forehead. He didn't speak until they reached the Jeep. "Can you drive a stick shift?"

"I'll manage."

In fact, as she started down the gravel road, the vehicle bucked like a wild pony. Beside her, Ben gritted his teeth.

"Sorry."

"I appreciate what you're doing."

"I wish it were a smoother ride."

It seemed to take forever to get back to the cabin. Finally Elizabeth pulled up by the front door. "Sit on the step," she told Ben.

"You going to change cars?"

"I'm going to stitch up your hand."

He stared at her as if she were speaking a foreign language. Without further explanation, she hopped down from the Jeep, fished her car key out of her purse, and opened the trunk of her car. Then she was racing back to Ben with her medical bag in her hand.

He eyed the gold letters on the black leather. Elizabeth Salvatore, M.D. "You're a doctor?"

"Yes."

"Your private little joke?"

She helped him out of the Jeep and onto the steps where she could sit next to him. Then she unwrapped the T-shirt, glad she could focus on his hand rather than his face. "There wasn't any use starting an argument last week. Besides, I agree with a lot of the things you said about doctors."

"I'll bet."

"There are too many illnesses we still can't treat effectively. That's as frustrating to me as it is to you."

Ben snorted.

"But we can sew up a ripped palm." She took his hand and set it in her lap. "I was going to tell you yesterday. All you had to do was inquire about what I did, after I asked you."

As she cleaned the wound, he muttered a curse. She didn't know whether he was responding to the pain or her gibe.

"Where do you work?" His voice was tense.

"Children's Hospital."

"At least I'm not going to run into you there."

At what hospital would she run into him? Elizabeth wondered as she retrieved a hypodermic from her bag.

"What's that for?"

"Local anesthetic."

After numbing the hand, she got out a suture kit and set to work. It took twelve stitches to close the cut.

"Your own doctor can give you a tetanus shot. The stitches should come out in about ten days."

"Yeah." Now that the emergency was over, he stretched out his legs and leaned his head back against the cabin door.

"You should be lying down. But I needed a strong light to see what I was doing and there wasn't enough in the cabin."

"I'll survive."

Elizabeth finished packing up her medical supplies. "I guess the best thing would be for me to drive you back to the city."

"I think the best thing would be for you to drive yourself back to the city."

She angled her face toward his. "I can't leave you here like this."

"The hell you can't."

"Ben..."

"Listen, Dr. Salvatore, the quicker we end this little interlude in the woods, the better."

Elizabeth swallowed tightly. "Just tell me your address, so I can take you home. There's no way on God's green earth you can drive without ripping the stitches out of your hand."

"I'll get a ride."

"With whom?"

"My secretary."

She cocked her head to one side. "You said you were in construction."

"I am. My uncle and I have a construction company."

"You do? I thought—"

"My company is none of your business."

"Granted." She made an effort to get the conversation back on track. "But I was under the distinct impression that there's no phone out here. How are you going to contact your secretary? Send up a smoke signal?"

He glared at her. In his present state, he hadn't considered that little detail.

"We'll take my car. You can send for the Jeep later."

"Our damp clothes are going to make a mess of your pretty leather seats."

"I'm not worried about that."

He didn't argue with her again until she was heading for the turnoff to the highway. "Okay, Lizzy, you can drop me at the city line, and I'll get a cab."

"Don't call me Lizzy. And don't be ridiculous. I'm not going to leave a half-naked, injured man somewhere on the street. I'll drop you at a friend's house or at home. Or what about your uncle?"

"He's on vacation till tomorrow."

The next part of the ride back to the city was accomplished in silence.

"What exactly are you angry about?" Elizabeth asked at last, pretty sure that she couldn't make things worse by engaging Ben in conversation. On the other hand, she did keep her eyes glued to the road.

"When I deal with a person, I like to know where they're comin' from."

"So do I."

"Well, as far as you and I are concerned, it's not going to be a problem much longer."

"I've been as straight with you as you were with me."

He snorted, and she wasn't sure what else to say until they reached the first Lexington turnoff. "Where to?"

His lips were drawn in a thin line. Finally he opened them wide enough to give her terse directions.

Twenty minutes later, Elizabeth found herself driving through one of the city's most expensive suburbs not far from the Lakeside Golf Course. All the houses were custom-built. All were on large lots. Many were hidden from the road by a thick screen of trees.

"The next right," Ben muttered.

Elizabeth turned in between stone gateposts. The house itself, an impressive modern structure of fieldstone and wood siding, was at the end of a long, curving driveway.

Ben opened the door as soon as her car pulled to a stop. "Thanks for the medical treatment."

Elizabeth swallowed. "Ben, can't we talk?"

He ignored the question. "It's been fun, darlin'. But since I didn't ever plan on bringing you here, you'll understand if I don't feel up to inviting you in."

"This is stupid."

"My thought exactly."

All at once her throat was so constricted that it was impossible to speak. Yet she couldn't stop herself from reaching across the console and laying her hand upon his bare arm. Although the gesture wasn't an attempt to keep him from going, he froze.

Elizabeth didn't breathe. She knew his lungs weren't working, either, because the broad expanse of his naked chest was immobile. She couldn't pull her gaze away from the dark golden hairs that spread in a circular pattern around his nipples and narrowed toward his flat stomach. It was as if someone had hit the Stop-action button on a VCR with the two of them caught in the freeze-frame. It wasn't a scene on videotape, however. It was reality.

The moment took on a life of its own—like the first time in the cabin, when she'd held him in her arms like an injured child. So much had happened between them. Or maybe nothing had really happened. Maybe it was all in her mind. Yet she was helpless to break the contact by herself.

She felt Ben's body give a little shake. When he started to withdraw, she pressed her palm against the firm, warm skin of his arm. For just a heartbeat, her fingers smoothed across blond hairs. The thought of never touching him again brought a sharp pain to her chest.

As if seeking the safety of separation, he moved out of reach. Her hand dropped to the car seat.

"Goodbye, Ben," her mind whispered as he made his slow way toward the front door.

Maybe he'd change his mind. Her body tensed. But he didn't turn around.

After the door had closed, she drove away. Tears blurred her vision, making it hard to see where she was going. She told herself it was ridiculous to be crying for the end of something that had never existed—that had never had a real chance to exist. You didn't build a relationship with a man in never-never land. You didn't build a relationship with a man who wouldn't talk about himself. But she had to stop at the bottom of the driveway for several minutes before she felt sufficiently in control to pull out onto the road.

MONDAY MORNING Elizabeth was at the hospital early, making rounds and looking for extra work so her thoughts wouldn't be drawn back to the weekend. When she checked Ellen Jackson's chart, she was delighted to see how well the girl was doing. Ellen's progress lifted her spirits considerably. At least something was going right.

The teenager had just finished breakfast. Because her roommate had gone home that morning, she was alone in the semiprivate room, writing in a green notebook between bites of scrambled eggs and grits.

"Got a minute?"

Ellen closed the book and set it on the nightstand. "I was just working on my journal."

"Do you write in it every day?"

"Not every day. But a lot."

"That's a good habit to get into."

Ellen laughed. "It's a good way to let off steam. And tell people off."

"Do you tell me off?"

"Not you!"

"I'm flattered. And I've got some good news," Elizabeth added, bringing the conversation around to the reason for her visit. "You're doing so well, I'm going to let you go home a few days early."

For a moment Ellen's face lighted up with pleasure. Then her expression changed.

"What's wrong?" Elizabeth asked.

Ellen pushed around a piece of scrambled egg on her plate. "Nothing."

Elizabeth tried to read her patient's expression. "Aren't you feeling well enough to leave?"

"Oh, I feel all right. Now. But how long is it going to last this time?" the girl questioned, clearly unable to keep a mixture of worry and anguish out of her voice. "I mean, I'm just going to get sick again. And again. And again."

Elizabeth knit her fingers in her lap. One of the biggest dangers with adolescent CF patients was that they'd give up and stop fighting the disease. She'd seen it happen too many times. Once a kid decided it wasn't worth the effort, the way downhill would be open.

"Let me tell you a true story about another girl," she said. "Her name was Elizabeth, as a matter of fact. Elizabeth Evans Hughes."

"Did she have CF?"

"No. Diabetes."

"That's not so bad. All you have to do is take insulin."

"That's true now. But when Elizabeth Evans Hughes got sick, they hadn't discovered insulin yet. So having diabetes was a lot worse than having cystic fibrosis is today. Once you were diagnosed, the life expectancy was only about a year or two."

"When was that—the Dark Ages?"

"1918. Back then, the only way to treat diabetes was to starve the patients. I mean serious starvation. Kids got so weak and listless they could hardly walk around."

"Oh, gross."

She'd gotten Ellen's attention. "Elizabeth got sick when she was twelve. She was a very courageous little girl who stuck to her diet and did everything the doctors told her. By the time she was fifteen, she was five feet tall and weighted fifty-four pounds. Most people would have just given up and stopped fighting."

"But she didn't die," Ellen said with conviction. "Or you wouldn't be telling me this story."

"That's right. Her parents heard that a doctor named Frederick Banting in Toronto had discovered insulin. The trouble was, at first he only had a tiny supply, so he couldn't treat very many people. But he agreed to take Elizabeth on as one of his first patients—maybe because her father was famous. He was the governor of New York and then a Supreme Court justice. By the time Elizabeth and her mother arrived in Toronto, Elizabeth was on a 400-calorie-a-day diet, and she was down to fifty pounds. She couldn't have hung on like that for much longer. But as soon as she started taking insulin, it was like a miracle. Within a few weeks, her calorie intake was up to normal, she was full of energy and looking forward to the future. Insulin changed her life. She went on to graduate from college, get married, have three children, and live into her seventies."

Ellen's eyes were bright. "I want to do all that. Except that there isn't any cure for CF."

"There will be. It's just a matter of time, now that they've discovered the gene that causes the disease."

"When?"

"Oh, honey, I wish I could say for sure, because I know you're tired of getting sick and ending up in the hospital. I know it's discouraging—and frustrating. But it may only be a year or two before they come up with a new drug therapy that will actually clear the lungs."

"Do you really think so?."

"I hope so. But in the meantime I'm asking you to help me keep you as healthy as we can. I can't do it alone." Elizabeth felt tears in her eyes as she spoke.

Ellen swallowed. "I don't want to be a quitter."

"Good."

"But sometimes, you know, it's so hard. You look at other kids and think how lucky they are."

"I know that, honey." She reached out to put her hand over the girl's. "And I can't tell you for sure that a cure is right around the corner. I can't even pretend to really understand how difficult being sick is for you. But there are hard things in everybody's life."

"Like when your husband died?"

Elizabeth lifted her eyebrows in surprise. "Yes, like that. How do you know about my husband?"

Ellen shrugged. "You hear things, you know, around the hospital."

"Yes."

"What happened to him?"

Last week Elizabeth would have changed the subject. Now she found she didn't need to. Somehow, talking to Ben really had made a difference. "An automobile accident. When he died, I wasn't sure I wanted to live. But I finally decided I didn't want to be a quitter, either.''

They were both silent for a moment. Then Ellen sucked in a little breath. ''Dr. Salvatore, I feel so close to you sometimes.''

''I feel close to you, too, honey.''

''If there's stuff I can't talk to my mom about, would it be all right—? I mean, would you mind if I—?''

''Ellen, any time you need to talk to me, just call. Or come in.''

''Thanks.''

Elizabeth left the girl's room feeling as if she'd won a major victory.

Helping Ellen brought her immense gratification. However, as she closed the door to her office, she acknowledged that she was following the same pattern that had created problems in her own life. Back in Baltimore, she'd gotten so wound up with her patients that she hadn't had enough emotional energy left over for her marriage. She hadn't even realized what was happening. Only when Jim had sat her down for a long talk one evening had she admitted he was right.

Now she sank into her desk chair and stared toward the shelves crammed with medical books and journals. She didn't really see them. She was remembering the past.

Every time she thought about that talk with Jim, she was overwhelmed with a sense of her own stupidity. That night they'd made love with a tenderness and passion that had been like a renewal of their marriage vows. Over the next few weeks, they'd decided to have the baby she'd been too busy to consider. She felt a chill sweep over her at the memory of what she'd lost. The accident had changed everything.

She'd loved her husband and was still appalled at the way she'd taken him for granted. After his death, she'd known she had to get away from the city where they'd lived. She'd come to Kentucky a different person from the young Baltimore doctor who'd thought she could have it all. She hadn't been willing to take the risk of messing things up again with another man.

Ben Rittenhouse had blindsided her when she was at her most vulnerable, and somehow she'd started building fantasies. Maybe it was because she'd sensed right from the first that he didn't want to get involved with her. Paradoxically that made him both safe and a challenge.

Elizabeth leaned back in her chair and sighed. What was she worried about now? she asked herself. Any choice in the matter had been taken away from her.

ELLEN STARED at the chair where Dr. Salvatore had been sitting. Then she reached for the green book on the bedside table. Inside, on the first page, were the words Private and Personal—Do Not Read. She flipped to the last entry. She'd been complaining about gross hospital food and nurses who came in at three in the morning to see if you were asleep and woke you up. Now she picked up her pencil and sat tapping it against her lips.

Sometimes in the hospital you get into the mood where you feel sorry for yourself, because they're always sticking you and poking you and thump-

ing you. But deep down you know that's not
what's making you upset. You know you're really worried because kids with CF don't live all
that long.

I just had a talk with Dr. Salvatore. She was
trying to buck me up because she knew I was de-
pressed about my health. The stuff she said
helped. It's my responsibility to hang in there.
And if I don't make it, I'll know I gave it my best
shot.

Tuesday Elizabeth threw herself into her work—
principally with two new patients. One was a six-year-
old boy named Eddie Lakefield. The other was a
bright, articulate little girl named Lorie Stiff, who had
just been diagnosed. At their age, the CF symptoms
weren't so bad. And she prayed that before the
youngsters started having serious problems, medical
science would have come up with a solution for them
as dramatic as insulin had been for Elizabeth Evans
Hughes.

Just as she was winding up her talk with Eddie's
mother, Elizabeth was paged to the phone and found
a frantic Perry Weston on the other end of the line.

"Elizabeth, thank God!"

"Perry, what is it?"

"I got a call from Cliff Morgan a couple of minutes ago. You know, the head of the Morgan Foundation. They're not due to make a decision on the
grant until next month, but he suddenly wants to come
in and have lunch with me."

"That's good."

"Maybe it's bad. Maybe he wants to kiss us off nicely. Maybe he'll offer us a few thousand dollars as a sop. And something else—he said he wants to meet you."

"Me?"

"Have you been holding out on me or something? Making contacts with the grants people?"

"Perry, I don't know Cliff Morgan. And I've been too busy with my patients to cultivate the grants people."

"Well, maybe someone mentioned you to him."

"All right, I'll meet you for lunch."

"Come to my office at twelve."

Elizabeth kept a blue knit dress and a pair of high heels in her locker for just such occasions. At ten to twelve she slipped down the hall, changed, and applied a little makeup. There was no harm in helping Perry get the grant money by being charming—and she saw the two waiting men look up appreciatively as she opened the door to the chief of staff's office.

"Elizabeth, so glad you could make it. I'd like you to meet Cliff Morgan."

Elizabeth shook hands with a tall, muscular man with gray hair who somehow didn't look much like a foundation head.

"We haven't met before, have we?" she asked.

His smile was warm. "I'm mighty sure I'd remember a woman as attractive as you."

"Why, thank you," she murmured.

"I've heard about your work. You have a right fine reputation, and I wanted to meet you."

The trio started down the hall to the staff dining room.

"Dr. Weston has been telling me about your amazing results with CF children."

"It's not just me. There's been dramatic progress in treatment in the past few years. Now that they've found the gene that causes disease, there's a good chance of developing a cure."

Morgan sighed. "I wish I could be as optimistic about my brothers."

"Do they have cystic fibrosis?"

"No. Huntington's Disease."

"Oh, I'm sorry." Elizabeth knew Huntington's Disease was also of genetic origin. But unlike CF, most victims didn't begin showing symptoms until well into adulthood. The disease usually attacked certain nerve tissues and the cerebral cortex, resulting in jerky body movements, intellectual deterioration, psychosis—and finally paralysis and death.

"I guess I'm old enough to figure I don't have it, thank the Lord. You don't know what it's like, watching someone going downhill like that."

Elizabeth murmured a sympathetic response.

They entered the dining room, and the hostess showed them to a table. When the waitress had taken drink orders, Morgan went on with his story.

"But that's how I got interested in genetic diseases. For a long time after my older brother got sick, we thought he was crazy. The same thing happened with my grandfather."

"Years ago, no one suspected Huntington's was a neurological disease," Elizabeth agreed. "The medical profession made assumptions—sometimes tragic assumptions—based on the current knowledge."

Morgan nodded. "But the doctors finally made a diagnosis with my older brother, Jed. Of course, with the younger one, we had a much better idea about what was happening when his personality started to change."

"Did either brother have any children?" Perry asked.

Elizabeth knew he was thinking that they'd have a fifty-percent chance of inheriting the disease.

"Just one—my nephew."

"Does he—?"

"Too early to tell. I pray for that boy."

What was it like, waiting to see if you were slowly going to lose your control over your body—and control over your mind? Elizabeth wondered. And knowing just how terrible it was going to be, because you had watched it happening to someone you love? Would you risk getting married? Having kids?

She glanced up to see that Cliff was looking at her as if he were following her thoughts. She flushed slightly.

"It was my nephew who insisted on setting aside a portion of the profits from our business to finance charitable contributions to medical institutions," Morgan continued. "We're still a small foundation, just getting started. And we pick our projects carefully. Most of our grants have been in the area of Huntington's research, for obvious reasons."

Elizabeth could see that Perry was holding his breath and felt the same sort of tension. Whatever she might think of Perry personally, Morgan Foundation money would mean a lot to Children's Hospital.

"My nephew and I both looked at your funding request. In fact, he talked to me about it yesterday." Morgan paused. "We're both impressed with the counseling program you've proposed."

She saw Perry take a nervous sip of his drink.

"I'd like to have something in Kentucky comparable to what they have at say, Johns Hopkins or the Mayo Clinic. Not just for families at risk for HD, but for other genetic diseases, too."

"That's what we were thinking," Perry managed, his voice several notes above its usual tenor.

"Suppose we give you half a million to get that counselling program started."

Perry's usual polish deserted him, and his eyes practically popped out of his head. "That's— That's a lot more than we asked for."

Morgan's smile widened. "Yes, it is."

The waitress came back to take their orders, and the discussion continued during lunch. Elizabeth was pretty sure Perry barely tasted his food. She knew she didn't taste her own.

She left the meeting feeling elated. But the euphoria didn't last. She wanted to tell someone about the Morgan Foundation grant. Not just anyone. Ben Rittenhouse. But he'd made it abundantly clear he didn't want anything more to do with her.

CHAPTER SIX

CLERKS from Hospital Records brought requested patient charts directly to examination rooms or physicians' offices. However, the staff was responsible for returning the records to a rolling cart near the secretary's desk. Anyone who didn't attend to the task promptly received a bright green reminder slip from the head of the records department.

Elizabeth was just gathering up a set of charts that needed returning before she went home, when the phone on her desk rang.

"Dr. Salvatore," she answered crisply, clasping the folders against her chest with one arm.

"Lisbeth." The familiar voice still had the ability to stroke her like a caress. Today it was edged with uncertainty.

The folders cascaded to the surface of the desk, scattering papers in all directions. Elizabeth sat down heavily in her padded leather chair.

"Ben." It took her several seconds to manage more than that one syllable. When she spoke again, it was impossible to hold her voice steady. "I didn't think I was going to hear from you."

"I know. I, uh, finally came to the conclusion that I wasn't being very mature, stompin' into the house like that."

"Oh."

"I want to explain some things to you."

"What?"

"I guess I'd rather not go into it over the phone."

"All right."

"I went out yesterday and brought your things back to the cabin. I was thinking, maybe tomorrow you could meet me out there and pick them up."

Elizabeth opened her appointment book. "I could get away around four."

"Then I'll see you after five-thirty."

"Wait. How's your hand?"

"Fine. My doctor says you did a wonderful job of sewing it up."

"I got an A in sewing in junior high school. It was just a matter of transferring the technology."

Ben laughed. "Listen—I've got to get going. Got some things to take care of."

She would have liked to prolong the conversation but after a brief exchange of goodbyes set the receiver carefully into the cradle. Then she leaned back in her chair and clasped her hands around the padded armrests. Her fingers stroked across the leather finding the tiny lines where the covering had been folded and pulled almost smooth over the foam rubber.

Today was Wednesday. What was so important it couldn't wait until the weekend?

It was almost like the times when the parents of one of her patients were worried about getting bad news and insisted on an early appointment so they wouldn't have to sit around stewing. No, that was silly, Elizabeth told herself. She was reading too much into her brief conversation with Ben. Yet as the rest of the evening and the next day dragged by, she suspected more and more that she felt like one of those parents, waiting for a distressing interview with Dr. Salvatore.

Because some test results were late coming back from the lab, Elizabeth's final appointment lasted longer than she'd anticipated. She'd brought a pair of jeans and a T-shirt to the hospital. Now she didn't want to take the time to change. The two-piece, jade-green dress she was wearing under her white coat would be fine, she told herself. Her white moccasins might get scuffed up, however, so she changed into a pair of old loafers that she kept in her locker. The combination looked a bit odd, she decided, as she gave herself a quick inspection in the full-length mirror on the door of the staff locker room, but it would have to do.

It was almost twenty after four when Elizabeth finally left the hospital. The traffic on the Mountain Parkway, however, was fairly light, and she made reasonable time, although she had to keep herself from pushing the car past the speed limit.

Ben's Jeep was already parked under the trees when she pulled off the access road to the cabin. Opening the car door, she looked toward the primitive log building and thought about the modern stone and wood house where Ben lived during the week. It had to be a lot plusher inside than this humble abode.

Ben had told her coming to the forest was like stepping into another world. Did that mean he was trying to escape anxieties and responsibilities? Or did this place bring him a sense of renewal? She suspected it was a little of both.

She stood for a moment, her eyes fixed on the rough logs, then heard a dull cracking and a splintering sound. Several seconds later, she realized it was coming from somewhere to her right. It sounded as if someone was chopping wood. But it couldn't be Ben. Not with a half-healed gash in the palm of his hand. He'd split the stitches open.

Curious, she walked around the cabin. About fifty yards from the front door was a large woodpile and a chopping block. Dressed in jeans and a powder-blue knit shirt that exposed the tan skin of his forearms, Ben was standing with his back to her, an ax in his right hand. His left hand, the one he'd hurt, hung at his side.

The wheat-blond hair at the back of his neck curled slightly, and Elizabeth could see that it was damp with perspiration.

He was chopping wood. It must be awkward work. Why was he doing it now, when he wouldn't be needing the fuel for months?

Probably she should let him know she was there, she thought. Probably he wouldn't like to discover her watching him when he was unaware. She opened her mouth to speak but closed it again when he put down the ax, picked up a sawed-off log with his right hand, and set it upright upon the block. She had assumed the maneuver would be clumsy. Now she realized that even one-handed, he had a grace and economy of movement that she found fascinating. Muscles rippled when he reached for the ax again and swung it over his head, still using only his good hand. The tool came down with surprising force and accuracy, smashing the log into the block with a thud, then bit-ing through its heart. The two pieces fell apart and toppled to the ground. Ben was reaching to pick one up when Elizabeth found her voice.

"Are you sure you should be doing that?"

Ben set the piece of wood on top of the pile. Then he turned slowly. "I was starting to wonder if you were coming."

"I couldn't get away any sooner."

He continued to look at her as if she were the one who'd requested the meeting.

"Are you sure you're not going to hurt yourself?" she repeated, at a loss for what else to say. She'd thought he wanted to talk about something important. He certainly didn't seem in a hurry to get on with it.

"I need the exercise."

"Let me see how your cut's doing."

Almost reluctantly he held out his arm.

Elizabeth crossed the ten feet that separated them. Taking his hand, she turned it palm up and lowered her eyes to the gash that slashed across the palm. Although it was knitting nicely, the skin was still slightly swollen, so that her neat black stitches were partially hidden.

"It's healing well."

He stood with one leg rigid, the other slightly bent. She remembered that stance. It was a sign of tension.

"You did a good job."

"Any pain."

"Not if I remember to keep it still."

She nodded, although she wasn't simply evaluating the healing process. She was equally aware that she was holding Ben's large, masculine hand; his flesh was warm and damp from his recent exertions. The musky, male scent of his body teased her nostrils.

When she raised her eyes to his, for just a second she caught an unguarded yearning in their blue depths that stole the breath from her lungs. Then he pulled his arm back, and she had the sensation that he was willing all expression out of his face.

"How was your meeting with Cliff Morgan?" he asked, his words clipped.

"He gave us—" She stopped abruptly. "How do you know about my meeting with Cliff Morgan?"

"I suggested he have lunch with you and Dr. Weston on Tuesday."

Elizabeth's brow furrowed. "What do you have to do with Cliff Morgan?"

"He's my uncle."

Her mind scrambled to process the new information. Why hadn't Morgan mentioned Ben?

"His brother, Jed Morgan, is my father," Ben added helpfully.

"But he told us his brother Jed has Huntington's Disease."

"Yes."

She stared at him uncomprehendingly, trying to take in what she was hearing. In medical school she'd memorized human anatomy, the symptoms of countless diseases and their treatment. Surely she had the background to understand what he was saying? This particular knowledge, however, refused to sink into the fibers of her brain. "I don't understand. Your name isn't Morgan."

"When my father first started getting sick, he was violent and erratic. A couple of times he beat my mother up. She got so spooked that finally she packed up our clothes and a few other things one day while he was at work. As soon as I got home from school, we went down to the bus station, and she bought tickets to northern Florida. We lived in Tallahassee. My mother took back her maiden name, Rittenhouse, although she didn't get divorced till later. Rittenhouse is my legal name, too."

Elizabeth could see him struggling to remain aloof, detached, matter-of-fact. Yet the hurt and sadness— and the anger—were there in his eyes and in his posture. She had a sudden picture of a bewildered little boy, ripped away from everything he knew and plunked down in an alien environment.

"Uncle Cliff kept looking for us. He finally tracked us down when I was nineteen," he continued in a flat voice. "He explained that my father was suffering from a physical disease, not a mental disorder, but Mom just didn't want to get involved again. I guess she figured there was no point in comin' back to what was left of the man she'd married." His Adam's apple bobbed. "But I missed my father. I mean, the closeness we had before he got sick. All the time we'd spent together out here. Building the cabin. Fishing. Palling around. So I came back to Kentucky."

"You didn't know what to expect, did you?"

He shook his head. "My father could barely talk coherently anymore. When I saw him try to walk and sort of dance across the room or not have enough muscle control to pick up a glass of water, I wanted to cry. But bad as that was, it wasn't the worst part."

When he hesitated, she sensed he was hauling up his next words from some deep well at the core of his soul.

"I started asking some questions about Huntington's. I found out it was hereditary—and that I had a fifty-fifty chance of ending up a basket case like my father."

"Ben—"

He shook his head and cut her off. "I want you to understand all of it. I guess I had some wild idea that I could outrun it. Or maybe pretend it wasn't lurking in the dark like a goblin in a haunted house, ready to jump out and grab me. That's why I lit out and joined the Marines." He laughed. "I didn't take a chance on the medical questionnaire. I lied about my family background. The corps gave me a feeling of belonging. I gave them everything I had. I was the best damn fighter that ever wore the uniform. It took about five years for me to admit that you can't run away from your destiny. So instead of reenlisting, I came back to Lexington. I think somehow it helps the old man to have me around, although it's hard to be sure now. He's just about paralyzed. And his mind...well..." The sentence trailed off, ending in a shrug.

"Oh, Ben. I'm so sorry." To her own ears, the words sounded ridiculously inadequate.

He didn't seem to notice. "After you said you worked at Children's Hospital, I sat down and studied the grant proposal Perry Weston had sent us. It was well thought out. Your testing program should help a lot of people. So I recommended to Cliff that we let you have the money."

"But..."

"Lisbeth, it was the only thing I could give you."

"No. Don't say that."

"After you dropped me at my house, I wasn't going to call you. Then I decided it wasn't fair to leave you thinking any of what happened last weekend was your fault."

"Stop. Please. Don't."

"There's something you need to understand. It's not you. I made up my mind a long time ago that there was only one way I could possibly live my life and still hang on to my self-respect. . . ."

She didn't want to hear any more. If he kept talking, she would scream. They were only three feet apart. She took a step forward.

Ben met her halfway. He had been fighting desperately to stay detached, impersonal, remote from this woman. He knew that if he gave in to the need to hold her and kiss her, he was lost.

In that first instant of contact, he knew he had been right. He was lost.

There was nothing detached about the sound that welled from deep in his chest when she took him into her arms. There was nothing remote about the raw hunger of his lips as they came down onto hers. And nothing impersonal about the way his good hand skimmed down her back and found the curve of her hip so that he could anchor her against himself.

His lips angled over hers, asking her mouth to open for him. There was no hesitation on Elizabeth's part. She wanted to taste him, experience him, blend with him.

When his tongue breached the velvety barrier of her lips to investigate the sweetness beyond, Elizabeth surrendered with a low moan of pleasure.

He muttered her name, the syllables almost obliterated by the urgent pressure of his mouth against hers.

She felt his body quiver, and any doubts about his wanting her, man to woman, were swept away by the waves of sensual tension that radiated from him. They caught her, too, and swept her along on a tide of feeling so powerful that she almost forgot to breathe.

His hands cupped her bottom, molding her against himself. She heard him groan and knew part of the reaction was from pain. In the heat of passion he had forgotten about his injured hand.

"Ben. Oh, Ben."

For a moment he held her tighter. Words tumbled from his lips. They were jerky and disjointed, more passionate than coherent. "Darlin', you look so damn pretty in that green dress. I've never seen you in a dress before. I wanted to kiss you that first time I held you in my arms. Down in that crevasse in the ground."

Her mind had stopped functioning rationally. There was only instinct, desire, the need to merge her being with his. He would take her into the cabin. They would make love on the wide bunk. And everything would be all right. She would make him understand that the things he'd just told her weren't as important as the magic of what they'd found together.

He had gone very still. She heard him suck a deep, shuddering breath into his lungs. Her eyes fluttered open. His were dark with passion—and something else that brought a cold knot of ice to her stomach.

"What is it?" The world seemed to tip and sway. But her heart was still pounding wildly from the sensations his kisses and caresses had aroused.

"I shouldn't have kissed you."

She didn't understand, and tried to tell him so with her eyes. Nothing had ever felt so right.

"Lisbeth, we can't."

He moved a few inches away, and the reality of his rejection sank in. When the warmth of his body left hers, she shivered. "So you're the one who makes all the decisions? I don't get a vote?"

He closed his eyes and bent to rest his forehead against hers. "I have to be the one."

She tried to pull herself out of his grasp. His good hand anchored itself to her shoulder.

"This isn't just about you and me right here and now. Although, God knows, I wish it were."

"What is it about?"

"It's about my somewhat murky future. I've read a lot about HD. It's subtle at first, you know. Maybe the people around you start to notice personality changes, coarsening of sensitivities, irritability, uncontrolled aggression. That's stage one. They say you can still hold a job in stage one. Maybe even stage two, if you switch to something that isn't very demanding. Stage three you probably need to be reminded to brush your teeth in the morning and shave. If you can still hold a toothbrush and shave without cutting yourself. The really grotesque physical manifestations come later."

"Ben, stop!"

He ignored her anguished plea. "The worst part is that the patient remains surprisingly insightful about what's happening to him. And the whole process is so damn slow. It takes years to die. But finally you're sort of like the husk of a melon, only all the substance has been sucked out.''

"You don't know that's going to happen to you. There's as much chance that it won't.''

"And as much chance that it will.''

"Ben, there's a test now. A way to find out if you have the gene.''

"I know. Since 1983. I told you, I've read just about everything there is to read about the damn disease. Unfortunately, the test was only about eighty-five to ninety-five percent accurate.''

"But now—''

"Now they've found a DNA segment more tightly linked to the Huntington's gene. They can test with ninety-nine percent accuracy.''

Elizabeth nodded. He really must keep up with the medical literature.

"Three months ago, I decided I couldn't stand waiting for the coin to hit the table so I could see if it was heads or tails. Even if the news was going to be bad, I had to know what was going to happen to me. So I applied to the testing program at Johns Hopkins in Baltimore.''

Her mouth had gone so dry she could barely speak. Did he already know the worst? Was that why he was struggling so hard to keep her at arm's length? "They didn't—didn't give you bad news, did they?''

"They haven't given me a nickel's worth of useful information yet.''

Her knees sagged, and she reached out to steady herself. When she realized she was clutching a handful of his shirtfront, she dropped her arm to her side.

"It's not like going in for a TB test," he went on, as if he hadn't taken any notice of her reaction. "First they make you go through a bunch of psychological and IQ testing—I guess so they'll have some bench-mark when you start going downhill."

"Not when. If."

He shrugged. "After they're satisfied that you're reasonably sane, they do the genetic studies. But they have to test the people in your family they know have the gene, too. And the people who don't have it. Otherwise they can't tell whether you've inherited the Huntington's marker. I suspect the problem right now is that my Aunt Ada is blocking their access to my Uncle Max."

"But why?"

"I think she doesn't want to admit he's really got the damn disease. He's still in the early stages, and that's how she's dealing with her sense of loss."

Silence stretched.

"Lisbeth, everybody has their own defense mecha-nisms, their own way of coping with something so terrible that it makes you want to curse God for al-lowing it to happen. I decided a long time ago that I wasn't going to leave anyone in the lurch the way my dad did. Or, God forbid, start beating up on a bunch of innocent people who happened to be trapped in the same house with me. Even if I don't get violent the way he did, I don't want to have anyone—who—who I cared about—see me falling apart bit by bit."

"Who you care about," she repeated softly.

He turned away, and she couldn't see his face. Af-ter a moment he reached for her hand. His fingers were strong and firm around hers. She felt that rock-like steadiness she had sensed the first time they'd met. Then she hadn't understood. Now she knew it was an outward manifestation of the control that had become second nature to him. Yet this afternoon his words betrayed the turmoil still raging inside him. "I'm too restless to keep standing here like this. Come on. Let's walk."

She let him lead her away from the cabin in a direction they hadn't gone before. Another time she would have looked around with enjoyment at the tall trees on either side of the trail and the delicate ferns carpeting the loamy ground. Now she barely took note of the sun filtering through the branches of the maple and sycamore trees.

"Ben, there are no guarantees in life—for anybody."

"I'm sorry if I gave you the impression I thought there were."

She was silent for several heartbeats. Then she asked quietly, "How old are you?"

"Thirty."

"My husband was twenty-nine when a truck came over the crest of a hill and plowed into our car. You've already had more time than he did."

"That's right. But up until the moment the truck hit him, he was looking forward to a long, happy life with you."

"You have all the answers, don't you!" she shot back.

"I've thought about this a lot. What do you think I do when I lie awake in the middle of the night?"

She remembered the night he'd sat at their campsite, staring into the fire. Now she understood. "I haven't had much time to marshal my arguments," she said in a low voice.

He gave her a considering glance. "It's not a debate."

"What is it?"

They rounded a curve to discover a giant rock bisecting the trail. Ben grasped Elizabeth's hand, and they made their way around it. They were deep in the forest now, and the air was cool and fragrant with the smell of pine.

"Darlin', I'm not used to talking about how I feel. In fact, it makes me damn uncomfortable, but I need to make you understand. The day we met I'd come out here because I was feelin' about as jumpy as a bullfrog on a bed of hot coals."

Elizabeth didn't try to interrupt. One thing she'd learned about Ben; he'd find his own way of telling her what he wanted her to know.

"I'd just come back from my third trip to Johns Hopkins. They'd taken blood samples already. So when I went up to Baltimore, I was expecting to find out the test results. Instead, they told me they weren't sure how long it would take. As soon as I got back to Lexington, I came out here to be alone."

"And you stumbled on me."

He squeezed her hand. "Yeah. There you were, down in that crevasse, so sweet and vulnerable. And so damn brave."

"I was scared."

"It was all so unexpected. Coming on you like that. You made me think of wood spirits and elves. I told myself I didn't want to get to know you. I told myself the best thing would be to turn you over to a forest ranger. But I just couldn't seem to make myself cut you loose.''

"I guess I felt the same way."

"Yeah. Well, I couldn't stop myself from asking you to come back the next weekend. Even though I knew it was a damn fool mistake, five seconds after I'd done it.''

"Why?" Her voice sounded so thin, Elizabeth thought, that it seemed to float away into the leafy quiet of the forest. Maybe if she could just keep the dialogue going—maybe there was a chance she'd make him see things differently.

"Because I knew it would be too damn easy to want all the things I've told myself I could never have." He leaned the back of his head against the rough bark of a sycamore tree. "That night after you told me about your husband, you went back to sleep so trustingly next to me. I couldn't keep my hands off you. First I had to run my fingers through your hair. Then I cupped my hand around your breast.''

His words brought a flush to her face and a wave of heat to her body.

"No wonder you woke up hot as a five-dollar pistol. Instead of making you feel better, I had to turn it around and make you the guilty one, because I couldn't handle my own feelings. Maybe if I'd just wanted you physically, it wouldn't have been so bad. But I wanted a whole lot more than sex. I still do.''

"Why are you telling me this?"

His lips parted and emitted a broken breath. "Because I want you to understand how hard it is for me to say that we can't see each other now. Maybe we never can. It all depends on finding out whether I'm going to end up like my father."

Elizabeth hunched her shoulders and cupped her forehead in her hands. It took her several seconds to realize how she felt. She had expected to be overwhelmed by sadness or despair. Instead she realized she was angry. Perhaps it wasn't fair or rational, yet somehow the emotion was liberating.

"Lisbeth?"

Slowly she raised her head. "I thought a lot of things about you, Ben Rittenhouse. I didn't realize you were a coward."

"I'm not!"

"What was it you called it? A defense mechanism?"

"Haven't you understood a damn thing I've been saying? I'm trying to protect you."

"Maybe that's what you'd like to think, but you're really trying to protect yourself. Isn't that what you've been doing all along? Not just with me. For years. With anyone and everyone who ever tried to reach out to you."

Instead of answering, he stared back at her, his cheeks flushed.

"You're afraid to get involved. Afraid to let yourself love. Afraid some other woman will let you down the way your mother did with your father."

"Damn you. Nobody talks to me like that."

Elizabeth pressed her hand to her mouth. He was right. Anger and frustration had made her speak out of turn. "I'm sorry," she whispered. Turning quickly, she started back up the trail.

CHAPTER SEVEN

BEN WALKED SLOWLY into the hospital room and stood glancing around as if he hadn't been there a hundred times before. Four institutional-green walls circumscribed the tiny universe. Deliberately he looked at everything else first—the closet door with the dent near the bottom, the leatherette chair, the oxygen tank—before letting his eyes come to rest on the shrunken figure lying between the metal railings that guarded the bed.

"Hello, Dad."

The old man didn't move or glance toward the door. It had been years since he'd spoken a coherent word. Years since he'd shown any interest in visitors. Now, in fact, there was no sign that he even knew he'd been addressed.

"How are you feeling?" Ben had given up expecting any answer. There were times he came to this room and sat silently in the chair beside the bed. This afternoon, the need to communicate was like steam pressure building up inside his chest. "The drive over was pretty good," he continued. "Not too much traffic."

He crossed the tile floor and stood beside the bed, studying Jed Morgan's still form. His father's jaw was slack, his eyelids half-shut. He might have been a statue, except for the breathing tube taped to his nose and the shallow rise and fall of his chest under the neatly turned-down covers. He couldn't last much longer, not like this, Ben thought.

Well, he would face the end when he came to it, just the way he'd faced everything else. "It's Ben, your son," he continued. "I've been thinking a lot about you this week. About old times. I was out at the cabin again. The one we built when I was eight." He laughed. "Well, you did most of the work. But remember how you told me I was your right-hand man? God, was I proud to be helpin' my dad with something so important. I guess I never said it before. But you were a great father before you got sick. That's why—" He stopped abruptly. *Stick to the good stuff,* he ordered himself.

"Do you remember the first time we spent the night out there? The two of us sitting around the fire, roasting apples. And all our big man talk about not letting any woman come out to visit us there? But all the time we secretly knew Mom would never agree to roughing it with us out in the woods, anyway." He laughed. It was impossible to keep his thoughts off certain subjects. "Well, after all these years, the joke is on me. There's this woman who likes coming out there to the cabin and roughing it. Her name's Elizabeth Salvatore. And she even likes sleeping down by the stream at that campsite we made."

Ben stopped talking again and dragged in a lungful of air. Although his head was still turned toward the old man on the bed, he knew his attention was elsewhere. "I didn't want to tell you about her before. It was something private. But it doesn't really matter now. God, she's beautiful. I guess you could say she's delicate looking. Fragile, even. But she's got strength. I think if you dumped the world on her shoulders, she'd try to carry it.

"But I didn't know that at first. Because when I found her I was frozen inside, like a mountain man staggering through an endless ice storm." He shuddered. "Then I looked down through this fissure in the ice, and there she was, waiting for me. It wasn't cold where she was. It was like springtime. Like warmth and light. Do you know how tempting it is to beg her to take away the cold? But she's right. I'm afraid to drag her into the Arctic with me," he admitted ruefully. How anguished he must sound!

The man on the bed didn't comment.

"I shouldn't have met up with her. It was just some damn ironic twist of fate. And I sure as hell shouldn't have let myself get involved. But I couldn't turn away from the pleasure of talking to her, the pleasure of touching her, the pleasure of kissing her." The room came back into focus, and he found himself gazing into Jed's eyes. Once they had been the same bright blue as his own. They'd been sparkling with life and humor. They'd been wise in their understanding of a small boy's needs. Now they were as dull and lifeless as stagnant water.

"In a way you were lucky." Ben punctuated the statement with a brittle chuckle. "I know it probably sounds crazy to tell a guy who can't move and can't think that he's lucky. What I mean is, if something like Huntington's is going to sap the life out of you bit by bit, it's better not to have a road map of what's happening. But it won't be like that for me."

Ben fell silent once more. When he looked down at his hands, he was startled to see that they were shaking. Heart pounding, he took several deep breaths and tried to will his body to calm, to steadiness. This was just a case of nerves, he told himself. Just a reaction to the terrible images he'd conjured up. Himself in that bed instead of his father. Slack jawed. Brain dead. But his mind didn't accept the logical explanation. For paralyzing seconds he felt as if the walls were closing in on him. Then, with a half-formed sob, he turned and bolted from the room.

OVER THE WEEK since her last visit to the cabin Elizabeth kept telling herself that she probably wasn't going to see Ben Rittenhouse again. Especially after the accusations she'd hurled at him. She told herself that with his attitude, it was probably for the best. She told herself there was no reason she needed to start doing research on Huntington's Disease. Finally she went to the hospital computer center and tied into Medlars, the information network designed to give physicians and other health professionals access to material on various medical topics. Within forty-five minutes she had printed out a wide selection of articles, both from medical journals and from publications directed at families of HD patients.

That evening she took the stack of material home. After fixing a tuna sandwich and some salad for dinner, she sat down at the kitchen table and began to read. She already knew something about HD. However, she'd never studied it in depth or from such a personal perspective.

The progressive neurological disease had first been described in 1872 by George Huntington. At first it was known as Huntington's Chorea, after the Greek word for dance, because of the jerky, twisting, uncontrollable movements of the muscles that HD patients often suffered.

The defective gene was as likely to occur in males as in females and could be inherited from either the mother or the father. Because the gene was a dominant one, it never skipped a generation, and the chances of passing the disease on to an offspring was fifty-fifty.

There was a long period of latency, during which no symptoms were present. Age of onset was usually between thirty and fifty, with those inheriting the gene from their father more likely to develop symptoms early rather than late.

Elizabeth pushed her sandwich away and for several moments sat with her eyes closed, trying to dispel the clogged feeling in her chest. Ben had told her he was thirty. Probably he'd read the same literature she was now perusing. Finally she gave up trying to conquer her tension and turned to another article.

There was a lot more material, some of it highly technical information about PET scan diagnosis of brain changes. It offered one note of hope. Measurable brain abnormalities did not precede symptoms. Which meant that if some kind of drug could be developed to retard the course of the disease and treatment were started early, the results would probably be excellent.

Realizing her fingers were gripping the edge of the paper, Elizabeth forced them to relax. The article had been written several years ago. Had researchers gotten any closer to finding an effective medication? She'd have to do some checking.

It was after midnight before she finally admitted her vision was growing too blurry to continue. Maybe she'd been hoping for some startling information that would have to change Ben's outlook on life, she admitted as she dragged herself down the hall to bed. The available literature had provided her with facts. Unfortunately it hadn't given her a beacon she could offer to Ben.

Sleep might have been a refuge from her troubled thoughts. Tonight, though, it played traitor again. This time her unconscious served up a new dream.

She walked slowly down the hall to the hospital room, dragging her feet, trying to hold herself back. No good. The door loomed in front of her. Like a magnet, it seemed to draw her forward. Against her will, her hand reached out. There was no sensation of turning the knob or crossing the threshold. Suddenly she was in the room, standing beside the bed.

She turned her head away. But it swiveled back. There was nowhere to look except at the man lying still as death, his eyes dull, his breathing shallow.

"No!" *The exclamation was part scream, part sob.* "No, Ben! No!"

Her own voice woke her. Or perhaps it was the sheer, black terror. For long moments she lay shaking, the covers pulled protectively around her chin.

I'm making progress, she thought, *fighting hysteria. I'm not having nightmares about my husband bleeding to death now. I'm having nightmares about a man who could end up mute and paralyzed in a hospital bed. The good part is that if they tell him he has the Huntington's gene, he says he never wants to see me again.*

SCHOOL HAD BEEN OUT for almost a month when Ellen Jackson came back to Children's Hospital—on a mission of her own.

As soon as she entered the building, she ducked into the ladies' room and smoothed her blond hair with a few quick strokes of the little plastic brush from her purse. Then she dabbed on some fresh lip gloss. Standing back, she tried to get a look at her Indian cotton dress in the small mirror over the sink. It seemed okay. Maybe she should have worn nylons and heels instead of sandals. No. Her legs were nice and tan, and she only wore nylons in summer when Mom insisted.

Ellen tossed her hair over her shoulders, hoping she looked mature. And hoping Dr. Salvatore wouldn't guess that her stomach was tied up like a pretzel.

It took her another few minutes in the bathroom to psych herself up. Then she flung the door open and practically flew down the hall. It was kind of strange coming to see Dr. Salvatore when she didn't feel sick or wasn't due for a checkup, she mused, hearing her leather thongs slap against the tile floor of the hallway. But there was no one else she could talk to. Good old Mom would have a conniption fit if Ellen tried to bring up the subject she wanted to discuss with the doctor.

At the reception desk, the woman in the white uniform asked for her name and medical number.

"Have a seat, dear, while I ring the doctor."

Ellen perched on the edge of an upholstered plastic chair. She hadn't exactly made an appointment, but she'd called yesterday and found out that Dr. Salvatore had a free hour this afternoon. She hoped dropping in would be okay.

Reading was beyond her at the moment. She was trying to concentrate on the ads in an old issue of *Glamour* when the woman called her name. "You can go right in."

Dr. Salvatore smiled warmly, momentarily erasing the worried look from her face. "When they told me you were in the waiting room, I was afraid you were feeling sick. But you look terrific. You're okay, aren't you?"

"Yes. I'm really good," Ellen assured her quickly. She leaned over, rapped her knuckles against the edge of the desk, and slipped into a chair.

"Well, it's great to see you. What can I do for you?"

"You said any time I wanted to talk to you, I could—we could . . ." She'd been planning to play the scene adult and sophisticated. Now she was stammering like a little kid who hadn't brought her homework to school.

"Of course."

Ellen willed her heart to stop pounding. "I got my license a couple of months ago. So I drove myself over."

"It's nice to be mobile."

Might as well cut the chitchat and get this over with, Ellen told herself. She took a deep breath and let it out slowly. "I wanted to ask you something I've been wondering about for a while. Is it possible for some-one with CF to get pregnant?"

Dr. Salvatore's answer stuck to the clinical facts. "Boys with the disease usually have a low sperm count. Girls don't have any reproductive problems. But pregnancy does put a tremendous strain on their bodies. A woman with cystic fibrosis who wanted to have a baby would have to consider things very carefully."

"Then, if I—if I wanted to have a—a—sexual relationship with someone special, I'd need to use birth control," Ellen said in a rush.

Elizabeth blinked, wondering if she'd heard that right. But no, from the strained look on Ellen's face, she knew she hadn't mistaken the real subject of the conversation—or the implications. "The simple answer is yes."

"Would you be able to write me a prescription for the pill?"

"Ellen, the pill wouldn't be a very good idea for you. And it wouldn't protect you against sexually transmitted diseases."

"Then what—?"

Elizabeth hoped she sounded unruffled. "Let's back up a little." She could see the sixteen-year-old across from her swallow nervously. "You met someone who means a lot to you?" she questioned softly. "A boy you really like?"

"That's right. So don't start off trying to talk me out of something I want." The girl's tone had gone from tentative to belligerent.

"I'm here to listen, not argue you out of anything."

"Yeah, well, lots of girls younger than me have boyfriends, but I've never had one before, you know. Now I'm going with Brian. He really likes me, and I like him."

"He's your age?"

"He'll be a senior next year, but he was in my history class. I was real excited when he asked me to the dance at the end of the year, but I didn't let myself get my hopes up."

"You're still going out with him?"

"Yes. He got this job as a lifeguard. When he's not on duty, we hang out together. Some evenings we watch TV at his house." Her chin jutted up. "Sometimes his parents aren't home when we're there."

Elizabeth was suddenly swamped by memories that had been buried for years. All at once she vividly recalled teenage evenings like that—alone in the den with a boy she really liked. Although her mom had always insisted that they keep the door open, that hadn't ruled out turning down the lights and sitting close together on the couch. Sometimes it had been awfully hard to stop herself from letting things go too far, but there was a line she hadn't stepped over until she'd met Jim. On the other hand, things were different for so many young people today, perhaps especially different for someone like Ellen.

"It's hard to make adult decisions when you don't have a lot of experience. But coming here to talk things over with me is a real sign of maturity. It makes me feel good—because it means you trust me."

Across from her, Ellen let out the breath she'd been holding. "I knew Mom couldn't handle this kind of discussion. Sex makes her nervous. I think she wishes I were still a little kid."

"She's just being protective."

The young woman nodded.

Under the desk, Elizabeth knit her fingers together, hoping she was handling things right. Giving sexual advice to teenagers was completely outside her specialty. All she could do was go on instinct and reach back into her own life for feelings and experiences. If there was ever a time to share her own first tentative yearnings toward love, it was now. "I remember the first guy I really liked," she said in a soft voice. "We went together during our sophomore years in high school, and we were so close. Then he went away to stay with his father in Seattle for the summer. For a while, we wrote to each other every day and talked on the phone, late at night, when the rates were low. But gradually he stopped writing and calling. It turned out he'd met a girl out there that he liked a lot. In fact, he decided not to come back to Baltimore at all. I never saw him again."

Ellen stared at her. "But you're so pretty and so smart. How could he do something like that to you?"

"Circumstances change. Feelings change. Relationships change. Especially when you're young." The words might have been dispassionate, yet Elizabeth remembered pain as she spoke. "At the time, I wasn't quite so philosophical. I felt like it was the end of the world. But it would have made me feel a lot worse if we'd gone all the way."

"Are you trying to tell me that Brian and I will break up?"

"Ellen, I know it's hard to think about the future when you're only sixteen, but it's not likely that the relationship is going to be permanent."

The teenager was silent for several moments, and Elizabeth felt a clot of tension swell in her chest.

"I do think about the future. But not the way you mean. You said I was pretty healthy right now. That still means I have to take twenty-five pills a day and keep on schedule with my thumping sessions. We both know I could get a lot sicker. If I went around coughing and sick all the time, no guy would want to hang out with me." Ellen gulped. "Or, you know, if I had another hemorrhage or something like that, I could die."

"Oh, Ellen." Elizabeth scrambled out of her seat and rounded the desk in a few jerky strides. Bending, she wrapped her arms around the girl's shoulders and pulled her close. The way a mother holds a daughter, she thought. Only she didn't have a daughter. Her fingers smoothed their way over Ellen's narrow back and through her long, silky hair. She looked healthy, but clutching her slender body made Elizabeth all too aware of her fragile physique.

For just a moment the girl held herself stiffly. Then she gave a little sigh and pressed her face into Elizabeth's midsection. They weren't doctor and patient any longer. They were simply two women, giving and receiving comfort. Strange, Elizabeth thought. She herself needed comfort as much as she needed to give it.

Finally Ellen tipped her head up so she could look at Elizabeth. "You can't promise I'm going to live—

the way that girl Elizabeth Evans Hughes did. Can you?''

For the second time that week the line came to her. *There aren't any guarantees in life.* This time she didn't want to say the words, but when Ellen so obviously knew the odds. ''Oh honey, I wish I could.''

''Then try to understand how I feel—just a little,'' she whispered.

''I do. Better than you know.''

''You're not sick.''

''I'm close to people who are.'' Elizabeth fought to keep her own emotions from overflowing. When she felt a bit more in control, she moved to the chair beside the girl. There was no broad wooden desk between them now. No barrier. ''There are things I want you to think about when you're deciding what to do. You haven't been dating Brian for very long. There's no hurry to rush into anything with him. Don't grasp at something just to have a particular experience. Give the relationship a chance. Find out if it's really right for the two of you.''

Ellen nodded. Elizabeth swallowed. This was a pretty heavy subject and getting heavier by the minute. But there was more she felt she had to say. ''Sex all by itself is just a biological process. What gives it joy and raises it to a profoundly moving experience between two people is emotional commitment. Two people who care about each other. Who love each other. Without that, you just have something pretty mechanical.'' She looked and saw that Ellen was hanging on every word. *Oh God, let me be doing this right,* she prayed silently.

"The worst thing would be if you went ahead for the wrong reasons and then felt bad about it—about yourself—afterward," Elizabeth added.

"I didn't think about how it would make me feel later," Ellen muttered.

"I'm willing to bet there are some good books at the library you could read. Books written for teens who want to know more about their bodies and their relationships with the opposite sex."

"Yeah. I wonder what Mom would say if she caught me reading them."

"Maybe she'd appreciate the opportunity to get into a serious discussion."

"Oh, come on."

"You might be surprised."

Ellen was thoughtful for several moments. Then she smiled. "I came in here thinking I had to make a decision right away."

"Sex is rarely an emergency."

Ellen laughed. "Really. I guess you've given me a lot to think about. Thanks."

"I'm glad you came to me."

The girl hesitated for a moment. "I wouldn't be going with Brian if it weren't for you."

Elizabeth blinked. "What do you mean?"

"Remember that day you talked to me about Elizabeth Evans Hughes?"

"Of course."

"You made me start thinking about how I want to live my life. I mean, not just let it happen to me. I was afraid to let Brian know I liked him. Then I asked myself what was the worst thing that could happen." She laughed. "All he could do was break my heart."

Elizabeth grinned. "I guess you're glad you took the plunge."

"Yeah."

The teenager stood up. So did Elizabeth, who held out her arms. Ellen came into them with no hesitation. This time they hugged fiercely.

"Take good care of yourself. And come back soon so we can talk again," Elizabeth said. "About anything that concerns you."

"I will," Ellen promised.

After the girl left, Elizabeth flopped back into her chair. Perhaps the hospital air-conditioning had gone into overdrive, because she felt goose bumps peppering her arms. Through the sleeves of her white coat, she rubbed them vigorously.

Bits and pieces of the conversation—and of the last one she'd had with Ben, out at the cabin—kept leaping from the corners of her mind. She'd taken refuge in reading about Huntington's. She'd deliberately put off the pain of doing any serious thinking about Ben and herself. All at once there was no place to hide from her thoughts.

Suddenly she couldn't sit still. Getting up, she paced to the window and stood looking down at the cars in the parking lot.

She was a woman in her early thirties. Ellen was still a teenager. But it was spooky how many parallels she could draw between the two of them. So many of the things she'd said to the girl could just as well have been applied to herself. She'd cautioned Ellen not to rush into an intimate relationship with her new boyfriend. She'd told her to wait and be sure that it was the right thing for the two of them. Only she hadn't exactly taken the sage advice she'd been dishing out. She'd been involved in a new relationship, too. With a man she'd known less than a month. A man who'd told her he might be carrying a fatal gene. He'd acted as if he were doing her a favor by sending her away. A lot of people would agree.

Yet, despite everything, the two of them together had seemed so right. If he'd taken her hand and led her to the cabin, they'd have ended up making love. But Ben had brought his rampaging emotions under control, like a stagecoach driver subduing a team of runaway horses.

She'd been hurt by his withdrawal. His rational explanations had made her blow her cool, as Ellen might put it. For the first time in years she'd reached out toward a man and asked for intimacy, and he'd turned her aside, without even considering the possibility that she had the strength of character to accept him as he was, genetic heritage and all.

Whatever happened, she and Ben had touched each other's lives in a fundamental way. He could never erase that fact, no matter how much he needed to control what happened next.

The problem was, he had forced her to play by his rules. She was used to making decisions, one way or the other, and accepting the consequences. How would she handle things if she had a real choice? she wondered. Would she still want a relationship, even knowing that he carried the gene that had struck down his father? Even knowing that she would lose him bit by bit, as surely as the earth turned and the seasons changed?

The draconian choice brought a sudden shudder to her body, and she was thankful that her thoughts were cut off by the ringing of the phone. Crossing back to the desk, she picked it up.

"Dr. Salvatore."

"Oh, Doctor, I was afraid you'd already left for the day. But I took a chance on calling. This is Mrs. Philips in the emergency room."

"What can I do for you?"

"There's a youngster here named Eddie Lakefield. His father says he's one of your new patients, and he's insisting that you see the boy. I tried to explain that the normal procedure would be to have one of the residents do an examination and decide if he needs to be admitted. But the father is being—uh—quite forceful."

From what she could pick up between the lines, Elizabeth had little trouble imagining the abrasive scene that had probably just taken place in the admissions office. Mrs. Philips was just a secretary, but was taking the heat from a worried, frustrated parent.

"No, I'll be right there," she reassured the woman. "Tell Mr. Lakefield I'll see them in the emergency room." She heard a sigh of relief at the other end of the line and hung up.

As she trotted down the hall to the elevator, Elizabeth mentally reviewed Eddie's records. What she recalled from her recent interview with the boy's mother was that his parents were divorced, and Mrs. Lakefield had custody. But now his father was bringing him in to the hospital. Probably he didn't have a lot of experience with his son's medical emergencies, which could account for his panic reaction. Or perhaps he was just the kind of guy who insisted on throwing his weight around and having his own way. She'd find out soon enough.

The emergency room could be partitioned off into small, more or less private cubicles by curtains that hung from ceiling tracks. She stepped through the door and noted that only two of the areas were closed off. Below one set of curtains she saw a pair of white trousers and knew that the patient was already being taken care of by one of the staff physicians.

Below the other set of curtains she saw a pair of scuffed boots and two lean, blue-jeaned legs, one rigid, the other bent at the knee. The image was achingly familiar. Ben. He often stood that way when he was tense.

She told herself she was crazy but couldn't stop her heart from pounding wildly as she hurried across the floor.

CHAPTER EIGHT

ELIZABETH FLUNG the curtains open and found herself staring at a man's lean hips and broad back. He was bending over the examination table and talking softly to a small boy.

"So the fox said to the raccoon..."

Hearing the curtains swish, he stopped in midsentence and spun to face her. She saw a flush spread across his cheeks.

One part of her mind was noting his reaction. The other part was eagerly taking in his appearance. Brown eyes. Dark hair. Well-cut nose. Easy to look at. But not Ben. Disappointment poured over her like a hot shower suddenly turned frigid. The reaction was all the more acute because it was irrational.

"I guess you must be Dr. Salvatore. I'm sure sorry I raised such a fuss to get you down here," he said awkwardly.

When she didn't reply, he went on, "I'm Kevin Lakefield."

Elizabeth automatically held out her hand. Kevin Lakefield. The name sounded vaguely familiar, she wasn't sure why.

They shook hands briefly. His grip was firm, but his eyes were haunted by shadows of worry and guilt. "Margaret left Eddie with me while she went out of town on a business trip. This morning he woke up coughing. I didn't think too much about it at first because he does that sometimes. This afternoon he looked flushed, so I took his temperature. It was 103°."

As she listened, Elizabeth brought herself back to reality. "You're right. We'd better check that out." She turned to the boy whose large brown eyes were swinging from one adult to the other. "How are you feeling, Eddie?"

"Not so great."

She warmed the stethoscope against her palm before pulling up the boy's shirt. "You know the routine. Take a deep breath and hold it for me."

The examination took about ten minutes. When Elizabeth finished, she sat down on a stool beside the table. "Well, Eddie, you have a slight respiratory infection. I think it would be a good idea to admit you to the hospital so we can fill you full of IV antibiotics."

The boy's face was suffused with disappointment. "I'm not gonna have to stay home from the beach next week, am I?"

"I hope not. The sooner we start the antibiotics, the sooner you'll start getting better."

Eddie didn't object. In fact he was quite cooperative, in the way of young patients who hope they can buy themselves some time off for good behavior.

Elizabeth could have gone home and left the rest of the admission procedure to the hospital staff. Instead she accompanied the Lakefields to the ward, talked to the nurse supervisor, and helped get the patient settled. It was seven before the IV had been started and

Eddie had been coaxed into eating some of the dinner a nurse's aide had brought.

Earlier the boy's father had been on edge. Now she watched the good-natured banter between the pair. They were giggling together about foxes and raccoons and bears and shooting her conspiratorial looks. Although Eddie might not live with Kevin Lakefield, the two of them seemed to have a warm relationship.

"Tomorrow I'll bring you a double burger and a shake for lunch," the father offered.

"All right!"

Kevin glanced at Elizabeth. "If that's okay with your doctor, I mean."

Elizabeth winked at Eddie. "If you don't tell the nursing staff, I won't."

"Why don't you watch TV for a while?" the senior Lakefield suggested to his son. "I'll come back to see how you're doing after I grab something in the cafeteria."

"Then you'll really get to find out how gross the food is here," Eddie informed him.

Out in the hall, Kevin turned to Elizabeth. "I want to apologize again for the fuss I made with the emergency room nurse. I was pretty worried, and guilty, I guess. I was feeling like I must have done something wrong. Margaret leaves him with me for a weekend, and look what happens."

"His getting sick wasn't your fault. Eddie is susceptible to respiratory infections. But if you'd like to make amends for something, it wouldn't hurt if you stopped in tomorrow and told the secretary, Mrs. Philips, why you were ready to tear the place apart."

"You're right. She probably thinks I'm some kind of gorilla."

Elizabeth laughed. "Probably."

"Your being so cooperative made me feel like a real heel."

"Don't be too hard on yourself."

"Yeah, well, I realize you didn't have to stay half the evening with Eddie. Thanks. Your family must hate it when you do this to them."

"I don't have a family, and I wanted to make sure Eddie was comfortable before I left."

"I'll bet you haven't had anything to eat since lunch. And here it is, way past dinnertime. Why don't you come down to the cafeteria and let me buy you something? It's the least I can do. I'm not just making a conciliatory gesture," Kevin added. "I'd enjoy the company—and a chance to get to know my son's doctor better."

About to issue an automatic refusal, Elizabeth gave him a considering look and decided she wouldn't mind postponing her solitary evening at home. "All right," she agreed. "If you'll tell me what's so funny about bears and raccoons."

"Just some bedtime stories I made up—about magic animals that changed themselves into people. They look just like us, except that they still have tails. So they give themselves away."

Elizabeth cocked her head to one side. Then she grinned. "Why do I get the feeling you were speculating about whether I had a raccoon tail under my lab coat?"

"Uh—something like that, I'm afraid."

Elizabeth's grin widened as the fanciful image captured her imagination. She was liking Kevin Lakefield better by the minute.

"Do you think Eddie will really be out of here in time for our trip to the beach?" he asked as they walked toward the cafeteria. "I've arranged my vacation around it. We've been planning it for a couple of months."

"I'm reasonably sure you're going to make it. However, I want to be certain he's better before I discharge him."

The evening rush was over, and the cafeteria line was short. After taking a quick look at the menu, Elizabeth turned to Kevin. "The baked chicken isn't bad. The split pea soup is actually pretty good. I'd stay away from the batter-fried steak and the liver and onions, if I were you."

"Maybe you could write food reviews for the *Lexington Herald-Leader.*"

"I think they're looking for something fancier than reports on hospital cuisine."

"Oh, I don't know."

Kevin took the chicken, mashed potatoes and green beans. Elizabeth opted for a light supper of the soup and a salad.

"Can't I get you anything else?"

"Really, this is fine," she insisted.

They took their trays to a table in a quiet corner, and Elizabeth found herself eating with more enthusiasm than she'd felt in several days. Kevin Lakefield was good company. It turned out they had something in common. Kevin was also from the north and had come to Lexington when his wife had moved back to

Kentucky to be near her family after their divorce. He'd made the move, too, so he could live near his son.

"I'm serious about the reviews, you know," he told Elizabeth. "You could probably write a pretty amusing piece for the paper on institutional food. But you'd have to visit a couple of the other hospital cafeterias and make some comparisons."

"In my spare time, you mean?"

"I guess you have a point. It's just that when a topic interests me, I naturally think about writing an article about it."

"You're a writer?"

"Yes. A reporter for the metro section of the *Lexington Herald-Leader*."

"So that's why your name sounded familiar. I've seen your byline."

"A lot of people don't read the names."

"Well, I do. Maybe because I was a staff writer for my high school paper," Elizabeth told him. "In college I got too involved with my science courses to do any more writing."

Kevin looked thoughtful. "If you have the inclination, I know the health editor is looking for some first-person articles, and your medical degree would give you a wonderful entrée. I could talk to Jerry if you're interested."

"I appreciate the offer, but I'd have to think about it," Elizabeth told him.

"What, you've lost that burning desire to see your name in print?" he teased.

"I can always volunteer to do more insurance forms."

After the main course, Kevin persuaded Elizabeth to join him for apple pie and coffee. Actually, it didn't take much persuading. She was enjoying both the conversation and the man.

"I'd like to check on Eddie before I go home," she told Kevin when they'd finished.

"Can I go back to the ward with you and say goodnight to him?"

"It's after visiting hours, but I don't think anyone will object if you're with me."

"One of the advantages of making friends with the doctor."

"Bribing me with apple pie."

He shook his head. "I haven't just been cultivating my son's doctor this evening. I've enjoyed having dinner with you. And it certainly wasn't because of the cafeteria food."

"I've enjoyed it, too," Elizabeth returned easily. They stopped in to see the boy. Kevin had brought a tote bag to the hospital, just in case, and Eddie had already unpacked a collection of miniature racing cars that he'd spread across the bed covers.

Elizabeth gave him a quick checkup, then waited while Kevin followed with a tender hug, being careful of the IV tube in his son's left arm. Once again she was struck by the easy warmth of the relationship. It wasn't always that way when parents were divorced. And it wasn't every father who made a long-distance move to be near his son.

Out in the hall again she said softly, "It must be hard not having him with you all the time, when the two of you are so close."

"Sometimes it tears me apart when we've had a great weekend together and I have to take him back to Margaret's. But I've convinced myself it's better for him living with his mother right now. And sometimes it's a relief not to have the major responsibility. Do you think that's selfish of me?"

"Not when you could move away and have a lot less to do with Eddie."

Kevin nodded.

They rode down in the elevator in silence. "Well, it was nice meeting you," Elizabeth said as they stepped out again on the ground floor.

"Nice meeting you, too. Are you coming to see Eddie tomorrow?"

"Probably around nine-thirty."

His gaze connected with hers and he gave her a little smile. "Then I'll make sure I'm here."

"You don't have to."

"I want to."

"All right."

As Elizabeth started for her car, she pondered their last words to each other. The exchange had been casual. Yet she was sure she hadn't mistaken the tone of Kevin's voice. It signaled male interest, and so had a lot of the looks he'd given her at dinner, she acknowledged, thinking back over the evening.

The realization made her stop and consider. He was an intelligent, engaging man—and a loving one, judging from his concern about his son. Dinner with him had turned out to be a welcome interlude in a difficult week. How had she reacted to him? She'd been relaxed. She'd even laughed. But she hadn't been thinking about him as a prospective date or anything like that, because going out with Kevin Lakefield wouldn't be fair to him, not when she'd be spending her time making comparisons to Ben Rittenhouse.

ELIZABETH WASN'T WRONG about Kevin. He did ask her out several days later, but she was able to tell him sincerely that although she liked him very much, she didn't think it was a good idea for physicians to date the parents of their patients. He took the turndown with good grace. But he made a point of keeping in touch. When he came home from his two weeks at the beach, he told her that the visit to the hospital had generated some feature story ideas that he'd like to discuss. Elizabeth agreed, and they set up an appointment for two days later.

She had just put down the receiver when the phone rang again.

"Elizabeth? This is Cliff Morgan."

"Cliff, what is it?" She could hear the strained quality of his voice. It sounded like Ben's, when he was grappling with a difficult subject. At the comparison, a harsh fist gripped the inside of her chest. She hadn't seen Ben since that afternoon at the cabin. How was he? Was everything going all right for him?

"It's about Ben," Cliff finally blurted, as if his thoughts were on the same wavelength. "He's missing, and I didn't know who else to call."

The fist squeezed tighter, almost cutting off Elizabeth's supply of oxygen. "What do you mean, missing?" she barely managed to ask.

"Then you haven't heard from him today or anything?"

"Cliff, for God's sake, stop beating round the bush!" Elizabeth gasped.

The man on the other end of the phone line sighed deeply. "His father—my brother Jed—died last night."

All at once Elizabeth realized that part of what she'd heard in his voice was grief. Grief for the finality of death. And grief for what might have been and never could be. "Oh, Cliff, I'm so sorry...."

"It's for the best." His tone was stronger now. "You and I both know that. But after Ben left the hospital last night, he disappeared. He's not answering his phone, he's not home, and he's not at work. I thought he might have gotten in touch with you."

"I haven't talked to him for almost a month. Not since he told me about Jed being your brother and having Huntington's."

"I knew he'd spoken to you. That was all I got out of him. He wouldn't tell me anything about the conversation. I don't like the way that boy keeps things bottled up inside."

"I don't, either. Why did you think he'd call me?"

There was a long pause at the other end of the line. "I guess I really didn't. Ben's too proud to reach out for help when he needs it. I guess what I wanted was for you to go to him."

"Then you must know where he is."

"Don't you?"

Neither one of them said it, Elizabeth reflected, but they were both almost certain where she could find Ben.

"What if he just turns me away?"

"You'll know that you tried. That's all anyone can do. Try."

INSTINCT had driven him out to the cabin. Instinct and the need to be alone. Or was it the need to banish loneliness? Ben didn't allow himself to consider the distinction.

He didn't want to think. If there'd been some way to simply turn off his mind, he would have embraced it. Instead he resorted to an old, familiar remedy. Punishing physical labor. He lifted the ax above his head and brought it down in a mighty arc. There was a tremendous thunk as the blade bit into the length of wood he'd hoisted onto the chopping block.

He remembered the last time he'd come out here to chop wood. Then he had worked with one hand at his side. Now both large fists were wrapped securely around the work-polished handle of the ax. The cut across his palm had healed well enough, so that there was no danger of reopening the wound. But the tender skin smarted as it rubbed against the handle. He welcomed the discomfort. It was another way to take his mind off far greater pain.

He willed himself not to think, but his mind was clear as a mountain stream. Images and snatches of conversation bobbed to the surface. His father and himself, putting up the cabin and collecting rocks to build the fireplace. The two of them fishing and pan-frying their catch.

Elizabeth, her dark eyes sparkling in the firelight as she roasted an apple over the campfire. Elizabeth, the way she'd looked that first morning, sexy and sweet and vulnerable, when she'd gotten out of her sleeping bag without her torn jeans. Elizabeth in his arms, warm and willing.

Teeth clenched, he pushed that tantalizing image away. But he couldn't banish the woman from his thoughts. Elizabeth, efficient and steady, stitching up the cut in his hand.

She was as much with him now as Jed had ever been. More, maybe. Against his will he felt himself calling to her from the tortured depths of his soul. The need only increased his anguish.

He wanted to see her. Hold her. Devour her mouth with his. Find comfort in her arms.

He didn't want to see her. Need her.

He cursed his weakness, his human frailty. Again he swung the ax. Again. Again. Again. He would work himself into exhaustion. Then, perhaps, he would be too numb to think.

FOR LONG MOMENTS after she replaced the receiver in its cradle, Elizabeth sat staring into space. She was terrified of risking any more runaway emotions where Ben was concerned. At the same time, she knew she'd never forgive herself if she didn't take that risk. He'd been alone for so long. Now that he was even more alone, he needed human warmth and comfort. Perhaps he even needed her, although she wasn't sure he could admit that.

Whether he could or not, she had to go to him.

Elizabeth checked the chart of the youngster she had been scheduled to see twenty minutes ago. Although the appointment was for a routine exam, she knew she wouldn't be able to concentrate on what she was supposed to be doing.

Pressing the button on her intercom, she buzzed her receptionist. "Helen, I've got to go out on an emergency. Could you get one of the residents to take over on my physical with Paula Sutton?"

"Of course, Doctor."

Once again she took Route 64 to the Mountain Parkway. The highways were clogged with rush-hour traffic, but she barely noticed.

When she pulled onto the dirt track that led to the cabin, she wondered for the first time if she and Cliff were wrong. What if Ben wasn't here? However, when her silver Acura Integra rounded the last curve, she saw the sun glinting off the Jeep, which was pulled up in its usual spot under the trees. Pulse pounding, she drew alongside, scrambled out, and turned toward the cabin.

Yet now she knew he was really here, unavoidable doubts assailed her. Ben had come out here to be alone with his memories and his sorrow. Did she have the right to intrude?

The cabin door was open. That as much as anything else pulled her forward. She took several hesitant steps across the clearing, then realized Ben wasn't inside. Somehow she hadn't registered the noise—the same clunking and cracking she'd heard last time. No, not exactly the same. More rapid-fire. More furious. More desperate.

She crossed the clearing and found Ben standing with his back to her again, the ax lifted above his head, both hands wrapped around the handle. As she watched, he brought the blade down with a savage swing. The log on the chopping block flew apart.

Quickly he reached for another, set it up and dispatched it with the same controlled fury.

"Ben."

He didn't bother to turn. "Get out of here, Lizzy."

She didn't bother to answer. Instead she circled to the front of the woodpile. Ben's face was etched with grief, his mouth was set in a harsh line, his eyes were red. Under the grief was defiance.

His pain was a knife slashing through her soul. As she came closer, the ax faltered in his rugged hands, but his expression didn't change.

"Go away. You're going to get hurt."

Physically? Was that what he meant? Was she going to get in the way of the sharp blade, when it came slamming down into the next stick of wood? Still, there was only one answer she could give.

"No."

He watched in silence, allowing her to advance a few more steps. Then, uttering a curse, he threw down the tool. It landed with a solid thunk in the dirt.

Elizabeth stared at the ax, remembering the respect with which he always treated his equipment. But not now. He had already turned and started back to the cabin, his long strides rapidly widening the distance between them.

When he reached the shelter, he slammed the door behind him. Elizabeth stared at the barrier. A rejection had never been so blunt or so final.

All the same, her own feet followed the path he'd taken. When she reached the cabin, blood was roaring in her ears, but she didn't even consider leaving. Instead she reached for the doorknob.

Once inside, it took her several seconds to adjust to the dim light. Ben was sitting on the end of the wooden bunk, his back to her, his shoulders slumped.

"What does it take to get rid of you?" His voice was raw.

"You don't have what it takes."

Without giving herself time to think, she crossed the room and took him into her arms, cradling his head against her breast.

It was like the first time she'd reached out to him. She felt his muscular body stiffen. Yet once again, he didn't have the strength to break free of her woman's grasp.

The first time she'd put her arms around him, he'd been a stranger, and she'd wanted to give him simple comfort. Now it was much more than that.

"Ben, don't shut me out. Not now."

For heart-stopping moments there was no reply. Then his iron control snapped like a guy wire under terrible tension. She felt his shoulders begin to shake with a violence that was almost frightening in its intensity.

"Ben, oh God, Ben! Let me help you!"

He didn't answer. He was incapable of speaking, of holding back the years of pain and anguish he'd bottled up inside his soul because there was no safe way to let them escape. Unleashed at last, the grief poured out of him like blood from a ruptured artery.

His face remained buried against her warmth and security; it was as if only her embrace made it safe to abandon control. Her arms never loosened their hold on his body. Slowly she eased onto the bed beside him so that she could hold him more securely.

Elizabeth didn't know how long she clasped him in her protective embrace, trying to absorb his pain. She was hardly aware of the soft, almost soundless syllables she murmured. She was more conscious of the physical comfort she tried to give him, of the way her hands stroked across his wide back and sought to knead some of the tension from his rigid shoulders.

He had held her like this in the dark hours of the morning, letting her cry out her sorrow. Now she tried to offer him the same unconditional acceptance. Anything he asked of her, she would give.

Gradually she felt the man in her arms grow quiet. Hardly daring to breathe, she waited for him to ease away from her embrace. She had given him the comfort one human being could give another. Perhaps that was enough. But he didn't break the contact. The hands that had hung at his sides came up to grasp her shoulders. The fingers that had been balled into fists tangled themselves in the curls at the back of her head.

She sensed the change in him, sensed his need. When his lips found the edge of her cheek, she turned her head, and their mouths melded as they had once before. This time there was a silent acknowledgment that there would be no stopping.

In that breathless moment, it was as if a whirlwind grabbed them, slamming them together. Suddenly only one course lay open. If they clung together, they might survive. If the wind whipped them apart, they were lost.

There were no words to convey the depths of his desire.

There were no words to convey the magnitude of what she was willing to give.

He couldn't kiss her deeply enough, couldn't touch her everywhere he wanted to at once. His trembling hands stripped off her clothes, even as she unbuttoned his shirt and worked his belt buckle free. Heartbeats after he first kissed her, they were naked on the bunk, his body pressing hers down, demanding entrance.

Masculine hardness probed insistently against feminine softness. When she tried to stifle a gasp, his eyes snapped back into focus.

"Lisbeth! My God, what am I doing to you?"

"Please, Ben, let me give you what you need."

"I don't need to hurt you. Never that."

She clung to his shoulders, afraid he was going to turn away. Instead he lowered himself to the bed and swept her into his embrace. "Darlin', if I just wanted sex, we would have settled the issue a long time ago. When I've dreamed of making love to you, I've dreamed of giving you as much pleasure as I was taking."

"Yes, that's what I've dreamed of, too."

As if by mutual agreement, they turned to face each other on the bed, and his hands spanned her narrow waist. He kissed her again. This time she felt as much tenderness as passion in the blending of his lips with hers. His fingers stroked her cheeks, the slope of her nose, the curve of her brows.

A tight knot broke apart in her chest as she saw the way he gazed at her. Eve might have felt this way in the garden when Adam first saw her, she thought with dreamy wonder.

Sighing, she allowed herself to savor gratifications long denied. Every sense was open to him. She feasted on his mouth, inhaling the pungent scent of his body, stroked her toes along the hair-coarsened length of his calves. If admission to paradise was limited, she would take advantage of every second she was granted.

"You'll never know how much I wanted you, needed you." His words were a balm, a caress, an erotic wind sweeping over her nerve endings. But words were only the beginning.

He began to touch her, too, as if he'd suddenly been given permission to seek his heart's desire.

When his hands came up to cup and caress her breasts, she uttered a soft little whimper of pleasure. Then his thumbs grazed back and forth across her hardened nipples, and the pleasure was like liquid fire flowing through her veins.

"I drove myself crazy, thinking about touching you like that," he muttered thickly.

Her breathing came in sharp little gasps, and he continued to indulge his desire.

"And like this." In the next moment, he bent his head, captured one distended nipple between his lips and began to suck.

Her fingers molded the back of his head, cradling him against her. She was aware of a deep, hollow ache inside her now.

When his fingers teased the insides of her thighs, her legs shifted restlessly.

"Please!" she gasped.

There was no question of denying what she—or he—wanted. His fingers moved higher, finding her hot and liquid and more eager than she'd ever been in her life.

"Can't you tell I'm about to go up in flames?" she exclaimed.

"Ah, God, darlin'. So am I."

His lips found hers, and he joined their bodies. This time they both gasped.

White-hot urgency slammed into him with the force of a freight train smashing through a brick wall. If he could just lose himself in her, drown himself in the ecstasy of making love to her.

Elizabeth sensed his need again, lifting her hips to meet his urgent thrusts.

"Darlin', I can't—"

"It's all right. I know. I know."

Climax took him with a soul-shattering force. Seconds later she was following him, rapture suffusing her being.

As Ben came back to himself he heard Elizabeth's small murmurs and felt her arms tighten around him. The possessive gesture was matched by the inner contractions of her body. At that moment he knew what it was for a man and a woman to belong to each other.

She cradled his head against her shoulder, stroked her hand across his perspiration-slick back. When he tried to shift away from her, she held him fast.

"I shouldn't . . ." The voice was thick.

"No. Stay inside me. I want you here."

Peace stole over him. A peace he hadn't felt in years. He let his eyelids close. There in her warm embrace, his body still joined to hers, he drifted into sleep.

CHAPTER NINE

WATERY MORNING LIGHT woke Elizabeth. She shifted on the hard bunk, wondering where she was. Then it all came back. Cliff's phone call. The cabin. Ben.

Last night he had needed comfort. More than that, he had needed the comfort only a woman can give a man. But he wasn't the kind of man who simply took. He had done much more than that. He had given as well as received.

They were still in the same bed, but sometime during the early hours of the morning he had moved as far away from her as he could. Now his back was pressed against the wall.

Vivid memories of lovemaking wafted over her, making Elizabeth long to snuggle against him—or simply stretch out her hand and lay gentle fingers against the blond stubble roughening his cheek. It wasn't the only feature of his face that drew her attention. Deep shadows smudged the skin below his eyes. And his lids were puffy. He needed his rest, she told herself and pulled back her hand.

There was another reason to deny herself the pleasure of reaching out to him. In her secret heart she acknowledged that uncertainty was motivating her as much as consideration. When he woke up, the fragile, almost magic shell that had encased them last night would shatter.

She tried to content herself with visual contact. She'd never had the opportunity to simply let her eyes roam over Ben. Now she lovingly studied his face. Despite his obvious fatigue, in sleep he looked so much more relaxed, younger, almost at peace.

One bare arm had worked its way free of the blanket. Elizabeth's eyes were drawn to the very masculine muscles and tendons. The instruments of motion, she thought, recalling medical school anatomy lessons. Yet no anatomy lesson had ever been so personal. That arm had held and enfolded her in the most intimate fashion.

Her gaze fell to his hand. The fingers were slightly curled now. Last night they had trailed down her flanks, cupped her breasts, stroked her most secret flesh. The memory sent a little shiver of awareness through her.

Her eyes returned to his face; he was awake—and watching her. For several heartbeats they simply stared at each other.

"How do you feel?" she finally asked.

"Like I've been flattened by a two-ton truck."

"That's a novel comment for the morning after."

"I guess I don't have too much experience with mornings after. I usually don't hang around until morning."

Elizabeth drew back to the other edge of the bunk. "Well, this is your cabin. That means I should be the one to leave." She started to swing her legs off the bed, but a muscular hand shot out and grabbed her wrist.

"Lisbeth, that didn't exactly come out right. I'm not trying to kick you out."

"Then what are you trying to do?"

The question hung between them like frozen puffs of breath on a winter morning. Then, uttering a muffled curse, he reached out and swept her into his embrace. She felt his arms tighten around her even as her own grasped him with strength born of desperation.

There was only silence in the little cabin, and the pounding of both their hearts. The next words seemed to be wrung from him, the anguished plea of a desperate man with nowhere left to hide. "God knows, I tried to drive you away. I ought to try harder. I just haven't got the strength anymore."

"Oh Ben, Ben, I told you, that's not what I want. Why won't you believe me?"

"I believe you. But I don't have any right to drag you down with me."

"Don't say that. It's a fifty-fifty proposition. There's just as much chance you'll escape." Her voice was muffled against his neck and shaky with the depth of her emotions.

"And just as much chance of my carrying the gene," he insisted doggedly.

"That doesn't give you the right to ask me to leave. Not when I want to stay."

"I'll say one thing for you, darlin', you've got guts."

"Guts is just another word for nothing left to lose."

He drew back and stared into her eyes. "God, what am I going to do with you, woman?"

"Hold me."

They clung to each other in a renewed silence. Finally he began to speak.

"Darlin', last night, admitting that I needed you was one of the hardest things I've ever done. That was a luxury I was never going to allow myself."

"I know, Ben, I know."

"But I can't make any promises."

"I understand that, too. Just let me do what I can. All right?"

"Do you mind if I talk about my dad?" His voice was very low, and she knew he was struggling with his sorrow.

"I want to hear about him."

It was several moments before he began to speak. "You know there's a sort of mythology in this country about the relationship between a boy and his father. I'm pretty sure you can conjure up the images because you've seen them in the movies or on TV. Maybe the best one is Andy and Opie, ambling across a field together, fishing rods over their shoulders." She heard him catch his breath. "In real life, nobody grows up like that. But for me it was close, for a little while."

She didn't interrupt.

"Looking back, it's almost like a dream memory. Or something I wished for but never got. Only I'm not just making it up. I've got pictures of the two of us. Pictures that prove the recollections. Before he got sick, he was like that. A wonderful guy. A great dad. He always had time for me. He taught me so much. About how to do things. About life."

She saw moisture glistening in his eyes. Instinctively she reached for his work-roughened hand and covered it with her softer one.

"I ran away once before. I told you. I joined the Marines right after Uncle Cliff brought me back. I shouldn't have cut out then. I shouldn't have cut out yesterday, either. There were decisions to make. Things that had to be done."

"I understand. I think Cliff does, too. You can trust him to make the arrangements."

"I was running from the memories. And the unfulfilled promise. The worst part is that I keep thinking that life could have been so damn good for him. Except it all fell apart." He swallowed convulsively. "There wasn't a dang thing he could do about it. No way to fight. His body was still here. But the man I'd loved was gone. Do you understand?"

"Yes."

"I tried to be there for him—to give him back some of what he'd given me. I'm not sure he even knew who I was for the last few years."

"You did what you could. You can't ask more of yourself than that."

"If the news from Hopkins is bad..." His words trailed off.

"We'll face that when it happens." *And, pray God, I can convince you not to run away if the verdict goes against you,* she added silently, realizing that she'd made a decision.

He seemed to sense her thoughts. More likely, he was responding to his own longing to be close to her, now that they'd found temporary sanctuary together. When she tipped up her face, his lips came down over hers with a kind of desperate fierceness. The kiss was long and urgent. Under the covers he pulled the length of her naked body tightly against his.

Hands stroked. Mouths merged. Hips rocked against each other. Then she felt his body grow very still. Under his breath he muttered a curse.

"Ben, what's wrong?"

"We can't. My God! Last night—" He broke off with another expletive. "We—What the hell was I thinking about?"

"I don't understand."

He moved away, and the air was suddenly cold on her heated body. He was a man who was used to denying himself, yet he kept one hand possessively on her shoulder. "Last night, when we made love, we didn't use anything." His expression grew hopeful. "Unless you're on the pill, or something."

She took the edge of her upper lip between her teeth for the briefest of moments. "Ben, there hasn't been any reason for me to be on the pill."

"Lisbeth, I made a vow a long time ago, when I finally understood what was happening to my father and what could happen to me. I will not pass this curse on to an innocent child. Contraception isn't hit-or-miss with me. It's something I always remember. And if I'm not prepared, things don't go very far. Except last night."

Elizabeth bent to press her cheek against the hand that covered her shoulder, as much to keep him from seeing her face as to reassure him. What he was saying made perfect sense. The problem was, life didn't always make perfect sense. "Last night neither one of us was thinking too clearly," she managed.

"I should have been. I told you, I always do."

"You're beating yourself again. If you have to assign blame, last night was as much my fault as yours." She swallowed painfully. "Maybe it was all my fault— because I came out here when you wanted to be alone."

"No, I wanted to be with you. I just couldn't ask."

She stroked her cheek against his hand. "If we're playing the odds, chances are nothing happened."

He looked somewhat pacified. "Darlin', I'm sorry, but we can't take the chance again until I can protect you. And I don't keep anything here at the cabin because I never bring women here."

A wry smile flickered on her lips. He was right. They could not, must not take the chance. The realization left her feeling empty, needing him more than ever.

"Ben," she breathed. She kissed the fingers that trailed across her lips, then surprised both of him and herself with a low, throaty laugh.

He looked at her inquisitively.

"A couple of weeks ago, one of my teenage patients came to me, asking if I could put her on the pill. To make a long story short, I ended up delivering a sex education lecture."

"I didn't realize that kind of counseling was part of your job."

"Neither did I, but it was obvious she needed to talk to someone. I couldn't let her down."

"What did you say to her?"

"I told her not to rush into a sexual relationship until she was sure it was the right thing for her and her boyfriend."

"Well, we're batting zero for one, so far."

She caught and held his gaze. "Ben, you and I aren't teenagers. Making love last night was the right thing for us."

She saw his Adam's apple bob.

"You don't agree?" she asked, hearing her voice quaver, afraid to hear what he might say.

His fingers cupped her shoulders. "Last night, making love to you felt more right than anything has in a long, long time."

Another shiver of awareness swept over her skin. "It was that way for me, too."

"But until we can take precautions..." His tone was resigned.

"Why don't you ask me about the rest of the lecture?"

He cocked his head to one side, his expression slightly amused now. "Okay. What else did you tell your teenage patient?"

"I told her to read some books from the library, but I think you and I have enough experience to figure out some alternate strategies on our own."

"Darlin', you really are something." The words were spoken with his lips inches from hers. When their mouths touched, she knew he was smiling.

He kissed her lightly, then with more ardor, as he pulled her back into his embrace.

Once again hands stroked. Voices murmured soft endearments. Last night they had been like swimmers, Elizabeth reflected, caught off guard by a raging current and swept out to sea. Now they plunged together into a deep, private forest pool, where light and shadow played over the surface of the water.

At the same moment each seemed to realize that finally they had time to embrace, had time to learn each other's most intimate secrets.

"Tell me what you like."

"Everything you do to me. I like everything you do."

"This?"

"Oh, yes. Yes, that."

"And this?"

The answer was a trembling sigh.

Soft caresses touched body and soul. By turns they were both exalted and gratified.

Afterward Ben held her against his side and nuzzled his lips along the line where hair and soft skin met. "I'll bet you didn't learn all that from a library book."

As her heart rate returned to normal, she felt surprised and a little shy when she thought of the way she'd thrown her inhibitions to the wind. Now her eyes were screened by her lashes when she gazed at his chest. "Oh, I don't know. You can pick up lots of good stuff from library books."

"Don't duck away from me like a mountain girl who meets a stranger on the road." He crooked a finger under her chin and tipped up her face. For a moment he simply looked at her, as if he were seeing her for the first time. Perhaps he was. "It made me feel honored to know how much you wanted to please me."

"Ben, I wanted you to know how I feel about us, and I couldn't do that by holding anything back."

She heard him swallow slowly and suspected he might not be able to reply. When his arms tightened around her with almost painful force, she had the answer she needed.

Later they got up and ate some of the dried fruit and cereal Ben kept in the cupboard. Then they washed with water he pumped from the well and heated over the fire.

They both moved slowly now, neither wanting to end the last few precious minutes of this stolen time together. Whatever happened now, things were going to change.

"I have to go back and find out what arrangements Uncle Cliff has made," Ben finally said.

"I'll go with you."

"Don't you have to work?"

"I'm going to call the hospital and explain that there's been a death in the family. They'll give me a few days off."

She watched him turn and begin to put away the food and knew that the relationship was coming to its first testing point. Until now, everything between them had been private. Although Cliff had figured out that they were more than casual acquaintances, nobody else knew. If she showed up at his side at the funeral home, his family would begin to wonder and speculate about the relationship.

She had already told herself that they couldn't spend the rest of their lives meeting in the woods, and welcomed the chance to let his relatives find out about the two of them. She suspected Ben was weighing the implications.

"I get the feeling you don't want to do this halfway."

"I don't want you to face the next few days alone. You've had enough of that in your life."

"How is it that you keep offering the things I can't ask you for?"

"I know how much I needed people around who—who—cared about me after Jim died."

She could see emotion shimmering in his eyes again and suspected he was embarrassed. Briskly she turned and began making up the bed.

Elizabeth heard him go out and waited several minutes before joining him. He had crossed to the woodpile and was stacking the pieces he'd split the day before. She watched him bend to the familiar task, knowing how much he needed the physical activity and the solitude. She was pretty sure she'd never be able to change the former. She hoped she'd be able to do something about the latter.

ELLEN WATCHED Brian Wilmore maneuver the long pole with the net on the end. Dressed in white lifeguard trunks, he was skimming leaves and other junk from the water. Although the pool was closed to the public before ten-thirty, Brian had fixed things so she could come in early. The privilege made her feel secretly smug. For once Ellen Jackson was getting to do something forbidden to everyone else.

Sometimes she still couldn't believe a guy as cool as Brian was dating her, when bathing beauties were practically lined up, trying to get him to notice them.

She was the skinny girl who pretended she burned to a crisp in the sun so she could keep her cover-up on. Unless she was actually taking a quick dip in the water.

He set the pole back in its holder along the fence and then waved at her. "Be with you in a couple."

"Sure."

Walking purposefully to the edge of the pool, he executed a perfect racing dive. Ellen couldn't repress a little stab of envy. He was so healthy, and he took it for granted. Most kids were that way. They felt invincible. It was like that line from "Fame" about living forever.

She couldn't even imagine what it must be like to feel so confident.

When Brian resurfaced, he began to stroke effortlessly through the shimmering blue water. Reaching the deep end, he grinned back at her where she sat on a beach towel spread across the municipal pool's prime real estate. It was understood that only the lifeguards' special friends ventured onto the grass in back of the high dive. The lifeguards joined them when they were off duty.

Ten minutes later Brian plopped down beside her on the towel. Ellen lowered the volume on the boom box that was permanently tuned to the city's most popular rock station. He was about to give her a hug when he checked himself. "Don't want you to catch a cold in a wet cover-up."

She nodded. At school she worked hard at making people think she was just like everyone else. But hesitantly at first, then with more assurance over the past couple of weeks, she'd told Brian something about her health problems, and he'd been fine about it.

"The great unwashed are going to descend on us in a few minutes," she said, changing the subject with one of their private jokes.

"Unless they stopped in the shower like they're supposed to."

"Don't hold your breath."

Brian covered her hand with his. "I hate to leave you alone." She turned her palm up and squeezed his fingers. "I'll be okay."

"Have I remembered to tell you how special you are?"

Ellen grinned. "About a million times. But I never get tired of it."

Just then, the boys' dressing-room doors burst open, and several ten-year-olds dashed onto the concrete. "Gotta go," Brian said and sprang to his feet. "Hey, you!" he called out. "No running, or you're gonna be benched for half an hour."

Ellen watched her boyfriend climb the ladder to the lifeguard tower. He was such a great guy, and the feeling of belonging to him was incredible. It was hard to believe she'd ever be this close with someone else. Or maybe Dr. Salvatore was right. Maybe you just didn't have the experience at sixteen to know how you were going to feel.

Reaching out, she turned up the volume on her radio again and let the insistent rhythm of the latest hit tune wash over her. When you got wound up in the music, you didn't have to worry about your problems for a while.

ELIZABETH COULD HEAR soft organ music playing in the background as she hesitated in the doorway of the funeral home's reception room. Despite her reassurances to Ben, she couldn't suppress a little self-conscious shake of her shoulders as her eyes swept over the small crowd of people who stood in clumps of twos and threes.

She imagined most of them were relatives or old friends of the family. A few looked as if they could be business associates of Ben and Cliff.

The senior partner of M and R Enterprises was talking quietly with a woman whose short, dark hair was threaded with silver. When he glanced up and saw Elizabeth standing in the doorway, a look of surprise captured his face. It was replaced almost instantly by something that was either gratitude or relief, she wasn't sure which. He touched his companion's arm and gestured toward her. They had both started in her direction when Cliff stopped short.

As Elizabeth's gaze followed the older man's, she saw Ben. Despite the sadness of the circumstances, she couldn't help admiring his appearance. A shower and shave had done wonders. He was wearing dark slacks, a camel-colored sports jacket and a soft white shirt. She'd never seen him dressed in anything but very casual apparel and was startled at the transformation. She'd grown to think of him as rugged and capable in a backwoods sort of way. Now she stood before a man who obviously moved with ease through a very different world.

For a moment they regarded each other as if there were no one else in the room. Then Cliff and his companion materialized at Ben's side.

His sweeping gesture included the couple.

"Lisbeth, you've met my uncle, Cliff Morgan. This is his wife, Carrie Morgan. Aunt Carrie, I'm sure you've heard about Dr. Salvatore."

"Yes, of course. You're at Children's Hospital, aren't you? Cliff has spoken very highly of you."

The two women shook hands.

"I'm glad you came, Dr. Salvatore."

"Please call me Elizabeth."

Elizabeth could see that some of the other people in the room had fallen silent and were watching the four of them with interest. Moving deliberately, she took Ben's arm. For just a moment he stiffened. Then he made an effort to relax and led her forward.

"Darlin', everybody is going to wonder who's with me," he whispered.

"I'm proud to be with you. I want your friends and relatives to know that."

A gray-haired woman and stoop-shouldered man were already coming forward. When they drew abreast, the woman gave the man a nudge.

"Mmm—who's the beauty you got there, boy?" he asked.

"Cousins Hector—Wilma—I'd like you to meet Dr. Elizabeth Salvatore."

The woman's face registered disappointment.

Elizabeth smiled in understanding. "It's not a professional relationship. I'm a good friend of Ben's."

"Oh, well, I'm glad to meet you. He's never brought a woman friend to a—uh—family gathering before." She turned to Ben. "We were sure sorry to hear about Jed."

Ben drew himself up. "It's for the best."

That was the reply he gave most of the people who approached with the twin purposes of offering condolences and meeting Elizabeth. She tried to catch all the names. Most didn't stick. But she did remember some. Cousin Harvey, a large man with a handlebar mustache. His sister Denise. Wilber Martin, who'd lived next door to Cliff and Carrie for years.

Many of those who stood talking for a few minutes were openly curious about Elizabeth. More than once she gave a brief account of how they'd met. But she could see that a number of the mourners were paying particular attention to Ben, studying his face, watching the way he moved, listening with sharp intensity to his words. Many hadn't seen him in years. Perhaps they were curious about how he was getting along.

Then the reason for the attention hit her like a fighter plane swooping out of the sky to drop a payload of deadly bombs. They weren't scrutinizing Ben simply because they wanted to know how he was taking his father's death. They were looking for little signs and symptoms that might indicate he had inherited the disease that had slowly killed Jed Morgan.

The realization formed a knot of ice in her stomach. Instinctively she slipped her hand into Ben's. He squeezed her fingers, but his face remained impassive. He must be used to this, she thought with a bit more insight into what his life was like. No wonder he had a strong preference for his own company.

Finally the line in front of them had exhausted itself. Except that Cousin Wilma was bustling back across the room. Elizabeth slid Ben a furtive glance, wishing she could spirit him away to some private place where they could be alone and just hold each other.

Too late. Wilma was upon them. "Well, the greeting's finally over," she announced. "I expect you want to see what a fine job the undertaker did with Jed, God rest him."

Before either of them could answer, Wilma had taken Elizabeth's arm. Knowing that forty pairs of eyes were on her, Elizabeth allowed herself to be led across the room toward the open casket that had been in her line of vision off and on since she'd arrived. Ben walked on her other side, and she reached for his hand. The crowd parted for them, and finally they were standing beside Jed Morgan.

"He looks so peaceful," Wilma murmured. "They can do wonders with the departed, don't you think?"

"Yes," Elizabeth answered automatically. A kaleidoscope of emotions swirled through her breast as she gazed at the folded hands and pale, wrinkled face that was old beyond its years.

Respect, pity, fear. It was more than that; she felt something terribly familiar. With a start she realized she was remembering the dream she'd had the night she'd done the HD research. Jed lay the way Ben had lain as she'd pictured him in that hospital bed.

Holding her breath, Elizabeth studied Jed Morgan's features. The resemblance to Ben was there. But she wouldn't call it striking. You would probably assume they were related. You wouldn't necessarily realize that they were father and son.

That last observation supplied more comfort than she had any right to feel, she acknowledged. She was praying that Ben hadn't inherited Huntington's from his father. But you didn't get HD because you looked like your parent. You got it because you had a defective gene in the distal region of the short arm of chromosome #4. Eventually, the doctors at Johns Hopkins would give Ben the verdict.

She looked up at him, seeing the tension in his shoulders.

"I wish I could have met your father. I mean, when he was himself."

He nodded tightly. "Darlin', I'm sorry. I have to get out of here."

Turning away with a jerky motion, he left her standing beside the casket.

CHAPTER TEN

CLIFF AND CARRIE APPEARED at Elizabeth's side; it was as if they'd known from the start that she was going to need them.

"Let's go somewhere quiet," Cliff suggested.

That was what she'd wanted to do with Ben. But he was doing that by himself, the way he did most things.

Carrie took her arm. The three of them made their way through the crowd of strangers and into the hall. Cliff opened a door and they stepped into a small room. The lights were low, the carpet was thick, the furniture was of overstuffed leather. Soothing music played softly in the background. All funeral parlors must have a room like this, Elizabeth thought. She could imagine widows coming in here alone to weep— or scream—and then returning to face once more the kind words of friends and relatives.

Elizabeth dropped onto one of the couches, sitting with her knees together and her hands clasped tightly in her lap.

Carrie patted her shoulder.

Elizabeth spoke the first words that came to mind. "You wouldn't have known he was Ben's father."

"Ben shouldn't have left you standing beside the casket," Carrie murmured.

"That boy doesn't have much experience with the gentle sex," Cliff observed; he dragged a chair across the room and sat down facing the two women.

It was an odd beginning to a conversation, Elizabeth thought, three random sentences that were only superficially related to each other.

"Oh, I think he's got plenty of experience," Elizabeth answered, trying to focus on Cliff's words. Then her face tingled as she realized how revealing her response had been.

"I mean he hasn't got a clue about how men and women ease each other's sorrow in time of trouble," Cliff replied.

Before he finished speaking, Carrie reached out to grasp his square hand, and the couple exchanged soft glances. How long had they been married? Elizabeth wondered. Probably thirty years or more. She could only begin to imagine what sorrows they must have weathered. Yet she could see one thing quite clearly; the experiences they'd shared had forged them together, like two links of a strong chain.

The middle-aged woman looked at Elizabeth and smiled gently as if she had followed her thoughts. "At the beginning, our life was sweet as a pan of biscuits drippin' with honey. Cliff and me felt like we had the whole world stretching out in front of us."

"We fell in love and married before we knew what was wrong with my older brother," her husband clarified. "We had planned to have kids—a whole house full of kids."

When Carrie picked up the explanation, Elizabeth knew they were sharing one of the most heart-wrenching decisions in their life together. "We talked about the odds, but back then there was no way to know if Cliff carried the gene. I wanted to go ahead, anyway. He was dead set against passing on Huntington's."

"She would have been a real good mother." Cliff's voice was full of mingled warmth and sadness. "You ought to see her with little kids. She really dotes on them."

"That's why I'm so pleased that Children's Hospital is getting the grant money," Carrie said. "I wish we had more to give."

"I think you give more than you realize," Elizabeth murmured.

Carrie looked embarrassed. Cliff's hand tightened on hers. "It's right hard when you have something like HD in the family," he mused. "But there's a good side, too. You know the woman who married you really loves you."

Carrie squeezed his hand.

"And you realize how precious life and health are. It makes you appreciate the little things, and live each day to the fullest."

Carrie looked at Elizabeth. "Child, don't let this old fellow make out like we've spent all our time dwelling on the sadness or worrying about the future. We've been good together, me and him."

Cliff cleared his throat. "I don't know how we got off on this tangent. I didn't bring you in here to talk about us."

"Everything you tell me helps me understand Ben better," Elizabeth responded. "And that's very important to me."

Carrie nodded.

"He—he—feels the same way you do about having children," Elizabeth added.

"I know that," Cliff told her. "I hope I didn't influence his decision."

"I'm pretty sure he came to his own conclusions."

Cliff shifted in his seat. "I tried to fill Jed's place with that boy. I know I came up short."

"You don't know anything of the kind," his wife corrected. "Ben was a good boy. He still is. But I realized pretty fast that he just wasn't going to let either one of us in on what he was thinking."

"You're not the only ones," Elizabeth put in softly.

Carrie gave her a sympathetic look. Cliff was clearly bent on working through his own thoughts.

"You know, I keep thinkin', maybe I made a big mistake trackin' Ben down and bringin' him back. He was such a happy little boy, and his father meant the world to him. I guess it was partly the shock of seeing how Jed had deteriorated that changed him."

"What do you mean?" his wife questioned.

"If I hadn't searched him and his mom out, he could have had a perfectly normal life. He could have kept that bright, shining image of his father."

"He'd already seen Jed fly off the handle."

"Yeah, well, he wouldn't have felt a black shadow stretching out to swallow him up," Cliff continued, anguish making his speech raw. "He wouldn't have had to keep runnin' all the time, tryin' to stay ahead of it. Only deep down he knew nothing he did was really going to make a difference. Huntington's would either get him or it wouldn't."

Carrie's eyes were riveted on her husband, and Elizabeth suspected she was hearing these self-accusatory thoughts for the first time.

Silently Elizabeth considered Cliff's words. She knew from being with Ben that he was a man with a great capacity for love. But his emotional growth had been chopped off, like a great tree in the forest, when only the stump is left.

"You did what you thought was best," Carrie told her husband loyally.

"Whatever happened after he came back, part of the damage was done when Jed started getting sick and Ben's mother ran away," Elizabeth added, hoping the observation gave Cliff some measure of comfort. "It was hard being cut off from his family. And I gather his mother wasn't a very nurturing woman."

Jed's brother sighed. "Lord knows, I tell myself all those things. And that Ben's not knowing his genetic heritage could have had terrible consequences."

Elizabeth swallowed painfully, understanding what he meant. What if Ben had gotten married, had children, and then later found out he had Huntington's?

Cliff continued. "But it's hard not to wonder—"

His sentence was cut off by a shout from the lobby.

"Where's—where's—Jed? I have a right to see my brother Jed!" a truculent male voice insisted.

"Damn! That's Max." Cliff sprang out of his seat and threw the door open.

The two women followed him into the lobby, then stopped short as they took in the scene. A small crowd had gathered around two men. The one with the handlebar mustache Elizabeth recognized as Cousin Harvey. He was reaching for the arm of a tall, lanky fellow whose flushed face was drawn into an angry, twitching mask.

"Nobody's tryin' to keep you from seeing Jed. It's all right."

"Leggo my arm, you son of a mule thief!"

"Now just settle down, Max," Harvey soothed. "You don't want to raise a ruckus in the funeral home."

Max. Elizabeth's brain processed the name even as she took in the confrontation. Ben's other uncle. The one who was in the early stages of Huntington's.

"Don't tell me to settle down!" Max shouted. The muscles in his face jerked as he tried to pull away, but Harvey held him fast.

"Max, please, please behave yourself!" a distraught-looking woman behind him sobbed. He ignored the frantic plea.

Physical restraint was clearly the wrong tack to take. Max's eyes blazed with blue fire. Swinging back his free arm, he hauled off and socked his cousin on the chin. The blow was awkward, but it connected with an audible crack. Despite his disability, Jed's younger brother was still a strong man.

"Max, no!" the woman wailed, tugging at his shirt. She was joined by the funeral director, who took in the violent scene with an expression of horror. For the briefest of moments he looked as if he might wade into the fray. Instead he turned on his heel and made a beeline for his office, where he swiftly closed the door behind him.

Harvey cursed under his breath and rubbed his jaw. "Why, you dang old coot!" he snorted and struck back. In a matter of seconds, the two men were going at each other like over-the-hill prizefighters, puffing and grunting with effort as they tried to score more blows. Harvey was by far the more coordinated. Max made up for lack of finesse with redoubled energy. The spectators who'd been drawn to the scene were obviously afraid of getting clobbered if they interfered.

A door opened at the other side of the room.

"That's enough. Both of you." Ben had materialized and was striding toward the combatants.

Elizabeth looked up with relief. Neither of the battling men paid any attention. They were now locked in a clinch and punching at each other's ribs and midsection.

"I'll get Max! You take care of Harvey!" Ben shouted to his uncle as he closed in on them. He grabbed expertly for Max and locked the big man's arms at his sides. Cliff reached for his cousin. Harvey got in one more good punch before the two were dragged apart. Max ended up on the floor. Harvey stood puffing beside him.

"Now listen here. Cool down, both of you," Cliff instructed.

"I *was* tryin' to calm him down!" Harvey protested weakly.

"We need your kind of interference about as much as a dog needs fleas!" The speaker was the woman who had been standing behind Max. Aunt Ada. Her eyes were red, as if she was on the verge of tears, but her tone was truculent.

Elizabeth, who had pushed her way through the small crowd gathering around the two men, saw Max swivel around and look at his wife, a confused expression clouding his blue eyes. One of his wiry brows was arched and twitching. He shook his head slowly, as if to clear his thoughts. "I guess I shouldn't have gone and hit him, Ady. I guess I should've remembered what you tol' me about mindin' my manners at the funeral home."

"Everything is going to be all right," the woman soothed, as she crouched beside Max and stroked his arm.

He hung his head like a little boy who'd been caught with his hand in the cookie jar.

"Why'd you bring him, Ada?" someone asked.

"Why don't you take him home?" another voice suggested.

A look of pain crossed her face, and she searched the crowd for the source of the comments. "Jed was his blood kin. His brother. I expect he's got as much right to be here as anyone else."

The words were sharp, but Elizabeth heard the defensiveness below the belligerence. She leaned forward and touched the older woman's arm. "Mrs. Morgan, I'm a doctor. Let me see if he's all right. And you, too." She nodded at Harvey.

"Come on, everybody," Cliff said in a brisk manner. "You didn't pay for a ticket on the forty-yard line."

There was a self-conscious rustle among the onlookers. Then people began to move away. Ben helped Max up.

"Let's go in there, and I'll make sure no real damage was done." Elizabeth pointed to the room where she and the Morgans had been talking before the disturbance.

Max grimaced as Ben led him in the right direction. Harvey wrapped his arms around his middle and disappeared through the doorway.

"If you don't need us, maybe Carrie and I should go back to the reception area and try to smooth things over," Cliff suggested.

"That makes sense," Elizabeth agreed. She didn't envy them the job.

She saw Ben hesitate. Now that the emergency was over, he seemed to be debating whether to leave the scene, as well. Finally he looked at her, although he didn't quite make eye contact. "Want me to stay?" he asked. "In case, you know, something else comes up."

"Yes. Thanks." Max was calm now, but nobody could predict what it would take to make him fly off the handle again. "Would you mind getting my medical bag from the car?"

"Right."

She handed him the keys, and he hurried toward the parking lot.

Elizabeth followed the combatants into the private room and closed the door. Harvey moved uncertainly to a far corner. Ada was huddled with Max on the couch. For the first time, Elizabeth took in the couple's appearance. Ada was wearing a dark dress that looked as if it had been washed and ironed many times. Her graying hair was wound in a tight knot at the back of her head, and her skin was networked with fine lines. The hands folded in her lap were rough and red. She looked like a woman who'd led a hard life—who was still leading a hard life.

Unlike most of the other men who'd come to the funeral home, Max was wearing a work shirt and cotton slacks. Like his wife, his face was lined and his hair was gray. He appeared to be years older than his brother Cliff, although Elizabeth had assumed that he was actually younger.

His wife spoke to Elizabeth. "You'd best take care of Harvey."

"All right." She looked up to see that Ben had come back with the medical bag; he'd entered the room so quietly that she hadn't noticed.

Harvey glanced sheepishly at Ben and gingerly lowered himself onto one of the easy chairs.

Elizabeth reached for the bag. "Thanks."

Ben's hand covered hers for a moment. "Thank you." The brief exchange conveyed a wealth of feeling, but there was no time for anything more personal. Besides, everybody in the room was watching.

Elizabeth turned back to Harvey and checked him over. "You're going to be okay," she reassured him when she'd finished her brief examination. "Just take it easy for a few days, and get some ice on that eye."

"Thanks, Doc," he mumbled. He tucked his shirt back into his pants and smoothed the top of his hair. "Appreciate it."

After he'd left, Elizabeth turned her attention to the couple on the couch. "You don't mind if I give your husband a quick examination, do you, Mrs. Morgan?"

The woman was silent for several seconds. "I guess you might as well go ahead," she finally agreed.

Elizabeth spoke reassuringly to Max. "You know I'm a doctor. Dr. Elizabeth Salvatore."

"Yes, ma'am. Dr. Elizabeth."

She smiled at him. "That's right. How are you feeling?"

"Tolerable."

"Good. We'll get this over with as quickly as we can."

"Yes, ma'am." Now that he had calmed down, his voice was barely above a whisper.

Elizabeth tried to be fast and gentle, but when she probed the ribs on his right side, he grimaced.

Ada shot her a worried look.

Max spoke up. "It's okay, Ady. I like the lady doctor. She's real pretty. And I know she's just doin' her job."

Elizabeth smiled at him. "You're a good patient." Then she turned to Ada. "No permanent damage, I think. But you might want to get an X ray to be on the safe side."

"Thank you," the older woman said stiffly. She was helping her husband button his shirt when there was a sharp knock at the door.

Elizabeth looked questioningly at Ben. He shrugged and began to turn the handle. Before he could complete the action, the knob was yanked out of his hand. Filling the doorway was a uniformed police officer.

He looked young and cocky, and stood in silence for several seconds, surveying the room as though he were letting the impact of his considerable presence sink in.

"Can I help you, Officer Templeton?" Ben asked, reading the nameplate on the front of the man's uniform. The question was polite, but Elizabeth caught the tightness in his voice.

"I was called by Mr. Jarvis to investigate a disturbance." He gestured, and Elizabeth caught sight of the funeral director, who'd headed for his office when the fight had started. As his name was mentioned, he shifted his weight from one foot to the other.

Elizabeth realized he must have rushed away to call for help.

"The slugfest is over," Ben assured Templeton. "It was just a family squabble. Everything's under control now."

The officer looked him up and down as though deciding whether to trust his account of the events. "You mind filling me in on the details?" The question was more order than request.

Ben glanced at Max and his wife. His uncle's eyes were squeezed shut, and he'd slumped against the cushions as if he were trying to minimize his presence. But his shoulders and face were twitching. "Jumpin' mother of Moses," Max muttered under his breath.

Ada sat stiffly beside Max, an arm thrown awkwardly around his shoulders.

"Let's go out in the hall where we can talk," Ben suggested.

Officer Templeton waited for a moment before backing out of the doorway. Ben followed him into the hall, and Elizabeth scrambled up and followed. She stood just to one side and a little behind him while he began to explain the situation in calm, measured tones.

"My uncle, the one on the couch, started the fracas. Sometimes he flies off the handle because he's— uh—sick with a disease that affects his mind."

"He's crazy?"

"No. It's a degenerative disease. Huntington's Disease."

"Like Alzheimer's?"

"Something like Alzheimer's. Only things usually progress a little slower, and there are physical symptoms, too."

"So shouldn't he be in a hospital or something?"

"He doesn't need to be hospitalized yet. Right now, his wife's able to take care of him at home. He wanted to come to his brother's funeral, but I guess he just couldn't cope with his grief."

That was as good an explanation as any, Elizabeth thought. However, she could see the officer wasn't entirely reassured.

"Perhaps I could offer a few words of clarification," she offered, stepping forward.

Ben looked around in surprise. Templeton shifted his attention to her for the first time. "Yes, Miss?" he inquired in a condescending tone.

"I'm a physician and a specialist in genetically linked disorders such as the one affecting Mr. Morgan." Elizabeth kept her tone both even and authoritative. Usually, when discussing medical terminology with laymen, she also kept her explanations simple. Now she took a perverse delight in leaning heavily in the opposite direction.

"I had just finished getting his medical history and conducting a physical examination when you arrived," she continued. "Mr. Morgan is suffering from a profound reduction in the enzymes synthesizing glutamic acid decarboxylase and acetylcholine."

"Decarboxyl—" Templeton quickly gave up the attempt to repeat the unfamiliar multisyllable words.

"Yes. But at the moment everything is under control. I'm sorry you were pulled away from more important duties." The last words were spoken with a pointed glance at the funeral director, who coughed nervously.

"You say you're a specialist?" Templeton mused.

"That's right, and I can assure you Mr. Morgan's choreoathetosis will not be a danger to anyone else here."

"Well...uh...then I guess you won't be needing me further." The officer took a step back.

"Thank you for your conscientious attention to the matter."

She and Ben stood without speaking until the front door had closed behind the policeman. Then Ben turned to her and shook his head.

"A profound reduction in the enzymes synthesizing glutamic acid decarboxylase and acetylcholine. That's certainly a five-dollar sentence, Dr. Lizzy."

"I notice you don't have any trouble with it."

"I told you, I've read up on Huntington's. It looks as if you have, too."

"Sometimes book learning comes in handy."

"Yeah." Ben glanced over his shoulder toward the little room where she'd conducted the examinations. "Maybe I'd better speak gently to Ada about removing Max from the premises until the funeral tomorrow so he doesn't turn you into a liar. I think that's the only way you can be sure his choreoathetosis won't pose a danger to anyone else here."

Ben wasn't gone long. As it turned out, Ada had already decided to take her husband home. In the lobby, she held tightly to his hand.

They stopped in front of Elizabeth. "I'm obliged to you," she murmured.

"Me, too," Max agreed. "If all the doctors was like you, I'd go more often."

"I'm glad I was here to help," she told both of them.

Ada looked from her to Ben. "You two are friends?"

"Yes. Good friends."

"Take care of him," she said with surprising feeling. Then she grasped her husband's arm. "Come on, Max. Let's go home."

"I want to stay."

"It's time to leave. Would you like a nice chicken salad for dinner?"

Max smacked his lips and allowed himself to be led toward the door.

For long moments Ben didn't move. "You were good with him," he said.

"I liked him."

"Oh, come on."

"No, really. I think I have a pretty good idea what he used to be like before he got HD."

Ben shook his head. "Is there any situation you can't handle with aplomb?"

"I can think of a few."

"I guess you've had your fill of the Morgan-Rittenhouse clan for the day. Maybe for the century."

"Ben, what you don't realize is that all kinds of crazy stuff goes on in every family," she said mischievously.

"Oh, sure."

"Take, for example, my cousin Megan's wedding reception. The neighbors called the police because they couldn't take any more of the raucous Italian celebration. Uncle Sal, who'd been guzzling champagne all afternoon, punched out the two officers who arrived on the scene, because they had the effrontery to defile the wedding reception with their presence."

"You sure you're not making that up?"

"Cross my heart. Actually it gets better. Aunt Lisa made everyone go down to the station house with her to plead for Sal's release. It was just the right strategy. I think they let him out to get rid of us."

Ben's lips flirted with a grin. "I'm still not sure whether you're putting me on. Maybe I should have a chat with your Uncle Sal."

"He doesn't remember much about the afternoon. But Aunt Lisa would be glad to confirm the details."

"I could call her. We could go into Jarvis's office and ask to borrow the phone."

"I don't think I want to press my luck with him," Elizabeth protested.

"We could go back to my house and make the call after dinner. Or maybe the two of us could go back there and forget about the call."

She looked up at him, very conscious of what the suggestion meant. An hour ago, when he hadn't been able to take the pressure of the reception room, he'd automatically walked away to be alone. Six weeks ago, when he'd been injured and angry, he'd disappeared through the wide front doors of his house with the finality of a car hurtling off the edge of a cliff. Now he was inviting her into his home.

CHAPTER ELEVEN

"I'D LIKE TO GO BACK to your house," Elizabeth answered. "Very much."

"Maybe we should make our getaway before another fistfight breaks out. Just let me tell Cliff we're leavin'."

Both Carrie and Cliff came out and hugged them goodbye, and there was a brief discussion of the next day's arrangements.

Ben and Elizabeth didn't touch as they exited the building. Now she couldn't help wondering if he was regretting his impulsive invitation. Or wishing his uncle and aunt weren't acting as if she was already a member of the family.

She expected to see the familiar Jeep, but Ben was driving a sporty little Celica. It was parked next to her car.

Before getting in, Ben reached for her hand and pressed her fingers. "You were terrific."

She felt some of the tightness squeeze out of her chest.

"I guess we have to go in our own cars." She hated the separation, yet it was probably the most practical approach. "You know the best route. Lead the way."

"Are you sure you can keep up with me?"

"Make certain I can."

So Elizabeth followed Ben, admiring the way he maneuvered the sports car through traffic.

Twenty minutes later she pulled into the circular driveway. The wood and stone house was as impressive as she'd remembered. This time Ben waited for her on the brick wall. The look on his face told her that he was just as aware as she of the last time they'd been here together.

Opening the door, he ushered her through a wide entrance hall that led to a living room at the back of the house. The space wasn't really large, but a cathedral ceiling gave it an expansive feeling. So did the wall of glass that made the maples and sycamores outside part of the decor.

The room itself was one of the most appealing Elizabeth had ever seen. Built on several levels with thick carpeting and substantial furnishings in neutral colors, it was oriented toward a huge stone fireplace that was a fancier version of the one out at the cabin. On either side were wide shelves that held entertainment system components as well as compact disks, video- and audio tapes, books and magazines.

Something about the ambience struck a familiar chord, but it wasn't until Elizabeth stepped onto the thick carpet that she understood why. It was a completely controlled environment, in some ways like the little room at the funeral parlor, where she'd talked with Cliff and Carrie and then examined Max and Harvey.

You could relax here in wonderful comfort. You could unwind from a hard day at work. But you could also scream out your frustration, and no one would hear you.

"Is this your design?"

Ben was standing in the doorway with his hands in the pockets of his slacks. "Mmm-hmm."

"More than just your design. You built the fireplace, didn't you?"

"I had some help with it. I did the shelves by myself. What do you think?"

She chose her words carefully before turning to face him. "It's a place where I could spend a lot of time."

"I think that can be arranged."

He came down to stand beside her. His simple statement told her that another protective layer had been shed. She wanted to strip away all the crusty layers he'd built up, until the tender core of his soul was exposed to her. Then she would heal his spirit. If he would only let her.

Ben broke into her reverie with a more mundane consideration. "I tempted you here with dinner."

"Not exactly."

"Not hungry?"

"Of course I am," she lied, silently chastising herself for almost missing the opportunity to make sure he got a balanced meal. "It doesn't have to be anything fancy."

"That's good, because I just realized the larder is a little bare."

"We'll manage."

"Even if it has to be a can of burgoo soup?"

Elizabeth raised her eyebrows questioningly.

"Burgoo is an old Kentucky tradition. Usually it's served around election time. Out in the hills, it's a bad idea to inquire about the ingredients. Unless you're partial to possum or squirrel."

"I'll pass."

"The canned version is pretty tame by comparison."

"Let's see what else you've got."

After taking stock of the pantry and the freezer, they settled on hamburgers, broiled on the deck outside the kitchen door. While Ben got the gas grill ready, Elizabeth made a pitcher of iced tea, stuck two potatoes into the microwave, and put together a simple salad of lettuce, cucumbers and tomatoes.

They ate on the deck in the gathering dusk. The bites of food were punctuated by minutes of silence. But neither of them was uncomfortable. When there were things to say, they talked.

"I used to have long, one-sided conversations with him, you know," Ben said slowly, testing the words as he spoke them. He didn't need to add that he was referring to his father.

"Just because he couldn't answer didn't mean he couldn't understand what you were saying. In the past ten years, they've learned a lot about the effects of HD on the intellect. Huntington's is different from other degenerative neurological diseases like Alzheimer's, where the patient doesn't even recognize his own children. Some of the intellectual decline seen previously may actually have been hastened by the medications given to suppress involuntary body movement."

"Well, you did say you'd been reading up on the subject."

Elizabeth flushed. "Sorry, I didn't mean to sound like a medical school lecturer."

"Why were you reading about Huntington's?"

"I wanted to know everything I could." She changed the subject. "You'll miss those conversations with him, I expect."

"Yeah. Do you think it's strange, talking to a man who couldn't answer back?"

"You needed to communicate with someone."

"Maybe I picked him because I knew he couldn't blab."

"You can talk to me, and I won't blab," she reassured him quickly.

"I know. But you'll analyze, make judgments, wonder if I'm being honest."

"Everybody does."

"Jed didn't."

"He would have, if he could. And he would have told you how proud he was of you. He would have told you how happy he was to have you for a son. He would have said how much he appreciated your visits."

Ben didn't try to deny her observations. Instead he reached for her hand. "You know the right things to say."

"I have a lot of experience talking to people after a loved one has died."

"Mmm."

She wasn't sure if the acknowledgment had come out the way she had intended. "Usually it's a little easier to keep my perspective."

She saw him swallow. "I keep thinking—about—last night and this morning out at the cabin. I mean, about what's right."

"You're talking about our making love so soon after your father died?"

He nodded.

She understood the reaction. "When death comes close to someone, they often need to reach out toward life. That doesn't mean they're showing any disrespect for the dead."

"Disrespect. I couldn't quite say the word, but that's what I was thinkin'."

"Going on with your own life doesn't mean you loved your father any less."

He considered her statement. "You told me that in the two and a half years after your husband died, you didn't want to get involved with anyone else."

The man had a good memory for the wrong details.

"Yes," she admitted.

"That wasn't good for you."

"I know. It's just that I didn't feel as if I deserved to go on with my life," she admitted, wishing that the focus of the conversation hadn't suddenly shifted to her.

"My God, how could you ever think such a thing?"

"Ben, I—I've made mistakes in my life. Things I regret more than I can tell you."

He waited while she found the courage to continue.

"When I said my husband had been killed, I didn't tell you that I'd made a mess of our marriage. The horrible thing is that we—we—were just getting things back on the right track when it happened."

"Are you sure you have things in perspective? I can't speak from experience, but I suspect it takes two people to make a mess of a marriage."

"Not necessarily. Not when one of them is so wound up with being Dr. Perfect that she doesn't devote much time to the care and feeding of her relationship."

He was silent, unsure of what to say.

"Meeting you changed things." Her voice was barely above a whisper.

"If I wasn't so selfish, I'd tell you I wished it weren't me."

"Ben, you're one of the most unselfish people I've ever met. If you were selfish, you'd have lived your life a whole lot differently. You'd probably be married. Maybe you'd even have kids. You might have kept your HD risk a secret. Some people do, you know."

"I can't imagine doing something like that." He stood up abruptly and began to clear dishes from the table.

Elizabeth watched for a moment before starting to help. She was grateful that he wasn't going to press her with any more questions.

In the kitchen, she started to rinse the plates, but he turned off the water.

"Leave them."

"Okay."

They went back into the living room. Elizabeth wandered over to the shelves and looked at the objects scattered among the books and albums. Several sports trophies from Ben's Marine days. A small calendar from a construction supply company. Idly she picked up a squared-off wooden tube with a rubber band threaded through one end. The other end was fitted with a notched stick that slid into the tube like a plunger. What was it?

Ben had apparently been watching her. "Darlin',
that's just a simple Appalachian toy. Let me show you
how it works."

He pulled out the rod; and Elizabeth saw Ben grin.
She observed carefully as he slid it back into the
holder. then he grasped the knob of the rod between
his thumb and finger and pulled it out about an inch.
The stick snapped back into the tube as if grabbed by
the rubber band.

"Want to give it a shot?" he asked.

"Sure." Trying to imitate Ben's hand motions, she
made an attempt to hook the stick onto the rubber
band. It didn't catch. After several minutes of fumbling, she was scowling and Ben was still grinning.

"A simple Appalachian toy, is it?"

"I'll be glad to show you how it works."

"Not on your life."

Elizabeth carried the little torture device across to
the sofa and sat down, tucking her legs under her. She
wasn't exactly unhappy that they'd found this toy to
focus on.

Ben followed. They sat together, within reach but
not actually touching. She felt her awareness of him
heighten; it was like tuning in a radio to beautiful,
distant music, making it stronger and clearer.

Elizabeth's hands played with the little wooden case
and plunger, trying to find the right combination of
moves. "Any time you want to give up," Ben teased,
"I'll let you in on the secret."

She shook her head. "Elizabeth Salvatore never
gives up."

"I've noticed."

"Show me again."

He demonstrated once more, giving the plunger a resounding snap. Then he watched her try to imitate him. "Lizzy, you're going to hate me when you finally figure out how this nasty little sucker works."

"I'll remember that."

Elizabeth knew the easy banter was therapeutic. She watched Ben lean into the cushions, watched him take off his shoes, wiggle his toes, and stretch his long legs. By degrees the tension seeped out of his shoulders. As she played with the wooden rod, they talked. About the plans for the funeral the next day. About the good times with Jed. About her family. About her work. About his.

"How do you always know what I need?" he finally asked, his voice lazy and relaxed for the first time since she'd gone to the cabin after Cliff's call.

"Because it's the same thing I need." She grinned at him and manipulated the wooden rod in her hand the way he had. It snapped back into the tube with a smart little click.

Ben's brows arched. "Lizzy, I thought I had you buffaloed, and you've been playin' me for a sitting duck all along."

She couldn't keep laughter out of her voice. "Not all along. Only part of the time."

"Come here." He reached for her. She moved into his arms. Tipping her face up, she clasped her hands around his head to bring his lips down to hers. It was a long, lingering kiss that had been building between them all evening.

By mutual agreement they eased down on the couch until they were lying facing each other.

Her fingers stroked his face. His lips made gentle forays against hers. They gazed into each other's eyes for long, heart-stopping moments. Then slowly, slowly they began to give each other infinitely tender pleasure.

A PILE of pink message slips and hospital memo sheets stared reproachfully at Elizabeth from the middle of her desk when she returned to her office on Monday. Almost instantly she felt guilty, and began to thumb through the bids for her attention. For the first time since she'd come to Kentucky, she'd forgotten all about Children's Hospital and her patients. Ben had needed her more. No, it was a combination of Ben's needs and her own. She wasn't going to lie to herself.

Most of the weekend messages were routine. One detailed memo informed her that another young patient had been admitted with an acute infection. Despite her resolve, she felt another stab of remorse. Then she took a deep breath. Dr. Elizabeth Salvatore couldn't be on duty every minute of every day. Nobody could and have a personal life. Well, her personal life with Ben was just as important as anything else. Maybe more important. She looked down at the notations on the sheet. Dr. Cross had handled the admission as well as she would have done herself.

The next memo informed her that Kevin Lakefield had called. When she saw his name at the top of the page, she closed her eyes, suddenly remembering she'd had an appointment to meet him to discuss some story ideas—on the evening she'd gone out to the cabin. She'd been so focused on Ben that she'd forgotten all about Kevin. Now an apology was in order.

Quickly she dialed his office number.

"Lakefield," he answered on the second ring.

"This is Elizabeth Salvatore. Is this a good time to call or should I—?"

"Elizabeth! Are you all right?"

"Yes. I'm really sorry about the other day."

"They said there'd been a death in your family."

"Not my family, exactly. My—" She stopped. *My lover? My boyfriend?* She hadn't put a label on the relationship. She wasn't sure what it should be. "The father of someone I care about."

There was a brief pause at the other end of the line. "I take it you're not referring to a woman friend."

"No."

"That first night when we had dinner in the cafeteria, I had the feeling that you were already spoken for."

"Yes." Ben hadn't said anything yet. The unexpressed commitment had been hers. "Sort of. It's kind of complicated."

"And I have the feeling you're not going to tell me about it."

"It's not exactly material for a newspaper article—which is what I thought you wanted to talk about."

"Touché."

"I've got some time, if you'd like to run your ideas by me."

"I guess that emergency admission of Eddie's started me thinking about kids with chronic illnesses. And about how ineffectively I was coping before you showed up to take charge."

"I'm glad I was there."

"Yeah, well, one idea I had would be to interview parents of sick kids and learn how they cope. What are their daily lives like? What kind of support mechanisms exist in the community? What happens when medical insurance won't pay the bills for long-term care? It would be an extended feature piece—probably for the Sunday magazine or the Life-style section."

"I like the idea."

"I was also thinking about another feature where I'd interview some youngsters. Not Eddie's age, but older ones, who could tell in their own words what it's like to keep interrupting their lives for hospital visits."

Elizabeth thought over the proposal. "Those are great ideas. Do you want any other suggestions?"

"Shoot."

"Instead of interviews, what about—maybe this wouldn't work—but what about having teenagers actually write something for publication? They could tell what their everyday life is like. What they have to cope with at school. How chronic illness affects their family life. Their friendships. What they're afraid of. What gives them hope."

"Elizabeth, that's a fantastic angle. If you can find kids who are articulate enough. Or perhaps I could do the piece as a mixture, with some interviews and some first-person experiences."

"I have a girl in mind, one of my patients. She's very sensitive and very good at expressing herself. In fact, I know she writes, because she keeps a journal. She'd be perfect."

"Let me clear the idea with my editor and I'll get back to you."

"Okay. I'm sure some of the other staff physicians would have suggestions for teenagers you can use. Do you think it would be possible to pay the teens who contribute? That would be a good way to make them realize they were taking on an important responsibility if they accepted the assignment."

"I think we could pay them at our usual free-lance rate. But I'll have to run it by my editor."

"Then let's get back in touch."

"Okay. Why don't I start doing some preliminary work for the article on parents? You could give me some names for both pieces."

"I'd have to make sure the patients—and their families—don't mind their being contacted."

"Of course."

Elizabeth was excited about the idea. As she hung up, she told herself not to be disappointed if the editor shot it down. She was astonished when Kevin got back to her twenty minutes later with a go-ahead for the project.

"I think about fifteen hundred words would be a good length for the personal experience sections. Or even a bit longer, if the pieces are exceptionally good. The focus would be on what you suggested. The kids' lives. Their problems. How they feel about their illness. It's not going to run until after the piece on parents of patients, so the kids will have a couple of months before they have to turn in the assignment."

Elizabeth took down the specifics.

"I'd like you to give me some names as soon as possible," Kevin concluded.

"Why don't I contact the girl I was thinking about myself? And I'll give you some other possibilities later in the week."

"Great."

Elizabeth hung up with a smile on her face. She was about to return a call from Perry Weston, when the phone rang. She picked up the receiver.

"Dr. Salvatore."

"Hi."

"Ben!" Phoning her in the middle of the day was uncharacteristic. Her heart skipped a beat, what did he want?

"Is this a bad time to call?"

"No."

She heard him clear his throat. "I—uh—just wanted to talk about this evening. We didn't make any plans. You aren't busy, are you?"

"I'm not busy."

"I could stop on the way home and get some steaks and you could come over here again. Or we could go out, if you want."

Such a simple statement, but it meant a lot, coming from a man like Ben Rittenhouse, who wasn't in the habit of making plans to be with anyone for the evening.

"I'd like that."

"Which?"

"Either." She didn't really care where they went or what they did. Just that they did it together. "Or we could eat at my place. Why don't you let me fix dinner this time?"

"Okay. If you promise not to go to a lot of trouble."

"I promise."

"Lisbeth."

"Yes?"

"I feel damn good."

For the second time that morning, Elizabeth hung up the phone, smiling.

In the early afternoon she talked to Ellen Jackson about Kevin's feature article idea.

"Really?" the girl squeaked, then began to cough.

The sound grew muffled, and Elizabeth pictured her clamping her hand over the phone. She waited for the spasm to pass. Excitement or stress could easily trigger a fit of coughing in CF patients.

"A newspaper article," Ellen finally managed. "Me. What would I write about?"

Elizabeth gave her Kevin Lakefield's specifications. She was interrupted several times when the girl coughed.

"Are you having breathing problems?" Elizabeth asked.

"No. No. I'm okay."

Elizabeth wrinkled her brows. CF kids didn't have any choice about being admitted to hospital for bleeding episodes or respiratory infections. But sometimes they got run-down and came in for what the staff referred to as a "tune-up." If Ellen needed to get her body back on track, she was maybe resisting the idea.

"Dr. Salvatore, do you think people would be interested in what I think about life and stuff like that?"

"Yes," Elizabeth assured her.

"How do you know I can write an article?"

"You told me you keep up your journal all the time."

"That's private stuff. I wasn't planning to show it to anyone."

"I understand, but the fact that you're interested enough to work at it is an important indication. The difference is, you'd have to think about what would work for publication. But I know you'd do a good job," she said softly, "because of the things you've told me when we've talked."

"If you really think I can do it, I'll try."

CHAPTER TWELVE

KENTUCKY MIGHT HAVE BEEN a border state during the Civil War, but Elizabeth had come to love the Southern charm of Lexington. For example, she'd never have found the grande dame of a house where she lived now in Baltimore. It was red brick and built in the Greek Revival style with a cupola and a triangular portico held up by Ionic columns. About twenty years ago, the owner had subdivided it into apartments. Elizabeth had half of the second floor, which gave her a large living room, two bedrooms and a spacious kitchen. All had high ceilings, crown molding, double-hung windows and wide oak floors.

Her Queen Anne furniture complemented the style. But she hadn't done much decorating. As she got ready for Ben's visit, she looked around critically, wishing she'd bought drapes to hide the roll-down shades. Well, she couldn't do much about the decor before dinner. She'd just have to try and impress him with her culinary skill.

The doorbell rang at seven, and Elizabeth realized she was as nervous as a teenager waiting for her first date. Impressing Ben had sounded good a couple of hours ago, except that she'd hardly done any real cooking in ages. Well, it was hard to mess up veal marsala. Then she'd started worrying about whether

Ben liked veal—and whether she still remembered her mother's recipe.

The look on his face when he inhaled the aroma coming from the kitchen put her mind at rest about the food.

"I have the feelin' I've been feeding a gourmet cook trail mix and roasted apples."

"Hardly a gourmet," she protested modestly. "But all Italian girls learn to cook, practically as soon as they can hold a wooden spoon." As she finished the explanation, she noticed that Ben's hands were full. In one he had a bouquet of pink roses. In the other was a small box wrapped in pink and silver foil.

He must have realized she was staring at the presents; Elizabeth saw him shrug and flush slightly. "I never brought a woman flowers before. I wanted to bring them to you."

"Thank you. They're beautiful. I love roses." She reached for the bouquet, then busied herself finding a vase and filling it with water. Although she was deeply touched by the gesture, she suspected that Ben didn't want any profuse thanks.

When she turned to face him again, the pink and silver foil box had disappeared. Without making any comment, she went back to her dinner preparations.

They ate in the dining room, which was furnished only with a table and chairs. She knew Ben noticed the bare white walls and the uncovered wooden floors. He never missed much. But he didn't say anything. Apparently they were both trying hard to make the other feel comfortable.

After dinner, she brought coffee and bakery cheesecake to the living room.

Ben leaned on the couch, started to kick off his shoes, then hesitated. He glanced at Elizabeth.

"Go ahead. I'm not very formal around here." She slipped out of her own shoes, joined him and began to cut slices of the rich dessert.

Ben accepted the plate and a cup of coffee, which he sipped slowly.

"This is a great old house," he mused. "It's a real find."

"But you're wondering why it looks like I just moved in."

He laughed. "Yeah."

"It's just been a place where I ate and slept and read medical journals. I spent more time at the hospital than I did here."

"Oh."

They were silent for several minutes.

"I keep thinking that deep down you don't really believe the things I've been trying to tell you," she finally said.

"What do you mean?"

"I needed you as much as you needed me." Elizabeth scooted across the sofa and snuggled beside him. "We were both ready for something good to happen."

"There's another way to look at it. In the Marines, in basic training, friendships get forged pretty quickly," he told her.

"Are you comparing our relationship to basic training?"

"Not exactly. I was thinking about how sharing traumatic experiences bonds people together."

"I share traumatic experiences with people all the time."

"And sometimes you get close to them."

"Yes." She thought about Ellen and Kevin Lakefield. And Billy Pierson, the boy whose death had sent her fleeing to the forest. If she felt an affinity for someone, it could blossom quickly under the stress of a hospital crisis. But it certainly didn't happen with everyone. In fact, she usually tried to stay detached.

"I happened along in the middle of a pretty bad experience for you."

"That's true. I had about decided I wasn't going to get out of that hole in the ground."

"Maybe you were responding to being rescued."

"Maybe that was part of it. A rather small part."

His arm slipped around her shoulder and held her close. He looked quizzical. "Why me, darlin'? What did you see in me?"

She grinned. "Are you fishing for compliments? Well, you must realize you're a very good-looking man. And you're strong. Not just physically. You have strength of character. You don't panic."

"Sometimes I do."

"Maybe, but you didn't that day you got me out of that hole in the ground. Or when Uncle Max started fighting Cousin Harvey," she added, before he could come up with some other objection. "You know how to do a lot of things well—everything from driving a car to cooking over an open fire and building a cabin."

"That's how you see me? All that stuff?"

"Yes."

His breathing spilled over. "No one ever said those things to me before."

"Because you didn't ask what they thought. Because you wouldn't let them."

He shrugged.

"Do you think I'm not being honest? Believe me, Ben, I am."

"I'm gratified."

"Don't let it go to your head."

"The truth is, I've worked my butt off to be knowledgeable and competent. I guess I know about everything there is to know about woodsmanship. And I'm damn good at the construction business, too."

"That's something to be proud of."

"It was a way to try and control the future," he admitted. "I told you everyone has his defense mechanisms. For me part of it is—if you keep your body and mind in tip-top condition, Huntington's wouldn't dare sneak up on you. And if you do end up with the disease and you've pushed yourself like a coal train chugging up a mountain, maybe the deterioration won't be so fast. Do you understand what I mean?"

She turned so that she could get closer to him. "I understand."

"I've never said stuff like this to anyone. I keep telling you things it was never safe to admit."

"Anything you say is safe with me."

"Being able to talk about it kind of lifts a weight off my chest. The funny thing is, I didn't realize the dang thing was there."

She stroked her cheek against his shirtfront.

"But it's more than that. Maybe I finally want someone to understand why I've kept people at a distance for so long."

"I want to understand everything about you. Everything that makes Ben Rittenhouse the man he is." She shifted to press her face more tightly against him, enjoying his familiar touch and scent and the new intimacy he was offering her.

"Sometimes I have this dream. I'm swimming upstream against the current," he said in a low voice. "I'm a good swimmer, so I make pretty fair progress. But eventually I get tired. I keep swimming, anyway. But I feel myself getting weaker and weaker and I know I'm going to be swept away, so I try to grab on to a rock. It's slippery the way wet rocks get, and my fingers keep sliding off. I claw at it, but I just can't hold on."

Elizabeth squeezed her eyes shut, glad he couldn't see the tears glistening behind her lids. You didn't have to be a psychiatrist to know what the dream meant. Well, he'd rescued her from a bad dream once. Maybe, just maybe, she could do the same for him. "Hold on to me. I'm not slippery."

His arms tightened around her and they clung for long moments. Then she felt him move slightly; he reached into his pocket. "I bought you something else."

"You don't need to buy me things."

"I like to. That's something else new for me, too." He took out the pink and silver box and offered it to her.

Elizabeth's fingers weren't quite steady as she pulled off the wrapper. Inside was a fine silver chain, from which hung an exquisitely detailed dogwood blossom.

"It's beautiful," she breathed.

"Do you really like it? I would have gotten you gold, but I've never seen you wear gold."

"I love it. The dogwoods were in bloom that first day in the woods."

"Yes. I must be getting soft and sentimental in my old age."

"It's been a long time since anyone was soft and sentimental over me. A woman likes that."

He opened her collar and fastened the chain around her neck.

"How does it look?"

"Good."

I wish I could give you a ring. I wish I could tell you I love you, Ben thought. Instead he said, "I want to make love to you."

I want to tell you that I love you. Elizabeth wouldn't say the words. Not until he'd heard from Hopkins. It didn't matter what the verdict was. Either way, she wanted him to know how she felt. But it wasn't the right time yet. She lifted her face for his scorching kiss.

ELLEN'S HEAD NESTLED against Brian's shoulder, but her body was tense.

"What is it, babe?"

"I'm trying not to cough."

"That can't be good for you."

Sometimes she won out against her body. Tonight she couldn't hold back the spasms any longer. Her chest began to heave, and she turned her head away from Brian.

He kept his hand on her arm.

When the coughing fit passed, he stroked her hair from her face. "You haven't been feeling real good lately, have you?"

"I'm messing up our plans for the evening."

"Don't worry about our plans."

"I hate being sick like this."

"I wouldn't like it, either."

"Why do you put up with me? I mean, with a girl who can't do half the stuff everybody else can?"

"Don't you understand by now? You're a lot more special than everybody else."

"Oh, Brian. I don't deserve you."

"I hate **it** when you bad-mouth yourself like that. You deserve so much. More than most kids—who just think the world owes them a good time."

Her eyes misted. "You're pretty special yourself."

"Will you tell me the truth if I ask you a question?" she asked.

"I always tell you the truth."

"Is the reason you haven't made love to me because I'm sick?"

"What the hell kind of question is that?"

"Is it?"

"No."

"That's not much of an answer."

"It's hard to talk about stuff like this."

"It's hard for me, too. But talking about how we feel—is a way to get closer."

"Yeah. All right." He cleared his throat. "Guys try to make it with girls. That's a goal when you're dating someone. At first with you, that's what I was thinking about. I know I was pressing you. I'm glad you made me back off."

"At first I thought I wasn't going to be able to hang on to you unless I went all the way. Now I'm worried that you don't want me."

"Ellen, how can you even think that? I want you, all right. But I started to realize it was a big step to take when you really care about someone."

"Oh, Brian. I really care about you, too."

They sat in silence in the darkened room, their fingers linked. She sucked in an unsteady breath. "What if I had to go in the hospital for a week or something like that?"

"You *are* feeling sick."

"Not all that bad. But if I go in for a while, they can—sort of—regulate my health." She licked her lips. "I haven't been in the hospital since—you know—since just before we started hanging around together. If I did go in for a couple of days, would you come to see me?"

"Sure."

"You wouldn't feel funny about it?" she persisted.

"A little, maybe. But if that's where I have to go to see you, I will."

She relaxed against him. "Something exciting happened today. But maybe you won't like it."

"What?"

"This reporter my doctor knows wants to do a story about kids who have...uh...been in and out of the hospital a lot." Kids with chronic illnesses, she thought. Somehow she couldn't yet put it in those terms with Brian.

"Is he going to interview you?"

"He's going to let me write the article in my own words."

"Babe! That's great!"

"You don't mind?"

"Why should I mind?"

"Everybody will know I'm sick."

"Stop worrying about what everybody thinks. I don't."

Ellen gave him an impish grin and deftly changed the subject. "You taste so good." She turned and began to nibble along the line of his jaw.

"Babe, when you do that, you drive me wild."

"I know."

His finger stroked up and down her cheek. "Are you sure you feel good enough to fool around?"

"Be gentle with me," she whispered seductively, then spoiled the effect by giggling.

ELIZABETH'S home-cooked dinner for Ben was the start of one of the best months of her life.

She and Ben spent as much time together as they could, and Elizabeth was pleased with the way she was balancing the needs of her work at the hospital and her personal life.

Because Ben was the unattached partner in M and R Enterprises, he'd naturally slipped into the role of overseeing the company's out-of-town projects. Since he couldn't drop that responsibility, he had to make trips to San Antonio, Atlanta and Nashville to check on the progress of several buildings. But he always came back to Elizabeth as quickly as possible.

The weekends she wasn't on call, they went out to the cabin. When Ben was in town they met after work, either at his house or her apartment. Sometimes they went out to dinner, often at an out-of-the-way location where no acquaintances would intrude on their privacy.

One Thursday evening they drove out to Winchester, a small country town with several restaurants along the Kentucky River.

"Darlin', you've got to try the fried banana peppers and the catfish," Ben told her after the waitress had seated them on the broad, covered deck that faced a tributary of the river.

"Maybe the peppers."

"The catfish are farm raised. Come on, where's your sense of adventure?"

"They could be raised in a gold bathtub, but they're still the ugliest fish in creation."

Ben laughed.

She was grinning at him when her eyes focused on the limestone cliff across the water.

Ben saw her change of expression and turned to follow her gaze.

"Every time I see one of those, I think about—about when you found me down at the bottom of that fissure."

"I guess I do, too."

"There are a heck of a lot of them around here."

"Yeah."

The waitress had come up beside the table. "Are you ready to order?"

"We'll share the banana pepper appetizer," Ben told her. "And the lady will have catfish for her main course. I'll have the Hot Brown." When the woman had left, Ben turned back to Elizabeth. "You'll have to taste that, too. It's another Kentucky creation— from the Brown Hotel in Louisville. Cheese, country ham, bacon, turkey and a bunch of other fattening stuff."

Under the table he stretched out his foot so that it was touching hers. They sat for several minutes, simply enjoying the peaceful setting and each other.

"Living down here, do you miss not being near your family?" Ben asked.

"Sometimes. But sometimes I'm glad I don't have to worry about them." Elizabeth launched into a story about her high school graduation, and how she'd had to go around buying extra tickets from her classmates, so that she wouldn't hurt any relatives' feelings.

"I didn't have any relatives at my high school graduation," Ben confided. "It wasn't till the year after that when Cliff tracked me down. I was working as an apprentice carpenter, learning the trade."

The waitress brought their drinks.

"What about your mother?" Elizabeth asked Ben. "Why didn't she come to your graduation?"

He poured his beer carefully down the inside wall of the glass. "She had to work. That's what I remember most about the years when we were in Florida. Her at work and me at home on my own."

Elizabeth covered his hand with hers. "I guess she was doing the best she could."

"She made her choice—and she was never willing to admit there might have been another way. She worked long hours as a waitress and didn't have much time left over for me."

Ben was silent while the appetizer dishes were set down. Elizabeth knew there was more he wasn't saying and made a big production of taking a cautious bite of the banana peppers. "They're good. I was afraid they were going to be hot."

"I wouldn't steer you wrong, Lizzy."

"I'm not so sure about that. We'll reserve judgment until after the catfish."

Despite her initial enthusiasm, Elizabeth let Ben take the lion's share of the appetizer.

"I thought you liked them."

"I do. But I have the feeling they're the kind of dish that comes back to haunt the faint of heart in the middle of the night."

He laughed. "And you're sure my heart isn't faint. Or maybe it's that my stomach is cast iron."

"Right." She tipped her head slightly to one side. "Speaking of the middle of the night, have you noticed? No more nightmares."

"I hadn't thought about it. That's good. I mean you're sleepin' through."

"I think it has something to do with sleeping next to you."

His expression softened. "I make that much of a difference?"

"Yes." *So why don't you move in with me, and we can stop getting our clothes mixed up in each other's closets? Or I'll be glad to give up my apartment.* She didn't voice the thoughts. Ben wasn't ready for that. Maybe he never would be.

Instead she changed the subject. "Ever caught any catfish? I mean, ones that aren't farm raised."

"In the kind of murky waters where they swim, you're just as likely to end up with Kentucky coral draggin' on the end of your line."

"Kentucky coral?"

"Aluminum cans."

The main course arrived. To Elizabeth's surprise, the fish she'd almost turned her nose up at was quite tasty. "It's mild. A lot like flounder," she admitted.

"Oh ye of little faith," Ben teased. "Here, try some Hot Brown."

"We could share—half and half."

He considered the suggestion. "Sure."

They made the exchange while Elizabeth watched Ben through lowered lashes. He was different. More at ease than she'd ever seen him. Under the table she found his foot again and relaxed in her own chair.

Across the restaurant she saw an older couple watching them. When the woman caught her glance, she smiled. Elizabeth smiled back.

She could imagine what a casual observer might be thinking. They must make a happy-looking couple. Maybe the other woman was remembering her own youth. Maybe she was envious of the young people.

But the image was part reality, and part illusion. If only it were all real enough to grasp in her closed fist, Elizabeth thought. She squeezed her hands shut.

There were so many things she wanted to say to Ben, things she knew he still wouldn't accept.

If you go away, the nightmares might come back.

If you go away. She tried not to let the fear intrude. Usually she was successful. But it had a habit of ambushing her, whenever she happened to glance up and find Ben sitting with his hands cupped under his chin, staring into space like a small boy lost and alone and too stubborn to admit he was frightened. She was pretty sure she knew which dark path his mind had wandered down.

Every time she saw him like that, she wanted to rush after him, grab him by the shoulders and make him understand that she would travel whatever road he took. She would be there for him, no matter what happened. But she knew he would only accept the offer under certain conditions.

Perhaps if she told him how much she was willing to give up. No. She knew Ben's fears and his convictions too well. If she blurted out the confession, she'd send him running headlong for the hills.

FOR ELLEN, the month also had its good and bad times. The best ones were with Brian—or whenever she came up with a couple of good paragraphs for the piece she was working on for Mr. Lakefield. He wrote a big feature article himself about parents of sick kids, and she learned that his own son had CF. The questions he'd asked and the parents' answers gave her a couple of ideas for topics she wanted to cover. The problem was, she wasn't sure if she was brave enough to let her feelings hang out in public like that.

The worst times for her were being alone at night in bed, when she stared into the darkness, wondering if she was going to get better by just taking her medicine, choking down the diet supplements Mom was pushing on her, and being real conscientious about her thumping sessions—or if she was going to have to go back to Children's.

Sometimes she wondered why she was resisting so much this time. Deep down, she admitted it was all wrapped up with Brian. He'd said he could handle having a girlfriend in the hospital. Could he really?

By the end of July, however, she admitted that fighting to stay out of the hospital wasn't worth the effort. Her weight was down about five pounds. She wasn't sleeping well. And she was acting grumpy, even with Brian. So, after calling Dr. Salvatore, she let her mother drive her down to the admissions office.

"I'd like to keep you for at least a week and see how you're doing," Elizabeth told her after she finished a brief examination.

Ellen shrugged. "Sure, why not?"

"I know it's tough, spending part of your summer vacation in the hospital, when you'd rather be out having fun."

"Brian said he'd visit me."

"Brian—the boy you told me about?"

"Yes." Ellen cleared her throat. "I . . . uh . . . took your advice."

"And things are working out."

"Yes." Ellen changed the topic. "You probably think I should have come in earlier."

"I think you're mature enough to make the right decision for yourself."

Something about the words and tone of Dr. Salvatore's voice made Ellen stop thinking about her own problems for a moment. Raising her head, she studied the woman who sat beside the examination table. She'd gotten to know Dr. Salvatore pretty well. Today she looked different. Happy, sort of. But also kind of stressed out. "Are you all right?" Ellen asked quietly.

"I think that's my line." Elizabeth laughed, then Ellen saw her expression sober. "I've been trying to deal with some personal stuff."

"Oh. Do—do—you want to talk about it?"

Dr. Salvatore tipped her head to one side. "Thanks for offering. But it's one of those situations where you just have to wait and see what happens."

"Like waiting for results from a medical test."

Dr. Salvatore's shoulders jerked. "Yes. Actually a—a good friend of mine is waiting for the results of a medical test."

"Oh. I hope it comes out okay."

The doctor nodded. Standing up quickly, she turned back to the small desk in the corner of the examining room. "I'd like to get you settled upstairs, so I can make sure you're comfortable. Let's see, Stacy Sutton came in yesterday. You've roomed with her before. How about if I put you two together again?"

"Okay." Stacy was a different kind of experience. The last time she'd shared a room with the girl, they'd also shared a six-pack of beer that one of her classmates had smuggled in. If you had to be in the hospital, Stacy was as good a roommate as any.

Mrs. Bateman was still commanding the nursing station on the third floor. For some reason she was being sweet as honey this afternoon, Ellen mused as she changed into a light pink polo shirt and jade-green sweatpants. Strips of color from the pants were repeated on the shoulders and pocket of the shirt.

"Hey, I like that outfit," Stacy said approvingly. "It doesn't look like pj's. Maybe I'll get my mom to bring me down something like it. Uh—if you don't mind my copying."

"I don't mind. Let's start a new fad around here. We can be the Liz Claiborne and the Donna Karan of the hospital set."

Stacy giggled. "Maybe we can even get the nurses wearing them. Then they won't be able to tell the patients from the staff. All except old Batman." Stacy deliberately mispronounced the name of the head nurse. "She'll keep her bat cape."

Ellen grinned. The knit pants and shirt were as comfortable and convenient as pajamas. If a nurse tried to get her into one of those dumb hospital gowns, they'd be sorry. No way was she going to let Brian see her in one of those.

Last night, when she'd finally told him she was going into the hospital for a few days, he'd said he'd come see her after he'd finished at the pool for the day. Now that she was here, she wasn't absolutely sure she wanted him to come. But there was no way to get in touch with him.

She and Stacy were watching sitcom reruns, but every few minutes she kept glancing at the door. When she looked up around five-thirty, she found Brian standing half in and half out of the room. He was eyeing the IV bottle hanging by the bed.

"Brian."

His eyes followed the plastic tube down to where it was taped to her hand. "Does that thing hurt?"

"Only when I laugh."

Stacy interrupted the exchange. "Hey, gorgeous, welcome to stir! Don't just stand there. Come in and join the party!"

Ellen flushed. "My roommate's a little aggressive."

"Just friendly," Stacy corrected; reached out and turned down the TV volume.

Brian smiled a bit uncertainly at the two of them.

"You've been holding out on me," Stacy observed.

Ellen made quick introductions, being sure Stacy understood that Brian was more than a friend.

"You didn't tell me you were dating a hunk."

Both Brian and Ellen flushed.

He lifted his hand, and Ellen saw that he was holding an all-day sucker—the big flat kind with the face made of gum balls and candy lips. "I guess I should have brought two."

"I'll break off a piece for her," Ellen told him. "If she asks nicely."

He approached the bed and eyed her pink and green outfit. "I thought it was going to be all starched white in here."

"This is improv theater," Stacy told him. "You create your own hospital experience. Like if you two want to make out, I'll draw the curtains and turn up the volume again."

"We would like to be alone," Ellen said softly. She scooted over so he could sit beside her.

"You sure this is all right?" he asked as Stacy drew the curtains.

Ellen reached for his hand. "It's not exactly like being alone in the den at your house."

"Really."

"Thanks for coming."

"Thanks for letting me."

She looked at him questioningly.

"You didn't want me to see you here, did you?"

"I thought . . . maybe . . . you know . . ."

"The problem with you is that you worry too much."

Ellen settled more comfortably against the raised headrest and knit her fingers with Brian's.

RIGHT AFTER she'd admitted Ellen Jackson, Elizabeth found her own energy level dropping. At first she attributed the draggy feeling to the expanded schedule she was maintaining—and to the anxiety that hung over her relationship with Ben.

In principle, it was fine to agree that you wouldn't talk about the future. In practice it was damn hard. However, that was the way he needed to live his life. For the time being, if she wanted to spend time with him, her only option was to go along.

Then she woke up two mornings in a row feeling sick and shaky.

The second time Ben gave her a worried look. "Maybe you've been pushing too hard. You should stay home from work, darlin'," he suggested.

"I don't think it's anything major. There's a stomach virus going around the hospital. I could have a touch of that." Elizabeth smiled at him reassuringly and forced herself to slide her legs out of bed. Knowing that he was watching her back, she gritted her teeth and disappeared into the bathroom.

Behind the closed door, she willed her stomach to settle down. Splashing cold water onto her face, she peered at her reflection in the mirror. There were dark circles under her eyes. And her skin was pale. Before she emerged to make coffee and pop frozen waffles into the toaster, she brushed her hair and dabbed on a tiny bit of blusher. The color made her look better. But as she measured out two tablespoonsful of freshly ground Viennese Cinnamon, she acknowledged she'd been ignoring other symptoms that should have set off signal flares in her physician's brain. The smell of coffee sent another wave of nausea rolling across her stomach. She knew she wasn't going to be able to drink the stuff.

Elizabeth was aware of the exact minute when Ben came into the kitchen. Without turning toward him, she finished the breakfast preparations. He was going out of town on one of his business trips that morning, and she didn't want to upset his plans.

Sliding into the seat across from him, she cupped her hands around her coffee mug but didn't pick it up. Ben set down his mug and looked at her with concern.

"You're still kind of pale. Are you sure you're going to be okay? Maybe I should stay home and take care of you."

"Stop worrying about me. I'll be fine," she assured him with false cheerfulness.

"I'll call you tonight."

"I—I have a meeting at the hospital. I may not be back until late," she said, suddenly aware that she'd never deliberately told him a falsehood before. Doing it made something inside her chest knot, but she was beginning to suspect she wouldn't be able to face him that evening, even over the phone. She knew her own body. What was more, she knew the early signs of pregnancy.

Later that morning she stopped in at the hospital lab for a test, pretty sure it was just a formality. She was too busy during the day to call the lab for results and definitely didn't want to delegate the job to her secretary. But when five o'clock came, she couldn't go home without finding out for sure.

The clerk who answered the lab phone had no way of knowing that Elizabeth was inquiring about her own test. The young woman was clearly anxious to leave for the day. "I can have the report on your desk tomorrow morning," she offered.

"If the information is available," Elizabeth replied, "I'd like to have it tonight."

There was a deep sigh at the other end of the line. "I suppose I can get it."

Elizabeth waited for two and a half minutes, during which she had to clamp her teeth together to keep them from chattering. All day she'd felt like a rock climber who had lost her footing and slipped down the side of the mountain. For hours she'd been dangling precariously over a precipice, twisting slowly in the wind. Or was she hanging at the end of a pole over a limestone crevasse?

The phone clicked back to life. Her heart jumped wildly in her chest.

"You want Test #5302, right?"

"Yes." She could barely dredge up enough air to get the syllable out.

"The results are positive."

"Thank you," Elizabeth murmured, then gently set the receiver back in its cradle.

A baby. She was really going to have a baby. Although she'd thought as much, that wasn't quite the same as having her suspicions confirmed by a lab test. The new knowledge was so overwhelming that it momentarily wiped everything else from her mind. She was floating, weightless, about to drift toward the moon. Unreasoned joy expanded in her chest.

Then the bubble burst. Gravity slammed her back against the earth, pressed her down, squeezed the air from her lungs.

The familiar walls of her office seemed to close in around her. For several heartbeats she could only stand there, gasping for breath, fighting her panic. Suddenly her white coat was too tight, the fabric too stiff. Struggling out of it, she threw it across the chair.

Elizabeth didn't really remember pawing in her desk drawer for her pocketbook, flying down the hall to the staff exit, or dodging a nurse's aide pushing a little girl in a wheelchair. Rounding a corner she almost collided with Perry Weston.

Oh, God! Not Perry. Not tonight.

"Elizabeth! What's wrong?"

"I'm late for an appointment. Talk to you tomorrow," she gasped and brushed by the chief of staff.

A few moments later she climbed into her car and locked the doors. As if that could lock out the world. She pulled out of the parking lot and knew exactly where she was going.

CHAPTER THIRTEEN

ELIZABETH ROUNDED a cloverleaf and merged onto the Mountain Parkway, thinking it was strange to be rushing toward Daniel Boone National Forest when she knew Ben wouldn't be there. Yes, over the past few months the cabin had become a sort of focus for her life, as it was for his, and today the journey had its own sort of logic.

The baby had been conceived at the cabin. Against the odds, the first time they'd made love, they'd produced a new life. Ben had been so caught up by his emotions that he'd totally forgotten the rules he'd set down for himself.

She struggled to stave off tears. It was impossible not to think about those rigid, ironclad rules Ben lived by. They weren't capricious whims. They hadn't been created for the purpose of cutting him off from human joy. They were riveted into the bedrock of his integrity. She knew all too well what legacy he had vowed he would never pass on.

An hour later, Elizabeth parked in her usual spot and turned toward the clearing. She had intended to hurry to the cabin and shut herself inside, as if the little room were a castle keep. Instead she stopped and caught her breath at the sight that welcomed her. In a few short weeks the meadow had been transformed.

White yarrow. Yellow buttercups. A sprinkling of pink-tipped stalks that she couldn't name. A sea of wildflowers rippled gently in the light breeze.

Plucking a sprig of yarrow, she crushed a leaf between her fingers, releasing the pungent scent. Her steps were slow as she made her way to the cabin door, feeling flowers brush against her skirt.

She unlocked the cabin door, laid the yarrow sprig upon the table and turned to the wide bunk. Her fingers stroked the sleeping bags that she and Ben had zipped together and left unrolled for the next time they returned.

Even though the man she loved wasn't there, she felt very close to him at that moment.

"I'm going to have your baby, Ben," she whispered. "What would you say if I told you?"

All day long, while she'd waited to hear the results of the lab test, she hadn't dared frame that question. The silent cabin didn't answer, yet she was afraid she already knew the answer.

Her emotions took another wild slide, like a runaway log on a flume. Scrambling off the bunk as if it had suddenly scalded her skin, she ran to the door. This time she didn't even glance at the flowers. Instead she stood staring at the woodpile, sucking in several sharp breaths. *Careful,* she warned herself, *you're going to start hyperventilating. You don't want to make yourself faint. Not out here. Alone.*

The medical advice as much as the fresh air helped her get a momentary grip upon herself. With deliberate steps she headed down the trail she and Ben had walked together, the afternoon he'd first told her about his father.

"Ben . . . oh . . . Ben." The words were a sob of anguish.

The ground seemed to tremble under her, as if she
were caught in an earthquake, but the force that
rocked her was irony. The colossal irony that the thing
you'd wanted most could suddenly turn into the thing
you couldn't even dream of having.

"Remember when I had that nightmare?" she
asked, picturing the way he'd come to her and com-
forted her in the night at the campsite down by the
creek. "Remember when you held me, and I told you
about losing my husband? Oh, Ben, I didn't tell you
everything. I couldn't tell you I lost his baby, too."

Tears were streaming down her cheeks, but she
hardly noticed. "Ben," she continued, aloud, because the pain was too great to hold inside herself. "At
first I thought I didn't know you well enough to share
that much of myself. Then, that morning in the cabin
after we first made love, I knew you'd panic if you
thought you were tangled up with a woman who
wanted a child. But I didn't trick you. I swear it, Ben.
I swear it. I didn't plan this. I told myself you were
enough. Finding love again. Finding you. I didn't
know this was going to happen."

Her mind spun crazily, teetering between past and
present. She remembered how happy she and Jim had
been when they'd gone off on that last, fateful trip.
Happy, because their life together was back on the
right track. Happy, because she'd found out she was
pregnant. The child she'd been carrying had been a
pledge of their new commitment, a kind of renewal of
the marriage vows. Then Jim had been killed. In the
aftermath of the physical shock of the accident and the

emotional shock of her husband's death, she'd lost the one last thing that she'd wanted desperately to keep.

Now she was carrying another child. A child she hadn't dared plan. A child Ben didn't want. What if the baby was doomed the way Jed Morgan had been doomed—the way Ben might be? A fresh surge of agony threatened to carry her away in its undertow.

Nearly blinded by tears, Elizabeth stumbled down the path, barely feeling the ground under her feet, hardly knowing or caring where she was going. She almost crashed into the big rock that separated the trail, only averting disaster at the last moment. After that she slowed down. But only when the trail circled back toward the cabin was she able to get some sort of grip on herself.

Stopping by the front door, she clasped the weathered wood in one hand and leaned her forehead against the rough logs. She walked inside and sat down at the table. Picking up the yarrow, she ran the fragrant herb back and forth between her fingers. She had some decisions to make. The sooner she sorted things out, the better.

It was hard to think straight about what she wanted and what Ben believed he wanted. It wasn't just a question of desires. It was also a question of rights and obligations.

Ben was already going through a terrible ordeal. Finding out about this baby would be an even greater burden. But did she have the right to keep the knowledge from him? That was one question she wasn't sure how to answer.

Yet whatever her decision concerning Ben's right to know, their child existed inside her. It had a reality of its own. It was a tiny life.

Elizabeth closed her eyes and slid her palm down to her abdomen. It would be weeks before she started to show, yet she was acutely aware of her impending motherhood. Silently she began to pray for what every expectant mother has prayed for since the dawn of humanity—a healthy, happy baby, who would grow into a strong, productive adult.

But she wasn't like most women. She was a physician.

She'd already considered what it might be like to be married to a man with HD. She'd told herself she was strong enough to cope with that. Now she had to consider the risks and dangers for this particular child.

It was too much to face alone. She wanted Ben's strong, comforting arms around her, holding her, holding back sorrow and danger. He was, however, more than a thousand miles away, and was going to be devastated when she told him about the baby.

Elizabeth stood up and began to pace back and forth across the rough pine floor. Theoretically, in utero tests for Huntington's were impossible. But the same circumstances that applied to Ben applied to the baby. Other family members had to be tested to give a complete genetic picture.

As things stood, with Ben's future still in doubt, the new life growing inside her had a twenty-five percent chance of carrying the Huntington's gene. If it turned out that Ben had the disease, the baby's chance of inheriting it would be fifty percent—as Ben's were now.

In her work she'd counseled parents of children with genetic problems. She wouldn't have chosen to conceive this baby, not without knowing Ben's future. But the pregnancy changed everything.

Surprisingly, her thoughts turned to Ellen Jackson and the talk they'd had after the girl's frightening bleeding episodes.

She'd practically promised Ellen that one day doctors would find a way to conquer cystic fibrosis—just the way they'd found the key to controlling diabetes. Well, if that kind of optimism applied to CF, it also applied to another genetic disease—Huntington's.

She'd desperately wanted to give Ellen hope for the future so she wouldn't stop fighting. Now Elizabeth tried to arm herself with similar reassurances.

Her child might not even carry the Huntington's gene. But suppose she or he did? In all likelihood there wouldn't be any symptoms until the child was well into his or her thirties or forties. Surely in thirty or forty years medical science would have found a cure for HD? Or, if not that, at least a treatment that would allow victims to lead a normal life.

Again she slid her hand down to her abdomen. "I want you to be all right," she whispered, realizing she'd made her decision. "I want that so much. But if you've got the gene, we'll learn to cope with that."

The vow made her think about Ben again. He hadn't been able to prevent fear of the future from robbing the present of contentment. HD clouded his prospects. But his outlook on life had been colored by other factors, too. Like the instability of his childhood. His mother had spirited him away from his father and raised him without the support of any kind of family life. He'd been cheated of the warmth and love that could have given him a feeling of security.

That wouldn't happen with their baby, she promised herself fervently. She wanted Ben to help her provide a secure and loving home. She'd make him understand. She had to.

But what if she lost him because of the baby?

Elizabeth couldn't face that question. Not now. Instead she pictured the three of them surrounded by grandparents, aunts, uncles and cousins who would help give their child the right start in life. "One thing you have going for you," she vowed as she cradled her tummy against her palm. "No baby will be more loved than you. You're going to have a warm, secure childhood. I promise."

Elizabeth had come to the cabin to find some sort of comfort. She left wrapped in a kind of serenity. She wasn't foolish enough to think it would last, but at least she'd given herself the courage to go back and face the world.

BEN COULD HAVE GONE to a restaurant. Instead, after finally getting away from the construction site, he'd shut himself in his room and ordered room service. The tray sat in the hall outside his door, practically untouched.

His hand trembled as he reached for the phone. He tried to will it to steadiness. The attempt was only partially successful.

Elizabeth. He needed to hear the warmth and caring in her voice.

Maybe he should get used to doing without that crutch.

No. Not yet. You don't know for sure, he told himself. Yet deep in his chest he felt a kernel of fear begin to expand.

For the millionth time that evening he dialed her number. It rang. Eight, ten, fifteen times. He let the receiver drop back into place. He could have her paged at the hospital. No. She'd think something was wrong.

For long moments he sat on the edge of the bed, his head cradled in his hands. Then he crossed to the sliding glass door. Stepping onto the balcony, he looked at the twinkling lights of the city. The breeze ruffled his hair. How high up was he? High enough.

He leaned over the metal railing and gazed down at the sidewalk.

Once Elizabeth had called him a coward.

Was he? And what did that mean for a man in his position? Which was the coward's way out? To let nature take its course? Or to decide your own fate?

IT SEEMED as if Elizabeth had barely closed her eyes when the phone rang.

"Where were you?"

"Ben?"

"Were you expecting someone else?"

"My answering service, maybe."

"Oh, right."

She saw by the lighted numbers on the clock that he was calling at two in the morning. How long had he been trying to get her?

"Where were you?" he repeated.

"Remember I said I might have to be at the hospital?" That wasn't a lie, she assured herself. It was just a question. She couldn't tell Ben she'd been out at the cabin and why. Not over the phone.

"Yeah. That's right. The hospital. But I was worried about you, so I decided to give you one more try." His voice sounded strained.

"Are you all right?" she asked.

"You were the one who was sick when I left. How are you feelin'?"

So much had happened that the morning sickness seemed like weeks ago. "I'm okay. But you sound—"

"I sound like what?" he demanded sharply.

She felt an icy tide rising in her chest. For a second she wondered if he had somehow found out about the lab report and was reacting to the news. Then she shook her head. That was impossible. "I don't know, exactly," she said, struggling to answer his question. "I guess you seem upset. What's happening?"

"There are some problems with the building project. It's...uh...behind schedule, because the supervisor hasn't been doing his job. I'm going to have to stay on here for a few more days to get things straightened out."

Elizabeth wavered between disappointment and relief. The longer he stayed away, the longer she had to collect herself before she saw him again.

"I miss you," she said softly.

"I miss you, too." There was a strange note of uncertainty—or was it regret?—in his voice. She wanted to ask again if he was all right. She sensed that he didn't want to pursue that subject.

"Tell me about your day," he asked before she could give the matter further consideration.

"It was busy." She yawned several times as she told him about some of the patients she'd seen.

"I'm keeping you awake."

"It's okay."

"You need your beauty sleep."

"I'll be home earlier tomorrow."

"I...uh...may be tied up," he told her.

"Let me know when you're coming back."

"Okay."

After hanging up, Elizabeth lay in bed, staring into the darkness. It had been an unsettling conversation because of the things she couldn't tell him. She'd also sensed there were things he wasn't telling her. The air conditioning switched on, and the cool air brought a wave of goose bumps to her bare arms. Pulling up the comforter, she burrowed into the warmth her body heat had created under the covers. She wished Ben were there beside her so she could snuggle up to the reassuring solidity of his body. Whatever the future held, she needed him now.

THE NEXT MORNING Elizabeth was surprised to get a call from Perry Weston.

"I tried to speak to you yesterday."

She'd forgotten the little scene in the hall. "Sorry I couldn't stop. I had an emergency."

"Well, uh, it turns out I need a favor."

"Yes?"

"I'm scheduled to meet with Cliff Morgan to give him a progress report on the genetic counseling and education programs we're setting up. I'd expected to be able to let Morgan know who the director of the new programs was going to be. Unfortunately, the deal didn't jell."

"That's too bad," Elizabeth told him sincerely. Getting the program going was important to the community, not just the hospital.

"You and Morgan seemed to get on pretty well when we had that lunch meeting. Why don't you come along to dinner with us tonight?"

Elizabeth might have refused, but she did like Cliff. Being with him tonight would be a way to feel closer to Ben while he was away.

"All right," she agreed, wondering if she should fill Perry in on her relationship with Cliff. No, she didn't want to go into that now.

"We're eating at the Gratz Park Inn. I can drive you over after work."

"No, I want to go home and change. I'll meet you."

"As you wish."

BUILT IN the early part of the century, the Gratz Park Inn was a small, very elegant hotel within walking distance of Elizabeth's house. She had just entered the courtyard when she spotted Cliff getting out of a silver Lincoln. Mounting the steps, she waited for him under the green awning at the front entrance.

Seeing him suddenly made her feel a little shy. She couldn't help thinking about the baby. But she wasn't going to tell him. Not until she'd told Ben.

He ushered her into the Chippendale elegance of the lobby with a warm smile.

"Well, how in the world are you?" Cliff asked. His eyes reminded her of Ben's. She wanted to squeeze his hand. Instead she swallowed, searching for steady footing on an unknown path. "Well, I'll be happier when your nephew comes back."

His uncle nodded. "I feel guilty now about giving Ben all the out-of-town jobs."

"The arrangement made sense."

"Until he met you. The two of you should be spending as much time as you can together."

"Yes."

"That boy has gone through a lot of changes since the two of you got together."

"I know."

"I mean changes for the better."

"Sometimes I think so."

"You don't have to be modest about it. As soon as I met you, I knew you'd be good for him. Ben wants people to think he's tough as a rawhide knot. He needed a good woman in his life to smooth off the jagged edges."

"It works both ways. He's good for me, too."

Cliff looked as if he was considering his next words. "You ought to hear him brag on you."

"What?"

"He's always telling me about the great stuff you're doing at the hospital. How well you can cook. How you're taking to the cabin."

Elizabeth couldn't conceal her surprise. The news was so at odds with her image of the very private Ben Rittenhouse that she wasn't sure what to say.

"I told you, you've changed him," Cliff repeated.

She wet her lips and was about to ask if Ben had given Cliff any indication of what was bothering him about the trip to San Antonio. Just at that moment, Perry came striding across the lobby.

"Sorry I'm late," he apologized. "I had to take a phone call before I left."

Entering the green and beige dining room with its brass fixtures and flowered drapery, they were seated at a corner table.

Elizabeth was amused by the way Perry listened to the easy conversation between Cliff and herself. She could tell that Perry had gathered they had seen each other since the last meeting. She knew he was trying to figure out the connection.

"How is your brother doing?" Perry suddenly asked Cliff as he finished his chicken gumbo. "The one with Huntington's?"

"He died."

"Oh, I'm sorry."

"It was expected—a blessing, really."

"How is Max?" Elizabeth inquired.

"About the same, I guess. We don't see him and Ada much." Cliff turned to Perry. "Max is my younger brother. He also has HD."

Perry's puzzled gaze swung back to Elizabeth. "How do you know him?"

"I met him at Jed's funeral." She took a sip of water from the crystal goblet in front of her, suddenly in the mood to throw caution to the wind. Maybe she couldn't talk about the baby, but she could talk about his father.

"I'm—seeing Cliff's nephew, Ben Rittenhouse. We met before I knew he was related to Cliff. But Ben had told Cliff I was at the hospital. That's why he asked to have lunch with me that first time. He was checking me out."

Cliff laughed. "Actually, my nephew was the one who suggested we give serious consideration to your grant proposal."

Perry sat there, obviously sorting it all out, but didn't comment. Elizabeth could imagine what was running through his mind. She supposed he had decided he was going to have an easier time with the business discussion since Cliff and Elizabeth knew each other on a social basis. On the other hand, he had also just realized that she'd turned down his overtures in favor of another man.

"Well, uh," he finally said, "I guess we'd better get down to cases. I was hoping to be able to tell you we had named a director for the new program. But we're going to have to start interviewing other candidates."

"Have you thought about Elizabeth?" Cliff nodded in her direction.

"Me?" She knew she sounded startled.

"I've seen your ability handling people. And then there's all the stuff Ben has been telling me."

"Undoubtedly your nephew's opinion of Elizabeth is very flattering," Perry cut in. "However, I'm sure it's not based on any kind of professional judgment." He cleared his throat as if he'd just realized how his words might sound. "Besides, I'd hate to see Elizabeth give up clinical practice. She's too good at what she does."

Cliff folded his napkin. "Sorry if I'm steppin' on anybody's toes. It was just an idea. Maybe I should confine my role to providing the money."

"No, oh no. We'd love having your input on important decisions," Perry insisted.

Elizabeth could see that both men were sorry the conversation had taken that particular detour.

"I'm sure Perry will find an excellent candidate," she murmured.

The discussion continued for about twenty minutes more, although the tone remained a bit strained. Finally Elizabeth announced that she had an early day tomorrow. Actually, from the expression on Perry's face, she suspected it was going to be earlier than she had planned.

She was right. The chief of staff was waiting in her office when she arrived in the morning.

"I don't like surprises," he began.

"Perry, I wasn't trying to pull anything over on you."

"You should have told me you knew Morgan socially."

"Oh, really?"

"Did the two of you already discuss the directorship?"

"Of course not. I was as flabbergasted as you when Morgan came out with that suggestion."

He looked somewhat mollified. "You did sound shocked."

"I don't want to run a major hospital program. I want time for some personal life."

"Yes, well, I concur. Mmm... From the discussion last night, it sounds as if I have you to thank for the Morgan Foundation giving us that grant money." He didn't seem entirely pleased with the observation.

"I'm sure we had a good shot at the money, anyway."

"I hope so. I wouldn't want to think we got the grant because of favoritism."

"That's very noble of you. Was there anything else you wanted to discuss?"

"Did I hear all that correctly last night? You're involved with Morgan's nephew? A man at risk for Huntington's Disease?"

"Yes."

"Have you ever seen a patient in the later stages of the disease?"

"No."

"Maybe you should."

She raised her chin. "Why?"

"Don't you want a realistic idea of what you may be letting yourself in for?"

She put her hand on the doorknob. "I'm going to be late for my first patient."

He didn't move to open the door. "I thought you were an intelligent woman."

"Perry, please. Don't say anything we're both going to be sorry about." The look on her face must have told him more than any protest she could have made.

He shrugged and let her pass. She was pretty sure he was through asking her to lunch or to stop by his office at the end of the day. However, that was the way she wanted things between Perry Weston and herself—strictly business.

IT WAS GREAT to be home from the hospital, Ellen Jackson thought; she leaned forward in her desk chair, fingers poised over the keys of her typewriter. Great to be able to do what you wanted, when you wanted.

"Ellen, didn't you hear me say I'd fixed you a snack?" Her mother's voice interrupted her thoughts. "A turkey sandwich with cranberry dressing. One of your favorites."

Well, just about anything you wanted, Ellen amended. As long as you kept your calorie intake up and stuck to your therapy schedule.

The bedroom door opened, and Ellen quickly pulled the sheet of paper out of the machine and laid it face down on the desk. "Sorry, Mom. I was working on that piece for Mr. Lakefield."

"It's funny to see you typing in the summer. You've been spending a lot of time up here in your room."

"It's important to me."

"Eating is important, too. You have to keep your weight up."

Ellen smiled. "Yeah, I know. Give me just a little more time. I've got this idea I'm having trouble saying the way I want to."

Mrs. Jackson looked toward the sheet of paper on the desk. "Maybe I could help you."

"I don't want any help. I need to do it by myself. I'll be down in a few minutes, okay?"

She expected her mother to go back downstairs and let her finish the paragraph. Instead she remained standing in the doorway. Finally she cleared her throat.

"Is there something wrong, Mom?"

"I was hoping we could talk."

"About what? I told you, I don't need any help writing."

"Well . . . I'd like to talk about Brian."

"What about Brian?"

"Ellen, you get so intense about things. You're putting so much into that relationship. And you know he's going away to college next year."

"Come on, lighten up, Mom. Are you already worried about next year? Maybe he'll go to U of K right here in town. Or maybe even Transylvania University. It was good enough for Jefferson Davis. Maybe it's good enough for him."

"His parents can afford to send him out of town, so he'll probably go. I don't want to see you hurt. That's all."

"I'm not going to get hurt, Mom."

There was a long silence. Ellen cranked the paper back into the machine and began to type mechanically, hardly paying attention to the words.

When her mother finally closed the door, she jerked the sheet out again and read what she'd written at the top of the page. The stuff at the bottom was garbage. She'd just been pretending to work, so Mom would get off her case.

Yesterday I stopped in the park and stood there in the middle of the rose garden. Each rose is so pretty. Each one has petals soft as a baby's skin. Each one smells wonderful. And each one only lasts for a few days.

When you think about the history of the world, you realize people are like that, too. No matter how beautiful or sweet they are, each person is here for such a short time.

Was that a dumb way to start? Shouldn't she be talking about herself instead of flowers and the history of the world? What would Mrs. Finch, her journalism teacher, say about a lead like that?

She was still deep in thought when she heard another knock on the door.

Ellen groaned.

"It's okay, honey. I know this article is important to you. I'm leaving a tray out here for you."

"Thanks, Mom. Listen, I'm sorry I snapped at you."

There was no answer. Her mother had already tiptoed down the hall again.

ALTHOUGH Ben didn't come home until Friday around dinnertime, he'd called and told Elizabeth when to expect him. After opening the door, she stood there, taking him in. She'd been thinking about him so much. Now she couldn't get enough of the wheat-gold color of his hair and the blue of his eyes. Before she could look her fill, he grabbed her and folded her into his arms so tightly that she almost couldn't breathe. Her own arms came up to clasp him, reassured by the breadth of his shoulders and the solid muscles of his body.

She could have kept on holding him for endless moments. He felt good. He smelled good.

The buzzer sounded behind her.

"Got to get the chicken out of the oven," she managed. Her voice was rough and her eyes were misted, and she was glad of the excuse to turn away. Tension had been building inside her all week. Somehow she hadn't realized how bad it was until Ben stood in front of her.

He followed her into the kitchen and leaned against the doorjamb as she removed the beautifully roasted bird.

"That looks delicious."

"Did you miss me or my cooking more?"

"It's a hard decision." He didn't quite manage to bring off the humor in the line.

"I'm glad you're home."

"Yeah."

She suspected he was still being evasive about something. Instead of probing, she got the salad out of the refrigerator and handed him a bottle of dressing. "Here, why don't you make yourself useful?"

"Sure."

Ten minutes later they were sitting across from each other. Despite the tempting aroma of the chicken and the stuffing, neither seemed to have much of an appetite.

Usually after a trip, Ben told her stories about the people he'd met and the situations he'd encountered. This time he didn't have much to say and did little more than pick at his food.

Her own mental state didn't help things much. All week she'd sifted facts and options in her mind, like a prospector desperate to find gold. Reluctantly she'd decided that it just wasn't fair not to tell him about the baby. Perhaps it was her own inability to deal with deception. Not telling Cliff the news had made her feel funny, although she knew a lot of pregnant women didn't make the announcement this early. Not telling Ben made her feel bad, both about herself and their relationship. However, she couldn't just spring the news on him. She needed to lead up to the subject of pregnancy with some degree of finesse.

Elizabeth sighed and covertly studied the man across the table. He wasn't making things easy for her.

She took a quick sip of the fresh lemonade she'd made and put her glass down. She couldn't take much more of this. "Ben, why don't you tell me what's the matter?" she finally suggested.

"What do you mean?"

"Something's bothering you. Until we get it out in the open, we're not going to have a very pleasant evening." She held her ground against the hard glaze in his eyes.

"It's been a hard trip. I just want the chance to kick off my boots and relax."

"You're not relaxed."

He laid down his fork. "Nothing's bothering me—except your prying."

"Ben, I'm not prying. I want to be here for you."

"Dammit! Leave me alone! Do you think the fact that we're sleeping together gives you the right to conduct the Spanish Inquisition?" He pushed himself awkwardly away from the table. Chair and table leg collided with such force that the crockery rattled. Ben's lemonade teetered on the edge of disaster and fell to the floor with a crash. Elizabeth's tumbler was still swaying when she caught it.

Cursing vividly, Ben looked down at the broken glass and liquid spreading across the floorboards. Elizabeth suspected he was glad to have found an acceptable focus for his anger.

"It's okay. I'll take care of it," she said and went to fetch some terry towels.

Getting down on her knees, she began mopping up the mess.

"Be careful. Don't cut yourself." Ben disappeared into the kitchen and returned with the trash can. He began picking up the large pieces of glass.

"I've made a mess."

"It was an accident. It could have happened to anyone."

"It's more likely to happen to me."

She paused in midswipe of her terry towel. "What are you talking about?"

He took the rag out of her hand. "I'll finish cleaning up."

She waited while he completed the job and hunted for stray pieces of glass on the floor.

"Ben," she said softly. "I knew the first time I talked to you on the phone that something upsetting happened in San Antonio. Are you going to tell me about it?"

He shrugged. "Why not? The first day I was there, I was thinkin' about your being sick. Maybe I wasn't watching where I was going. I tripped and fell down some steps at the project."

"Oh Ben." She expelled a reedy note of air and reached toward him. "I'm sorry you were worried about me. Did you hurt yourself?"

"I banged my hip on the railing, that's all."

"That's what has you so upset?"

He clenched his fists. "A couple of hours later I got mad at the supervisor who's been screwing up the project. I chewed him up one wall and down another, and then I fired him."

"If he had it coming—"

"A calm explanation of why I was letting him go would have been sufficient. But when I saw the way the place looked, I blew up."

"Don't you think you're being too hard on yourself?"

"Am I?" His blue eyes bored into her dark ones.

Up till now she had been terribly dense. All at once she realized the point of the discussion, and her heart started to pound.

"Instead of knocking that glass over, I was pretty close to picking it up and throwing it across the room," Ben continued in a strangely calm voice. "You know, like my father."

"You didn't."

"It was tempting."

"You stopped yourself."

"I didn't stop myself from giving that supervisor the tongue-lashing of his career. I didn't stop myself from saying something pretty uncalled-for to you a few minutes ago."

She had been hurt by his gibe, but the anger had faded in the face of his upset. "Everybody flies off the handle sometimes," she said. "Everybody trips and stumbles on the stairs. I have."

"It must be wonderful to have the freedom to be clumsy." He looked down at the wet rags. "What should I do with these?"

"Let's put them in a plastic bag beside the clothes hamper."

She watched his broad shoulders disappear down the hall. They were hunched and still tense. He didn't have the freedom to be clumsy, as he'd put it. If he lost his footing, it could be an early symptom of HD. If he lost his temper, that could be an even more frightening harbinger.

If he found her watching him, he'd probably make something of that. Turning back to the table, she began to clear away the plates and the uneaten food. When he returned, he helped her in silence. While she put the food away, he stacked the dishes in the dishwasher.

Out of the corner of her eye, she watched him work. He moved with his usual efficiency and the economy of motion that she'd come to associate with him. When he finished, he washed his hands in the sink and dried them on the towel that hung on the back of the cabinet door.

She turned to him and caught his hands, unable to hold back what was in her heart.

"Ben, I love you," she said softly.

CHAPTER FOURTEEN

BEN'S WHOLE BODY jerked in reaction. Then he went very still. "No."

"You can't dictate my feelings. I've been trying to keep myself from saying the words because I knew you wouldn't accept them. I've come to the conclusion it's not going to make things any worse if I tell you."

"Oh, darlin', darlin'. You can't even leave me with my illusions."

"Your illusions. You mean you want to fool yourself into believing that we're not deeply involved?"

"I want to fool myself into thinking that I won't hurt you—that I haven't already hurt you."

"Come here." She held out her arms. She saw the silent struggle on his features. Love won. Even if he couldn't give it that name. He pulled her hard against him and clung to her.

"I missed you so much," she murmured, pressing her cheek to the edge of his jaw.

"I missed you, too. It was hard being away from you for so long. I wanted to talk to you. I wanted to hold you. Touch you."

With strong, sure fingers, he found her chin so he could angle her face toward his.

They went from warmth and closeness to frantic passion in the space of a heartbeat. His mouth sought hers. There was no holding back. He devoured her, consumed her, as though the week of separation had driven him over the edge.

But it was more than the separation. Much more. Somehow he needed to take her life force into himself.

She yielded freely, gladly, unselfishly. In the yielding she received as much as she gave. Her fingers tore at the buttons of his shirt. She needed to touch him, stroke him, make intimate physical contact.

His hands pushed up her knit top and fumbled with the clasp of her bra. When he cupped her breasts, she cried out with need and almost unendurable pleasure. Then he was bending to suck one taut nipple into his mouth, and she felt her body melt.

More, she needed more of him. This moment. Now. She had to make him understand how she felt.

There was no thought of breaking the contact. No thought of retiring to a more appropriate setting, of taking precious seconds to strip off their clothes.

Her fingers were clumsy as they struggled with his belt buckle and the fly of his pants. She felt his body rock with tremors and knew he was caught in his own dilemma. He could help her. But he'd have to let her go to do it.

At last he was in her hand, hot and powerful and pulsing with life. Her fingers closed around him, and he muttered something incoherent.

"Ben, you feel so good."

"That feels good. I'm going to explode."

"Yes."

Large hands at her narrow waist, he lifted her and set her upon the counter. With quick, desperate motions, he pushed her skirt up and dragged her panties down over her hips.

His eyes were wild and glazed by passion. Her body arched, anticipating his possession.

Suddenly he stopped and shook his head.

"Ben, please. Do it now."

He shuddered, struggling for some shred of control. "You make me crazy like nobody's ever made me crazy," he muttered thickly. "We need—I have to get—"

Her hands on his shoulders, she urged him forward. "It's all right. You don't have to worry about getting me pregnant anymore."

"You've taken care—"

"Everything's fine." *Depending on what you meant by that,* she thought with the last shreds of her own coherence. Her guilt at misleading him was wiped away when he thrust into her.

Both gasped; hot, moist femininity closed around hot, distended masculinity.

"Are you all right?" he asked urgently.

"Yes." Elizabeth had known passion in her life. She'd known passion with this man before. She had never known need this violent.

She had shattered into a million pieces when he'd first cupped her breasts. Now she called his name when he started to move inside her. It took only a few swift strokes to send her into oblivion. Again and again her body contracted around him.

His hoarse shout of pleasure seemed to surround her, just as her body surrounded his.

She sagged limply against him. His head sank to her shoulder. Ragged breathing seemed to fill the room.

They clung together, each overwhelmed by the intensity of what had happened between them.

"That was quite a finale to dinner," he finally muttered. She could hear laughter and wonder in his voice.

"And I thought the meal was a washout."

"It wasn't because of your cooking. The man you invited was acting like a storm trooper."

"He's forgiven, under certain conditions."

"What conditions?"

"That he carry a physician who's too limp to walk to her bed."

"Give him a minute to do something about his pants, or he'll trip and dump her on the floor."

He finished the job and swung her into his arms.

In the bedroom she shed the rest of her clothes and reached for her nightgown.

"Don't." His voice was gritty. "I want to feel you against me."

Under the covers they held each other gently, kissed tenderly. Then hands and lips began to brush sensitive flesh with more specific purpose. Slowly, with precious leisure and great sweetness, they began to love each other again.

Later, as she lay beside Ben in the dark, Elizabeth thought about the baby nestled inside her, and her eyes brimmed. While he'd been away, she'd told herself she'd come to a decision. The honorable decision. Tonight she had changed her mind. For the time being, at least, her honor was less important than his peace of mind. He'd see the baby as one more hostage to the future—just as he saw his whole life held hostage until he could get the tests from Hopkins completed.

She reached out and stroked his shoulder.

"Mmm?"

"I just needed to touch you. I didn't mean to wake you up."

"I wasn't sleepin'."

She was silent for several moments. "Will you get angry again if I want to talk about what happened while you were in Texas?"

"Go ahead."

She could hear his voice struggling for an even timbre.

"What purpose does it serve for you to always be watching yourself like a hawk, looking for any little sign that you're slipping?"

"If I were a singer, I could tell you it was an occupational hazard."

"What does that have to do with anything?"

"I've thought a lot about singers. I'm willing to bet they do it, too. Just when they're experienced enough to have all the technique down pat, the voice starts to go. But a lot of them keep performing, anyway. Either they know they're cheating their public, or they're fooling themselves."

"Yes."

"Then there are guys who make their living playing football. It's even worse for them. They have such a short professional life. They get to be thirty-five, and they start dropping the ball. Or their legs give out. Or the injuries catch up with them and they're on painkillers all the time."

"I don't want to talk about singers and football players. I want to talk about you."

"I'm just trying to make you understand that I'm not the only person on earth who watches himself like a hawk, as you so charmingly put it."

"What you're doing isn't good for you. Everybody stumbles. Everybody gets upset and lashes out. You're taking universal human frailties and making them into early symptoms of Huntington's Disease. Then when something happens that you think is a sign, you get uptight and that makes something else happen."

"That's not a bad analysis. Except that there's no way to prove that you're right."

She was silent. There *was* a way to prove she was right. If he could get the tests from Hopkins completed, he'd know for sure.

"Don't you watch me?" he asked in a barely audible voice. "For little signs that I'm slipping?"

"No."

"Other people do. Why not you?"

"Ben, being at risk for HD means you have a fifty-percent chance of not getting it. I'm betting we're going to roll a seven the first time out."

"A seven, huh? What do you know about playing dice?"

"My brothers taught me. We used to play a lot until I took twenty dollars away from Julius. He thought he was going to win the money back the next day. But I'd already spent it on a resort wardrobe for my Barbie doll."

Ben laughed. Then his tone sobered. "What if you're wrong about this particular bet?"

"I'll cope."

"Maybe I won't be able to."

"Don't say that."

She took him into her arms again. It was all she could do at the moment. For years the risk of Huntington's had been his lonely burden. It wasn't just his problem now. It was hers, too. And the baby's.

IF THERE WAS one unwritten rule of the medical profession, it was that physicians didn't step on each other's toes. Elizabeth would have been highly offended if some out-of-town doctor who happened to be a relative of one of her patients called up and told her how to manage the case.

Nevertheless, she was desperate enough on Monday morning to look up the phone number of the Johns Hopkins Huntington's Disease Clinic. After lunch, when she had an hour between patients, she called, identified herself, and asked to speak to the physician in charge of the testing program.

As it turned out, Dr. Frederick Manley was tied up in a meeting, so he wasn't able to call back until after five.

"Dr. Salvatore," he began. "Didn't you used to practice in Baltimore?"

"Yes, I did."

"I remember you chaired a session at the Hopkins conference on genetic diseases."

Elizabeth was astonished and flattered that she'd made so much of an impression on the man. "Yes, I moderated a panel at the conference," she told him.

"Prettiest moderator on the program."

So that was what he remembered—her looks, not her expertise. Or perhaps it was a combination of the two, she told herself wryly.

"Have you changed specialties?" Dr. Manley asked. "I remember you were working with CF children."

More than likely he'd had his secretary look her up in a couple of reference books before calling back, Elizabeth decided.

"I'm still doing clinical CF work," she acknowledged.

"Well, what can I do for you? Are you looking for participants in another workshop?"

That had been the last thing on her mind. However, the idea wasn't bad at all. "Well, we might be planning something down here next year after our new facility opens," Elizabeth told him. It would be a good way to showcase the hospital's programs to the medical community. They could even get some local publicity if Kevin did an article. Perry would like all that, she was sure.

She talked with Manley for a few minutes about possible workshop sessions. Then she took a deep breath and prepared to change topics.

"I was wondering if you might be able to do me a favor."

"If I can."

"You have a man from Lexington in your testing program. Ben Rittenhouse."

"Yes. Rittenhouse. I've interviewed him."

"His family foundation is providing the funding for our new program."

"Hmm, well… He never said anything about that."

"He's rather modest. But he's doing so much for us, and I know how anxious he is to get his own test results. I was wondering if there was any way to speed things up for him."

"Yes, I see. Just a moment, let me get his folder."

Elizabeth waited the longest five minutes of her life while Manley was away from the phone. She could hear a file drawer open and then papers being shuffled. Finally the physician came back onto the line. "As I'm sure you know, the test works by comparing the marker DNA in different members of the family. By tracking the marker, we infer the presence of the HD gene."

"Right."

"The specific relatives who need to be tested are determined on a case-by-case basis. Luckily we got a blood sample from Rittenhouse's father before he died. Which means that all of the family testing is completed—except for one uncle who apparently has the disease. We've asked for a blood sample from him several times, but the request has been refused. There's a notation in here, explaining that the wife is resistant to having her husband's diagnosis confirmed."

"Yes. That's what I understood. I was hoping she'd changed her mind."

"Perhaps you could bring some pressure to bear from that end."

"Perhaps I can." Elizabeth hesitated for a moment. "Assuming you get the sample from the uncle, how long would it take to get Mr. Rittenhouse his results?"

"If we expedite the process, a couple of weeks."

"Thank you for your help."

"No problem. Perhaps we'll be in touch later."

"Yes. I hope so."

The polite goodbyes over, Elizabeth hung up the receiver. Then, before she could change her mind, she got Cliff Morgan's home number from Information.

His wife, Carrie, answered.

"Why, this is a surprise! Cliff told me what a nice time he had with you at dinner the other night."

"Yes. I enjoyed getting together with him, too."

"I was planning to call you. Maybe you and Ben would like to come out to our house some Sunday afternoon for supper."

"I'd love to get together with you, but Ben's been sort of . . . uptight lately."

"Cliff told me he was stomping around down in Texas like a bear with a thorn in his paw," the older woman said softly.

They both knew what that could mean, Elizabeth thought as she rushed in with an explanation. "It's because he wants those test results from Hopkins. The wait is driving him crazy." *Oh, God, let that be the only thing that's wrong,* she prayed silently.

"I guess I can understand that," Carrie murmured.

Elizabeth moistened her lips, glad that the other woman couldn't see how tense she was feeling. "Carrie, I need your help. Could you give me directions to Max and Ada's house?"

"Max and Ada's! Why, child, you're not planning to go out there, are you?"

"Yes, I am."

"I don't think that's such a good idea. Folks in the hills and hollows don't take well to strangers. And Max, he...you know."

"It's the best idea I can come up with to help Ben. Carrie, I love him. And..." She longed to tell his aunt about the baby, but knew it would only complicate things. "It's very important to both of us," she murmured instead.

During the long silence on the other end of the line, Elizabeth held her breath.

"I guess I know what you're going through," Carrie finally said. "If there had been a test back when Cliff was Ben's age, I think he would have taken it." She sighed. "All right, I'll give you directions."

"Carrie, you don't know how much I appreciate this."

"Promise me you'll be careful. And call me when you get home, you hear?"

"I will."

"It's hard to find their place if you haven't been before."

"I'll manage." Elizabeth got out pencil and paper.

ELLEN LEANED BACK against the cushions of the overstuffed chair in her room and tapped a yellow school pencil against her lips. She was staring at the draft of the article she'd been pouring herself into for weeks. It was just about done now—unless it was a complete piece of junk.

When Mr. Lakefield had offered her the chance to write whatever she wanted, she'd been excited. She'd told herself there was plenty of good stuff in her journals she could use. All she had to do was pull it out and put a different slant on it. Except that when she'd started reading it over, she'd decided it was mostly whiny kid stuff.

So she'd started trying to put down some more mature thoughts. The problem was, when you only had fifteen hundred words, it was hard figuring out the most important things to say. A couple of times she'd almost given up.

Now that she had the whole thing almost finished, there was something else to worry about. At first she'd only been trying to get her thoughts straight and the sentences smooth. Then she'd started picturing the article in the newspaper. Going on the record was scary. Everybody in town would know how she felt. But somewhere along the line, putting herself into print had become important. Maybe because the words would still be there, long after she was. She swallowed. Maybe when Brian read the article, he'd understand how she felt. And her mom and dad. And Dr. Salvatore. Ellen wanted her to know how much she appreciated what she'd done for her.

A couple of days ago, a photographer from the paper had come out and taken some pictures of her and the family. They'd taken some shots of her with the hospital staff, too. That had made the whole thing more real. Too real. But she could still back out now, if she wanted to.

Her mind came back to Brian. Right now he was PO'd, because she'd told him two nights in a row that she couldn't see him because she was working on the article. It was almost finished. One more draft. Maybe she should put it away for a day or two and then come back to it.

When the phone rang, she ignored it.

Seconds later, her mother was calling her name up the stairs. Sighing, she reached over and picked up the extension on her desk.

"Ellen."

"Mr. Lakefield?"

"Yes. How are you coming along on that piece you're writing for me?"

"I was...uh...just trying to polish it up."

"Do you think you could let me see your draft?"

Ellen could feel her heart start to thump. "It's not ready."

"You could let me be the judge of that. Why don't you bring it down to the office and leave it with the receptionist in the feature section? After I read it, I can tell you if I have any suggestions."

Ellen gulped.

THERE HADN'T BEEN much rain during the past few weeks, and summer held the countryside in its dry palm as Elizabeth headed out of the city toward the hill country. Even the famous Kentucky bluegrass was losing its color, she noticed. She turned off the highway onto a dusty secondary road and passed a sagging, tin-roofed barn, its broad side brightly painted with an ad for chewing tobacco. In the adjacent field, an old blue pickup truck sat rusting near a dozen grazing cows.

This was a part of the state Elizabeth had rarely seen. At a crossroads a half mile farther on, a country store advertised Dr Pepper and souvenirs. It didn't look much like a tourist stop.

Carrie's directions led her through a small town, where the bank and the Church of the Brethren were the most impressive buildings. When the one traffic light stopped her for a minute, Elizabeth looked over at the pickup trucks and old cars lined up in front of the Food Town. The women bringing out full carts or heading inside to shop wore sundresses not unlike the one she'd selected for her visit. Most had at least one toddler or infant in tow.

They took their lives and their kids in stride, she thought, as she watched a mother calmly restrain a redheaded little boy who'd been about to dash into the road.

The scene made her wish that she and Ben were just a simple country couple living out here. Maybe they'd be worried about having another mouth to feed, especially if they were trying to make a living off the land. But they'd be joyful and optimistic about the baby, not terrified that there might be something wrong with their unborn child. Or the child's father.

Closing her eyes, Elizabeth gripped the wheel tighter. When a horn honked behind her, she realized that the light had changed and she was blocking traffic. Her foot bounced on the accelerator, and she started up again with a little jerk. Two minutes later she was on the other side of town and in the countryside again.

Now she began looking for the turnoff to Max and Ada's place. Carrie had said the road that led into the rolling hills didn't have a name. But she'd seen a cluster of mailboxes, about a hundred feet after a willow tree that had been half uprooted by a storm but was still growing, lying on its side.

She spotted the tree, sprawled like a sleeping giant, and started looking for the mailboxes. They were clumped together beside two deep, dusty ruts that wound between a field of ironweed on one side and scrubby oaks on the other.

She tried but failed to read the names on the mailboxes. Then she craned her neck and squinted up the road. It was the only one within sight of the willow tree. As she turned in, however, she couldn't help recalling Carrie's words of warning. And her admonition to be careful.

"I will," she muttered under her breath.

Soon Elizabeth was out of sight of the two-lane road. She spotted a few houses in the distance. But no people. Her car jostled along, only the occasional call of the birds perched in the oak trees and the sound of her own engine breaking the silence.

Since the road was just wide enough for one car, she wondered what would happen if she met someone coming the other way. One of them would have to pull into the field or back up. A driveway led off to her left. Then two more intersected the road on the right. The next turnoff on the left ought to be the Morgans.

When Elizabeth reached it, she hesitated. It was even narrower and more rutted than the road she'd been following. What was more, there was absolutely nothing to indicate that she'd find Max and Ada at the end. Elizabeth firmed her lips. She'd come all this way, and she wasn't going to go home empty-handed.

Almost as soon as she turned onto the new road, she left the bright sunshine for the dappled shade of a locust and maple forest. At least it was a lot cooler in the woods. Patches of sunlight winked into her face like strobe lights so that she was forced to drive slowly, leaning forward as she peered ahead.

Rounding a corner, she slammed on the brakes to avoid hitting a man standing in the middle of the road. It was hard to see him in the shifting light. An old railroad man's cap was pulled down over his eyes, partially hiding his face. He was dressed in faded coveralls and a T-shirt that had seen better days, and carried a rifle casually over his left shoulder. He made no move to get out of the way. Instead, as Elizabeth watched in shock, he purposefully lowered the weapon and pointed it at her windshield.

"Whoever you are, git out of that car!" he bellowed. "Git out of there now, 'fore I blast you right through the glass!"

CHAPTER FIFTEEN

SEVERAL WILD CHOICES flashed through Elizabeth's mind as she stared at the man with the gun. She could step on the gas and try to run him over before he shot her. No good for either one of them. She could back up and hit a tree—and probably get shot as well. Or she could follow orders. Although that might mean getting shot, anyway.

He made up her mind for her by taking a step closer to the car.

Gingerly Elizabeth reached for the door handle and stepped out into the deathly quiet of the woods. Even the birds had stopped singing, she noted with some tiny corner of her mind that was capable of focusing on anything besides the gun trained on her chest. She and the man stood less than eight feet apart. At that range, there was hardly any chance of his missing.

"This here's private property. What the hell you doin' bargin' up my road, missy?" he demanded.

Elizabeth tried to swallow past the sandpaper coating her throat. She'd thought she recognized him. Now they stood face-to-face and she was sure. It was Max. He'd been dangerously out of control at the funeral. With a rifle in his hand, he'd upped the ante considerably. Her eyes focused on the muscle jumping below his left eye.

"Max," she addressed him, turning up her palms in a gesture of consolation. "It's Elizabeth Salvatore. Don't you remember me?"

"I don't know no Elizabeth Salva—whatjacallit."

"You remember," she murmured soothingly, silently praying that she could jog his memory. "At the funeral home, when Jed passed away. Dr. Elizabeth. I made sure you were all right before Ada took you home."

He continued to stare at her as if he'd never seen her before in his life. The rifle twitched in his big hands. *Oh, God,* she thought. *It's not just his mind I have to worry about, it's the HD movements. What in the name of all the saints is he doing with a rifle, anyway?*

"Put the gun down. You don't want to hurt anyone." She struggled to keep her voice even.

His arm jerked. Now the barrel wasn't pointed straight at her chest. It was a bit off center.

"Jed's funeral," he muttered, his face strained in concentration.

"Yes. I'm Dr. Elizabeth," she repeated.

He nodded slowly. "Yeah. The pretty lady doctor. I told Ada I liked her."

"Yes."

He lowered the gun to the ground, and Elizabeth let out the frozen breath she'd been holding.

"What you doin' here?" he asked.

"I came to see you and Ada."

"A visit."

"Yes. That's right. A visit to you and Ada." She worked at reinforcing the friendly image, at keeping her voice from warbling out of control.

"Can't see the house. It's up that way." He pointed up the road. "Give me a ride, and I'll show you."

She hesitated for a moment. "Sure. But why don't you put the rifle in the back seat?"

"Yeah. Thanks. I was out lookin' for game."

She wiped her sweating palms on the sides of her dress and watched him climb through the passenger doorway and settle into the plush upholstery. How often did he roam the hills with a gun? she wondered. Were the neighbors in danger? Or did they know to watch out for him?

When she started the engine, the radio sprang to life. Apparently Max didn't like the classical station she'd been listening to; he reached out and turned the dial with jerky movements until he got something with a lively beat.

"That's better."

"I'm glad you like it."

Chickens scattered when they came out of the woods into a yard that was surrounded by a split-rail fence. A mule announced their arrival, and the door of the weathered wooden house several yards away flew open, almost as soon as the car came to a stop. Ada Morgan was wiping her hands on a dish towel as she hurried toward the driver's window. She was wearing a shapeless cotton dress covered by a white apron. Her gray hair was pulled into a fat ponytail at the nape of her neck. When she saw both Max and Elizabeth in the front seat of the car, she stopped and gawked.

Max opened the car door and jumped out. "A visit, Ady. Put the kettle on for tea. We're going to have a visit. Just like the old days. Can we have cake?"

Elizabeth got out more slowly.

Ada regarded her with considerable less enthusiasm than her husband had shown. Then she turned to Max. "You can get out the plates and cake and fill the kettle. But don't fiddle with the stove. You don't want to burn yourself again, do you?"

"No, ma'am."

Max rushed off toward the house, while Elizabeth opened the back door and gestured toward the rifle. "He forgot his gun."

"It's not loaded, if that's what you're worried about. I've got the shells."

"Good. I was concerned about his tramping through the woods with a loaded weapon." She heard the note of relief in her voice.

"Is that what you come up here for—to lecture me on lettin' someone in Max's condition run around loose?" The woman made no attempt to hide the belligerence in her voice, Elizabeth noted. But Ada's tension was betrayed by the way she twisted the dish towel in her hands.

"No." Elizabeth swallowed. She hadn't pictured the interview going quite this way, but Ada had just handed her an opportunity she couldn't turn down. "I came up here because I'm pregnant with Ben's baby."

She had the satisfaction of seeing Ada's mouth fall open.

"Ben doesn't know yet, because I don't think he could cope with the news. He's been on edge for months, waiting to find out from Johns Hopkins whether he's carrying the Huntington's gene. But the way it works, they can't tell him anything until Max is tested."

The door of the house flew open, and Max charged back into the yard. He bounced up and down as he regarded the two women. "What are you gals doin' standin' out here, flappin' your mouths? I got the peach cake on the table. Is it all right to fill the kettle?"

His wife gave him her full attention. "Yes, I told you it was all right to fill the kettle. We'll be right in."

Elizabeth heard the change in her voice. It was softer, almost caressing. What was also apparent was how much of her attention it took to keep him out of trouble. How was the woman managing by herself, up here in the middle of nowhere?

When Ada turned back toward Elizabeth, her tone changed again, abruptly. "Are you trying to decide whether to have an abortion?"

"I wasn't planning on getting pregnant. But now that I am, I'm not planning on having an abortion. No matter what happens."

"Then what do you want from me?"

"It's Ben's peace of mind I'm worried about. He's so tense now, he's about to fly apart into a million pieces. I want to help him. But there's not much I can do."

"That's the way I feel." The older woman's words were clipped.

Before Elizabeth could respond, Mrs. Morgan turned unexpectedly and started toward the house.

"Please. Wait."

"I have to go and see how Max is doin' in the kitchen," her hostess answered without looking around. "Usually he follows directions. But sometimes he gets into trouble."

Elizabeth's chest was tight as she followed Max's wife across the farmyard. Ada was the first person she'd told about the baby she was carrying. Now that she'd revealed her secret, she wanted some sort of resolution to the Hopkins problem. Either a yes or no. Apparently she was going to have to wait.

She caught the screen door that slammed toward her. Already inside, Ada walked rapidly out of view. Elizabeth stood for a moment, taking in the living room. It was neat and clean, but the appointments had seen better days. The wide pine boards were covered only by a rag rug. The sofa and overstuffed chair sported heavy plastic slipcovers.

The house was small. She had no trouble finding the kitchen, particularly since the aroma of peaches and cinnamon wafted toward her. The source of the tantalizing smell was the home-baked cake sitting in the center of the trestle table. The room itself was surprisingly charming, with sturdy pine furniture, a beamed ceiling, and a long window that provided a spectacular view of the mountainside behind the farmstead.

Max gestured toward one of the places that had been set with checkered place mats. "Take a load off your feet."

Elizabeth smiled at him and pulled out one of the straight-backed chairs. "Thank you, Max."

Since the frightening confrontation on the road, he'd clearly been eager to make her welcome. Elizabeth responded to what seemed to be his naturally outgoing personality, feeling that she was getting a glimpse of what he must have been like before Huntington's had begun to erode his mind.

Ada brought cups of tea to the table. Max smacked his lips as she cut the peach cake. As soon as he got his portion, he dug in, although his hand wavered, making it difficult for him to get a whole piece into his mouth. Crumbs scattered on the table. They all ignored the mess, although Elizabeth saw her hostess watching her for a reaction.

When Max reached for his teacup, Ada shook her head. "Wait till it cools."

"Oh, yeah. Right."

It was a strange tea party. The two women regarded each other warily, while Max clearly enjoyed both the food and the company.

Elizabeth forked up another bit of cake. "It's delicious."

"Ady's the best cook in the county," Max declared.

"And this room is so charming."

Ada glanced at her husband. "He built it onto the back of the house before we got married." She smiled, and her face took on a faraway look. "It was part of his way of courtin' me."

Max's chest puffed up with pride.

"He's like his brothers," Elizabeth murmured. "And his nephew, Ben. They're all excellent builders. They're all very talented."

"Cliff's the lucky one!" Ada shot back.

Max had finished his cake and tea. Getting up, he went to the window and stood looking out, shifting his weight from one foot to the other.

"You were going to pick snap beans for me," Ada reminded him. "So we could have them for supper."

"Right. Snap beans." He picked up the basket hanging by the back door. "Fill it to the red line." He glanced at Ada.

"Yes."

He went out, and they could see him heading for the vegetable garden.

"He'll be gone awhile," Ada said. "He's not very fast at pickin', with the muscle spasms and all. They get worse when he's concentrating on something." Hands locked together in her lap, she gave her uninvited visitor a direct look.

Elizabeth nodded sympathetically. "It's hard sitting by and watching your husband lose the things that make him what he is."

"It's not fair!"

"You love him." Elizabeth could feel a tug at her own heart as she spoke the words.

"Yes. I'm going to be here for him. As long as he needs me. I married him for better or for worse. In sickness and in health. I'm not going to let them stack him in some nursing home like a damn cord of wood, the way they did with Jed, because Cora cleared out and there was no one to take care of him."

"Unfortunately, Jed's wife wasn't as strong as you. Or as loving. And she didn't realize what was wrong with him. She thought he had some kind of mental illness, and that he'd be a danger to her or Ben."

"She was his wife!"

"Sometimes HD tears a family apart. Sometimes it brings out the best in people."

"I'm no saint."

"No. But you've got guts. And integrity."

Perhaps no one had told Ada that before. She looked at Elizabeth in surprise.

"Nobody has to cope with something like this alone. Not as it progresses. There are doctors and social service agencies that can help you. Plus, physical therapy has proved very helpful with HD patients. If you took Max in for a medical evaluation, there'd be things they can do for him. Things that would make him more able to cope. Physically and mentally."

"I didn't know that. I thought..."

"Don't cut yourself off because you wish Max wasn't sick. You don't have to go through this alone," Elizabeth murmured, conscious now that she'd told Ben the same thing. It had been hard to convince him, too.

Ada's thoughts had apparently also turned to Ben. "I married Max before I knew what would happen to him. But you don't have to let yourself in for all of this."

"I'm not a saint, either. It's not the way I would have chosen for things to happen." She hadn't planned to tell Ada the story of her life. Now she found she wanted the other woman to understand why Ben was so important to her. "My husband died two years ago in an accident. I saw him hit by a truck."

Ada sucked in a sharp gust of air as if she was imagining what that must have been like.

"The only way I could deal with the grief was to let my emotions get all frozen up inside me. I had my work at Children's Hospital. I told myself that was enough, that I didn't really need a personal life to be fulfilled. Then I met Ben. And the thaw started. I knew I'd found the right man. I didn't understand why he wanted to keep me at arm's length, because I could tell he was responding to me, the same way I was responding to him.''

Ada didn't interrupt.

''Finally Ben told me about Jed, and that he wasn't going to see me again until after he heard from Hopkins. He said he'd decided a long time ago that he wasn't going to get married or have children—that he wasn't going to do to some woman what his father had done to his mother. There was no way to change his mind without getting the results of that test.''

Ada nodded slowly.

''I got angry at him, because he insisted it had to be his decision. I told myself he was right, that we might not ever see each other again. Then Jed died, and I knew Ben needed me. I was pretty sure I'd find him out at the cabin that the two of them built. I guess you can figure out what happened,'' she continued in a low voice. ''He's never allowed himself to be spontaneous with women. But that night, neither one of us was thinking about being careful, and I got pregnant.''

Elizabeth's eyes were misted as she looked at Ada. So were the older woman's.

''I see why you don't want to tell him about the baby,'' she whispered.

''I told myself I had to. Then I decided I couldn't lay one more burden on his shoulders right now. But it would be so different if—if we knew that he'd escaped the gene. He'd be happy about us.'' She struggled to keep her voice from quavering. ''About the baby.''

''That's the good side. What if he's going to end up like Max and Jed?''

"I'll feel the way you do. It's not fair. Not when he's such an exceptional man. But I'll deal with that. And I hope he'll let me share the burden with him. But Ada, if it's going to happen to him, the clock is ticking. I want whatever time we can have together. I want him to know his child. If he has Huntington's, I could help him. The way you're helping Max. And I told you, they're doing research. By the time the baby would be likely to come down with the disease, they'll surely have a treatment that stops the process dead—or maybe they'll even have a cure." She knew that last part was her own wishful thinking. She had to cling to her faith in medical science.

"Tell me why Max has to be tested. Why can't they leave us be and just test Ben?"

"I guess you know that HD is carried by a dominant gene, so children with a parent who has Huntington's have a fifty-percent chance of developing the disease. They're referred to as being 'at risk.'"

Ada nodded.

"Researchers have discovered a piece of DNA that travels with the Huntington's gene during reproduction. It's called a marker for the gene. To find out which at-risk individuals will develop the disease, doctors have to compare their marker with those of close relatives with HD, as well as close relatives who don't have Huntington's."

"What kind of test is it?"

"Nothing invasive. It's usually a blood test, like the kind you probably had when you got married. Except that they take several tubes of blood."

"Finding out about Ben is important to you."

"It's more important to him."

"I—I have to think about it."

"I understand."

Elizabeth stood up. "Thank you for the tea and cake. I'll go out and say goodbye to Max before I leave."

"He likes you."

"He's a good person."

"Most people can't see that."

"That's their loss."

MARGARET JACKSON wished she could sleep in like everyone else on Sunday morning. Somehow her internal clock never let her stay in bed past eight. Slipping quietly out of bed so she wouldn't wake her husband, she went downstairs and fixed herself a cup of peppermint tea while she thumbed through the paper.

The lead story in the feature section riveted her attention. At the top of the page was a color picture of Ellen, sitting on the sofa in the family room. She hadn't even known the article was finished. And Ellen hadn't said anything about its being scheduled for this Sunday. Maybe she hadn't known.

She studied the smiling sixteen-year-old. Ellen looked beautiful, almost fragile. Like a princess who'd been locked away from the world. Had they done that to her? Kept her too sheltered and protected?

Half-afraid of what she might encounter, she let her gaze drift to the text below the picture. Ellen had been pouring herself into this article for weeks. What had she written? Was it any good? Was it true? Would it condemn her family? Her parents?

Full Speed Ahead—Slowly By Ellen Jackson

I can't be a cheerleader. But I win points for my school on the debating team. I can't be on the girl's soccer team. But I've had a couple of supporting roles in our school plays.

I can't do ten laps of the pool. But I can cup a rose in my hand and brush the baby-soft petals against my cheek, inhale the perfume, and let my eyes feast on the delicate color.

I've thought a lot about roses. Each one lasts only a short time. But each one is beautiful. Special.

People are that way, too. No matter what their limitations or their handicaps. Or how short a time they bloom.

Helen Keller wrote about flowers once. She could smell their fragrance and feel their softness. She couldn't see the colors or hear the wind rustling their foliage. But that didn't keep her from being one of the greatest women of this century.

Everybody alive has limitations. Some more than others. It's not your limitations that count. It's what you do with the gifts you have. What you make of the time that's been given you. How you affect other people. What you do with the talents you've been given.

My most obvious limitations come from cystic fibrosis. It's a genetic disease. My younger sister, Cindy, doesn't have it. And she won't get it, because you have to be born with it. You have to inherit the recessive gene from both parents.

When I was a little kid, it mostly affected my digestion. But as you get older, your lungs are the worst problem. They secrete thick mucus that makes it hard to breathe. You get a lot of lung infections. Sometimes your lungs even hemorrhage, which is pretty scary....

There are times when I've been afraid. Even times when I might have given up and stopped fighting. But there was always somebody to help me. Like the time my lung started bleeding, and my mom had to get me to the hospital. She was so calm and reassuring. She kept me from panicking.

Margaret realized she was trying to read through a film of tears. She stopped for a moment to get her emotions under control.

After the crisis was over, that was when I was really spooked. I'd lie there in my hospital bed and worry about the future. But Dr. Salvatore, my doctor, helped me get through that. I won't say I never worry now. Or that I love to cooperate with all the medical treatments that are necessary. But I think I'm handling it better....

She drew in a deep breath. Right here in black and white were all the things she'd been afraid to talk about with her daughter. All the things she'd thought Ellen was afraid to face. Everything was here for the reading. Not just for Ellen's father and herself. Other people, too. They'd get a better understanding of what it meant to struggle against chronic illness from the moment you were born. Yet it would only be second-hand for them, not a personal experience. It wouldn't make them think about the things they'd tried to do for their child. The mistakes they might have made. The opportunities they might have missed. Or maybe it would.

KEVIN LAKEFIELD was also up early. The article by Ellen Jackson was scheduled for today. He'd woken up, unable to get it out of his mind. Finally he'd gotten out of bed and retrieved the paper from the door-mat in the hall of his apartment building.

When he'd picked up the draft from the secretary's desk, he'd been reminded of the first article he'd written for his college paper. He'd wondered whether the piece was any good. So he'd simply buried it in the editor's In box, hoping it would make it into print. It had. With some judicious editing.

He hadn't done much editing on Ellen's piece. It had gone through just about the way she'd written it, with a little bit of polishing from him. But he hadn't changed the thoughts. Those were strictly Ellen's.

Opening the paper, he turned to the feature section. There she was, sitting on the sofa, looking every bit a teenager. You couldn't tell from looking at her how extraordinary she was. But you could from reading her article.

How did it read in print? He scanned the text, feeling the same power from the words that he'd felt when he'd read her typescript. The girl had a career in journalism ahead of her. He could probably get her a summer job while she was still in college. If her health held up. That was the big question.

Not just for her. For his son, too.

Putting down the paper, he tiptoed down the hall to the room where Eddie was sleeping. For long moments he stood looking at the tousled-haired little boy. Ellen had made him think about things he hadn't wanted to face—like Eddie's future, for example. And the time they had together now. Sometimes taking Eddie had been an obligation. Now he was wondering if he could get his ex-wife to let him spend more time with the boy.

BRIAN WILMORE slept late Sunday morning. His parents were visiting his older sister in Ann Arbor, Michigan, and there was no one down in the kitchen, rattling pots and pans, or listening to the Sunday morning public affairs programs.

Dragging himself out of bed at twelve-thirty, he poured himself a Coke and brought in the Sunday paper. First he read the sports section. Then his favorite comics. It was around one when he started thumbing through the rest of the paper.

He stopped dead when he came to the feature section. There was Ellen, right on the front of the page. At the top. He'd known she was all wound up with the article she was writing. She'd even canceled a couple of dates, and he'd gotten bent out of shape and hadn't called her since Wednesday. He hadn't thought her article was going to be such a big deal. The most important story. With her picture in color.

Brian studied Ellen's face. It might sound corny, but every time he saw her, she sort of took his breath away. He'd kind of forget how beautiful she was and then remember all over again. Some people didn't look as good in a picture as they did in person. Not Ellen. If anything, she looked better.

He'd been hurt when she wouldn't let him see what she was writing. Well, here it was in print for everybody in Lexington to read.

The introduction grabbed him by the throat and slammed him back into the kitchen chair.

He didn't lift his eyes from the page until he'd finished the whole article. It was all there. All the stuff she'd tried to talk to him about. All the stuff she'd kept inside. All the stuff he hadn't really understood, even though it had been right there in front of him.

He reached for the phone, then changed his mind. Instead he pounded upstairs, took a shower, and got dressed. Twenty minutes later he was pulling up in front of her parents' two-story colonial.

It wasn't until he rang the bell that he thought about the possibility she might not want to see him. Not after the way he'd been acting all week.

When she answered the door herself, they stared at each other tentatively.

"Brian."

His arm jerked. "Hi."

"I was hoping you'd call. I was afraid you might not want to see me."

"You?"

"I thought you might not like the article."

"Sheez! I slept late. I just read it. It was great, really great!"

"You really think so? You wouldn't lie to me?"

He held his gaze steady. "No."

She nodded.

"I'll bet your parents are all excited. Mine would flip if I had a story in the paper."

"Yeah."

Silence stretched again.

"Want to come in?" Ellen asked.

"Uh... Do you think they'd mind if you went out this afternoon?"

"I don't know."

"I'd like to be alone with you."

Ellen swallowed. "Give me a minute."

She was back sooner than that. "I just have to be home for dinner. You're invited too, if you want. Barbecued chicken on the grill."

"Sure. Sounds good."

They didn't talk much on the ride to Brian's. Inside, the house was dark and quiet. They stood uncertainly in the front hall, two feet apart, facing each other.

"My parents are in Michigan. Until Wednesday or Thursday."

"I remember they were going."

"I missed you this week."

"I missed you, too." She laughed self-consciously. "When I wasn't all wrapped up in the article."

"You put a lot of yourself into it."

"You really like it?"

"Yeah, babe, I really like it."

"I was worried you'd think it was too personal."

"It was like you were talking to me—saying things that maybe only I would understand."

"In a way I was." There was an intensity, an expectancy on her face as she lifted her arms around his neck.

He reached out to brush back a strand of her golden hair. It was incredibly soft. Like her skin. Like her voice.

His own arms came around to circle her tiny waist. She was so delicate. And strong. When he smiled into her eyes, she smiled back. Then he lowered his head, and their lips met in a long, sweet kiss.

CHAPTER SIXTEEN

BEN RITTENHOUSE had kissed Elizabeth goodbye and left her apartment around midnight. Cliff was sending him on another inspection trip, and he had to catch a 9:00 a.m. plane for San Antonio.

He'd packed when he'd gotten home. Now his bags were sitting by the front door, ready to go.

After fixing a cup of coffee he brought in the Sunday paper and read the headlines. A bank robbery. A train derailment. A drug bust. He wasn't particularly interested in the details. Instead, he turned to the feature section.

At the top of the page, the picture of a pretty blond girl sitting on a sofa was like a breath of fresh air. "Author Ellen Jackson Relaxes in Her Family Room," the caption read.

Ellen Jackson. Where had he heard that name? His gaze dropped to the headline. "Full Speed Ahead— Slowly. A Local Teenager Tells What It's Like to Live with Cystic Fibrosis."

Ellen Jackson. Now he remembered. Elizabeth's patient. The girl she'd spoken about a number of times. The one she obviously liked so much. She'd mentioned that Ellen had been asked by the newspaper to write an article on her life experiences.

When Elizabeth had told him about it, he'd seen it in very personal terms. He'd imagined someone asking him to write for publication about the disease that cast a shadow over his life. For him, spilling his guts in public was simply unimaginable. He was still getting comfortable with telling Elizabeth how he felt. Maybe he wouldn't even have done that, except that she never let him hide behind silence or a bad temper. That wasn't her way.

Of course, sharing the emotions he kept hidden from the world had been a prerequisite for entering the testing program at Hopkins. They hadn't agreed to take him on until they'd carefully examined his motives for applying. The interviewers had insisted on talking about his father, his mother, his childhood. His adult life. His relationships. Why he wanted the test. How he'd feel about a favorable outcome. How he'd handle it if it turned out he was carrying the gene. He sighed. He hadn't exactly lied to them. But sometimes he'd played fast and loose with the truth, when he'd been pretty sure they wouldn't like the answer.

He studied Ellen more closely, wondering if he could tell by her face why she'd written the article. She was smiling for the camera. If you weren't too observant, you'd miss the fact that she was sick. Even though she was. Cystic fibrosis affected you physically, right from birth. And it got progressively worse.

At least he hadn't been faced with that burden. One thing about HD, you had a normal life until you got the first symptoms—if you could call waiting for the ax to fall across your neck "normal life".

Spreading the section open on the table, he began to read.

...Sometimes they have pictures in the paper of people who have lived to be a hundred, as if that were some sort of wonderful achievement all by itself. I know I won't live to be a hundred, unless medical science comes up with some miracle cure for CF—the way Dr. Salvatore told me they did with diabetes in the 1920s.

The way things are now, maybe I won't even live to be thirty. But I'm going to do something important with my life. If I can't go for quantity, then I'll go for quality. And for making a difference. One idea I have is to help little kids who have to go in the hospital. It's scary when you don't know why you're sick or what they're going to do to you. Or if it's going to hurt. But I could write a book for them, telling them what it's like, so they'll know what to expect and they won't be scared, the way I used to be.

What had he accomplished beyond trying to maintain his integrity on a personal level? Ben wondered. What had done for anyone else? His Uncle Max? Elizabeth? Ben turned back to the article.

Don't think I'm not selfish. I'm as selfish as anyone else. I want to go to college. I want a career, probably as a writer. I want love. I want to have children. I may not get to do all of those things. But I'm going to try for every bit of happiness and joy that life can offer me.

God, what a combination of guts and determination, Ben thought. She certainly hadn't sat around feeling sorry for herself. She was making plans for the future. Even if it was a future that existed only in her imagination.

He'd never dared to think very far beyond the next day. Not even after he'd signed up for the Hopkins program. Not even after he'd come to an uneasy agreement with Elizabeth. But so much had happened recently, and he hadn't really let himself grasp the implications.

He sat with his hands clasped, knuckles pressed against his lips. Elizabeth. The wild card that had popped into his life. Reluctantly he forced himself to examine what he hadn't wanted to admit. Lately she'd been uptight. He'd sensed something was wrong, but hadn't pressed her because he hadn't been sure he could handle the conversation. Now he had to face the possibility that she might be regretting that she'd forced him into a relationship.

But it wasn't just Elizabeth he had to think about. It was also himself.

ELIZABETH couldn't help being worried when Ben didn't call her Sunday. It was a relief to hear his voice Monday night as she sat in bed with a medical journal spread across her lap, trying to read.

"Hi."

"Hi, yourself."

"What have you been doing?" he asked.

"Working. The usual. Except for reading the article I was telling you about, the one by Ellen Jackson. It was in the paper yesterday. I saved it for you, in case you didn't see it."

"I read it before I left."

"What did you think?"

"It was interesting."

"Oh, Ben, I'm so proud of her. I wrote her a note. She'll probably get a lot of fan mail." She went on about Ellen. But as she talked, she could feel a lump building in her chest. This was like the last time Ben had been away. Something wasn't quite right at the other end of the phone line. "Ben, what is it?" she finally asked.

"You, uh, remember my last trip, when it turned out I needed to stay and get the project back on track? Well, it looks like it would be better if I put in a little extra time down there again."

"How long?"

"Oh, maybe a couple of weeks. Maybe a little bit more."

The lump in her chest threatened to close off her windpipe. "Is everything all right with you?" she managed.

"Yeah."

She didn't think he was telling the truth. She knew there wasn't any point in pressing him over the phone.

"Lisbeth," he said suddenly.

"What?"

"I was lying to you about the article. I didn't just think it was interesting. It blew me away. That's... uh... why I'm not kickin' about having to stay down here. That girl made me realize I have to do some serious thinking. And I think it's better to do it alone."

Her whole body had gone rigid. "Can't we talk about it? Whatever you're worried about?"

"Darlin', don't press me. Just let me try to work my way through this."

"All right."

"I...uh...I may not call you for a couple of days."

Dredging up enough air to get out a single syllable, she replied. "Okay." But it wasn't okay. This was like the time he'd told her about Jed and insisted he had to be the one to make the decisions. Only now there was a lot more at stake.

"I'll miss you," she said in a low voice.

"I always miss you when I'm away."

That was something, at least. More than she might have gotten out of him a couple of months ago.

Elizabeth carefully replaced the receiver on the cradle and sat with her arms wrapped around her shoulders, hugging herself.

"FULL SPEED AHEAD— SLOWLY." That had been the title of Ellen's article. Ironically, it was just the opposite of the way Elizabeth was beginning to feel. First one week and then the next one dragged on. She simply wasn't making any headway. In fact, she counted it an achievement if she managed to slog through the days without sneaking a nap in the staff lounge between patient appointments. Once they'd had to page her on the PA system because she was late for an appointment.

As she sat picking at a dinner of chicken and pineapple salad in the hospital cafeteria, she told herself she understood the reasons for the feeling of inertia. All pregnant women were tired during the first trimester. But she had added burdens to carry around. If only Ada would come through, it might affect Ben's thinking. Sometimes she had crazy fantasies about sneaking back out to the Morgan property, waiting on the road, and ambushing Max. Only this time she wouldn't be afraid of the gun. She could tell him she'd come out to examine him again and then whip out a couple of syringes, take his blood, and express it to Hopkins. Only a stunt like that was completely out of the question.

Putting down her fork, she gave up the battle to eat a well-balanced dinner and reached for the bowl of red and green gelatin cubes. Usually she hated the stuff. For the past week, she'd been looking forward to it at the end of every meal.

Tonight she could only finish half the serving. Suddenly the smell of cafeteria food was just too much. Making a quick exit from the building, she hurried to her car.

The light classical station she tuned in didn't lift her mood. Silently she admitted that when she wasn't worrying about everything else, she was worrying about her body. It was starting to fill out, become more maternal. You couldn't really see it when she was dressed. Her waist was still slim. Only her breasts were larger, and her abdomen was just beginning to curve slightly. When she stood naked in front of the full-length mirror on the bathroom door, however, she was all too aware of the changes. It was hard to believe Ben wouldn't notice, especially since he wasn't seeing her on a daily basis now. Three weeks of changes would hit him all at once.

Whatever decision he came to in Texas, she couldn't just let him discover her pregnancy on his own. That meant she'd have to tell him as soon as he got back. Or she could talk to him about it on the phone the next time he called. The news might jog some kind of response out of him.

No, that would be using shock tactics. Which wasn't fair. Not even if the waiting and the uncertainty were driving her crazy.

Elizabeth tried to imagine what was going to happen. There were too many possibilities. The only thing she was sure of was that finding out about the baby would change things forever between Ben and herself. He might be so angry or threatened that he'd completely break off with her—if he wasn't already planning to do that. Would he think she'd tricked him? Or would he entertain the idea of marriage?

Her first burst of optimism had gradually given way to realism. Against her will, she'd started making contingency plans. If Ben bailed out, she'd stay in Lexington and try to change his mind. If she couldn't, Baltimore was a better place to raise their child— they'd be surrounded by all those uncles and aunts and cousins. But maybe going home was the wrong thing to do. That would be like giving up on Ben, once and for all.

Suddenly the whole situation seemed too much to cope with when she was so tired. Maybe if she went right to bed and slept for about ten hours she'd have a better outlook.

She could hear the phone ringing as she inserted her key into the lock. Ben! Or the answering service. The first possibility made her run toward the phone. The second made her press her lips together at the thought of having to go back out again.

"Elizabeth. I've been trying to get you."

For a moment she thought it was Ben. Then she realized she was talking to Cliff.

"What's wrong?"

"Ben called me. He asked me to give you a message."

The fine down on the back of her neck prickled.
"Yes?"

"We got a call at the office from Hopkins a couple
of days ago. They were trying to locate him."

He hadn't called. He hadn't let her know. But he
was giving her the message now—through Cliff.
"And?" The question came out as a little gasp.

"Ben's in Baltimore. They've scheduled an appointment for him tomorrow morning."

"Oh." The tiny syllable didn't begin to convey what
she was feeling. She had the odd sensation of floating, as if the solid kitchen floor had dropped away
beneath her feet.

"He's catching a flight for Lexington at two in the
afternoon, and he wants you to meet him out at the
cabin."

"He wants me to meet him," she repeated, as if she
didn't really believe the words. "At least he's going to
share the verdict with me—whatever it is." The words
came out in a reedy little gasp.

"Elizabeth, whatever happens, I want you to know
that you've been the best thing that ever happened to
him."

"Maybe not."

"Definitely yes."

When she didn't answer, silence stretched. Finally
the man on the other end of the line cleared his throat.
"Good luck."

"The odds are even, Cliff. I have a fifty-fifty chance of ending up in heaven—or in hell." Her throat was raw, and she swallowed painfully.

Carefully hanging up the phone, Elizabeth prayed silently in the darkened kitchen, although she knew that the matter had been decided thirty years ago at the moment Ben Rittenhouse had been conceived. Either he'd inherited the Huntington's gene from his father or he hadn't.

Sleep was out of the question now. The meager dinner she'd eaten rumbled in her stomach like the contents of a rock-tumbling machine. And her heart felt as if it was going to pound its way through the wall of her chest. Over and over she reached out to pick up the phone again, then pulled her hand back. Ben was in Baltimore, alone in some hotel room, sweating out the dark hours of the night just the way she was. Cliff must know where he could be reached. But he hadn't volunteered the information. Which meant that Ben wanted to be alone tonight. Just as he'd wanted to be alone over the past few weeks.

At least he was willing to see her tomorrow. She hugged that knowledge to her heart. That meant something, although she wasn't sure what, she admitted with a little gulp. He'd asked her out to the cabin once to tell her about Jed and to say goodbye. Breaking off the relationship could be his intention now. Maybe that was what he wanted, no matter what happened.

She paced back and forth, wishing she could turn off her churning thoughts. If it had been safe for the baby, she would have taken a sleeping pill and embraced blessed oblivion.

SOMETIME during the early hours of the morning, Ben had actually managed to doze off. He woke up cold and alone. As he had done every night since he'd been away from Lexington, he reached across the bed for Elizabeth. She wasn't there. He cursed.

At himself. He was the one who'd decided what would be best for both of them. The way he had before, he admitted ruefully. He'd tried to hold out. It had taken a little over two weeks before he'd given up and admitted that the forced separation wasn't helping. Then, when he'd been about to tell Cliff he wanted to come home, the social worker from Hopkins had called. She wouldn't give him any information over the phone. He had to come to Baltimore to hear whether he was a doomed man or not.

His appointment wasn't until ten. What was he going to do until then? For the millionth time, he looked across the room at the glowing green numbers of the clock. Then he swung his legs out of bed and went to stand by the window, the way he'd done in other hotel rooms. He wished this one had a balcony, so he could step outside and feel the wind against his face.

Across the street, twinkling lights defined the rooflines of the shopping pavilions that had revitalized the harbor area. By breakfast time, the buildings would be bustling with tourists. Now the waterfront was deserted, which suited him fine, he thought. He reached for his pants and jammed his legs inside. A solitary walk along the brick quay was as good a way as any to make the time go faster. He closed the door to his room and thought about Hopkins. In a few hours he could call the Huntington's Disease Project and say he'd changed his mind about getting the results of the test. No, that was the coward's way out. He'd come this far; he wasn't going to turn tail now.

Ben crossed the deserted hotel lobby and exited into the humid Baltimore morning. A few minutes later he reached the waterfront. His solitary footsteps echoed on the pavement as he walked beside the dark water, staring at the small craft bobbing in the gentle waves. It should have been a soothing scene, but his shoulders were tight and his stomach was tied in fisherman's bend knots. Breakfast was going to be out of the question. Probably he couldn't even choke down a cup of coffee—not just because he was waiting out the last few hours before he got the test results, although, God knows, that was bad enough.

Since he'd come back from the Marines, he'd followed his own rules. It was like the old joke. The right way. The wrong way, and the Ben Rittenhouse way. But over the past few weeks he'd found himself questioning every smug assumption he'd ever made about his life. He'd told himself he'd come to a decision down in San Antonio. Did he really have the guts to share it with Elizabeth?

SLEEP HAD BEEN IMPOSSIBLE. All night Elizabeth had felt as if she were standing on the edge of a high cliff that was crumbling away under her feet. Soon she might tumble off the edge and fall into oblivion. Or a sweet wind, heavy with the scent of wildflowers and pine, might sweep her to safety. It would magically pick her up and carry her off to the land of milk and honey.

At seven in the morning she thought about canceling her office hours for the day. Then she decided that it was better to keep her mind occupied, as long as she could function efficiently. Somehow she managed to concentrate on her patients, although she knew she wasn't giving them her best. Even when she tried to block it out, the anxiety was always there below the surface.

Finally she gave up and cleared her afternoon schedule. Shrugging out of her white coat, she left it on the back of her chair. Her bare arms felt chilly in the air conditioning, so she hurried down the gray-carpeted corridor. It felt good to step out into the sunshine.

What a beautiful day! she thought as she passed the beds of pink and yellow petunias that flanked the brick sidewalk. She hadn't been paying attention to the weather when she'd come in. Now she stopped for a moment, took a deep breath of fresh air, and raised her face to the jewel-like blue of the sky. It was a perfect day for getting good news. Maybe that was a good omen.

Her first stop after the hospital was the grocery store. Standing at the checkout counter, putting steaks, apples and marshmallows onto the moving belt, she started to laugh at herself. The typical female instinct, responding to a crisis by laying in supplies. Or was she storing up more good omens? Food she and Ben had enjoyed together. As her laughter escalated, she realized people were staring—and that she was in danger of slipping over the line from mirth to tears. It took her several moments to get a grip on herself. As soon as the clerk had put her bags into the cart, she made a hasty exit from the store. She'd already packed a travel bag early in the morning, and the ice chest was in the trunk. Instead of going back to her apartment, she headed for Route 64. If she wanted to cry, she could do it down by the stream, where only the birds and chipmunks would hear.

She'd thought she'd set her things in the cabin and wander into the woods. But once she'd lugged the ice chest inside, she knew she was too exhausted to put one foot in front of the other and not fall onto her face. Maybe if she just lay down on the bunk for a while, she'd feel better. Then she could change out of the dress she'd worn to work and into a pair of slacks and a shirt.

Elizabeth hadn't known she was going to drift off to sleep. Or that her dreams would send her tossing restlessly back and forth across the bed. Or that she'd wake up, her hair mussed and her light cotton dress plastered against her body, the hem twisted around her hips.

Disorientation was her first conscious sensation. Then she realized that the light from the doorway was blocked by a pair of broad, masculine shoulders. Ben. Her heart leaped into her throat. How long had he been standing there, watching her sleep?

"I didn't mean to wake you. I didn't want you to see me like this." His voice was low and thick.

Her anxious gaze found his face, and she saw that his eyes were red and his cheeks were streaked with tears.

Struggling to a sitting position, she held out her arms.

CHAPTER SEVENTEEN

BEN'S STEPS gathered momentum; he crossed the room so quickly that the impact of his body meeting Elizabeth's pushed her back into a prone position. Her arms went around him, and she held him fiercely.

She felt him trembling, felt his hands steal around her to tangle possessively in her hair and stroke up and down her back. If she knew anything at this moment, she knew that he needed her. That was the only important reality. She twisted around and lifted her face to him so that he could see the love she sensed was shining in her eyes.

"I love you, Ben. I love you."

"Oh, God, Lisbeth, darlin'." The words were blurred and indistinct as his lips moved over hers.

He clasped her shoulders tighter, and the kiss built in intensity.

Sometimes their lovemaking had been sweet. Other times they'd drawn out the lazy delight of giving each other pleasure. And there were glorious and desperate times, like these, when they seemed to be caught up by some primal force beyond their control.

There were no words to describe the power of what was happening between them now. Tenderness and passion. Desperation and the sweet, loving celebration of what one man and one woman could become to each other. They kissed and touched, sighed and murmured.

Finally Elizabeth's need coalesced into a simple goal. Holding Ben naked in her arms. Feeling him move inside her.

Fingers worked at buttons and fastenings. Arms lifted garments over heads, legs kicked away unwanted encumbrances. Finally there was nothing between them but passion, crackling like forks of lightning in a black-velvet sky.

He pulled her into his arms, clung to her, rocked against her. Close, but not close enough. He rolled her onto her back, separating her legs with one of his.

Her eyes were squeezed shut. On a sigh, she savored the gratification as she felt him enter her.

"Don't move, darlin'. Please don't move."

It took her several heartbeats to realize that he was completely still above her.

"Lisbeth, look at me."

Her lids fluttered open. He was braced on his hands, looking down with an intensity that almost robbed her of breath.

"When you woke up and saw me standing in the doorway, you held out your arms, the way you've always done."

"Yes."

"You didn't ask what they told me at Hopkins, darlin'."

Suddenly this moment suspended in time had become the most important of her life. "You want to tell me now?"

He nodded and swallowed convulsively, but his gaze didn't leave hers. "I don't have the gene." He tried to keep his voice from cracking and failed. "I don't have it, Lisbeth. I've escaped."

"Oh, my God! Ben! Oh, Ben!" She was crying. And laughing. And touching his face, as if she could hardly believe that her prayers had been answered. She was reaching for his lips with hers, clasping her arms around his shoulders, even as she felt him begin to move inside her with sure, claiming strokes.

The words he'd spoken were as much a spur to her ardor as the thrusting of his hips against hers. She moved with him, around him, taking everything he offered her with unbounded joy. They were free of the terrible specter that had hung over him. They were exalted.

They moved in perfect harmony, driving each other to fulfillment, holding each other as sweet, piercing spasms wracked their bodies.

Fresh tears wet her cheeks; she was still hardly able to absorb their good fortune. But the tender, feminine core of her understood the truth of Ben's words, and unbounded happiness overflowed from her heart. The nightmare was over.

Ben tried to shift his weight away from her. She couldn't bare to be parted. Not now. "Stay inside me. Like the first time."

He kissed her cheeks, her brow, her lips. "I love you, Lisbeth. I've loved you for a long time, but I'm finally free to say it."

"Ben, I love you. I wouldn't have left you. No matter what they'd told you at Hopkins."

"I know." His blue eyes were shining. "But this way is a hell of a lot better."

"Yes. God, yes." She sighed with enormous contentment, closed her eyes and nestled in his strong embrace.

"I can still hardly believe it, you know," he muttered, echoing her thoughts.

"Believe it."

They clung together fiercely.

"Ben, why were you crying?" she finally asked, her cheek cushioned by the springy hair of his chest, her voice barely above a whisper. "When you were standing in the doorway, looking at me."

He shifted to one side so he could tip her face up to his. "It's pretty complicated. A whole bunch of emotions, one right after the other. I opened the door and found you sleeping on the bunk and thought how beautiful you are. First I just wanted to stand there, watching you and marveling at how everything was suddenly different."

She moved against him, burrowing closer, acknowledging the truth of his words.

"I got all choked up, thinkin' about how I could finally offer you the things a man ought to offer the woman he loves. Then I saw you were thrashin' around and knew you were having one of your bad dreams—only now I was probably part of it." He shuddered. "Or maybe I was the cause of it."

"I don't remember what I was dreaming."

"I wanted to take you in my arms and tell you everything was going to be all right. That's when I noticed the way your dress was clinging to your body."

Air seeped from her lungs. "Ben...I..."

He stroked a gentle finger against her lips. "Shh— Let me finish. When you opened your eyes and saw me, I was thinking what a bastard I've been to you and what you must have been going through the past few months. Pregnant with my child. Not knowing whether I had the gene. Not knowing whether I'd walk away when I found out about the baby."

She gulped.

"You did think I might walk away, didn't you?" he asked.

"Yes."

"It happened that first time we made love, didn't it? When I needed you so much that I wasn't thinkin' about protecting you."

She nodded. "I wasn't thinking about anything but loving you, either."

"And when you found out, you were afraid to tell me."

"I knew I had to tell you when you came back from this trip. I thought you wouldn't be able to see, not if I kept my clothes on."

"Honey, didn't you realize you were going to have to be damn quick?"

She gave him a sheepish smile.

He grinned broadly. Then he was laughing with a freedom she'd never heard before, and her own happiness swelled.

"Maybe most people wouldn't notice," he went on. "But they probably haven't spent as much time as I have admiring your figure. I was thinking you'd filled out. Then I spotted that pretty little potbelly of yours, and I thought my heart was going to stop."

"Oh, Ben."

"It's almost too much to take, you know. Like my heart's going to burst wide open. Finding out that I'm finally free of the family curse. Finding out that I'm going to be a father. All in one day.'' His blue eyes held a hint of mischief as they probed hers. ''The only way to top it would be to find out I'm also going to marry the woman I love.''

''Is that a proposal?''

''You're damn right.''

''In that case, I accept.''

He clasped her joyfully. Then he began to kiss and stroke her again. But there was a bit of hesitation in his touch.

''I won't break.''

''I guess I don't know the rules with a mother to be.''

''Until she gets big as a house, the rules are she can handle all the lovemaking she wants.''

''Good.''

Much later they dressed and walked arm in arm down toward the creek. The trip took twice as long as usual. Ben, ambled along, stopping to look at trees, listen to birds, pick things up—or turn and stroke his hand against Elizabeth's middle.

''I've never seen you so...'' She searched for the right word.

''Happy,'' Ben supplied. ''Contented. No. Maybe it's free.'' He turned and wrapped his arms around her, as if he suddenly needed to anchor himself. ''It's still hard to believe, you know. After all these years, I'm really home free.'' He sucked in a draft of air. ''Rationally, I knew I had a fifty-fifty chance of getting HD. Emotionally, I was sure I was going to be one of the unlucky ones.''

"I know. I kept trying to get you to see the other side of it."

"I just couldn't let myself dare to hope. Make plans for the future. After I met you it was worse."

"I know. You were so strong. Too strong. Like the mountain rock."

"Maybe I seemed that way. But you made me want all the things I told myself I couldn't have. Want them so badly I could taste them. Then I had to keep trying to drive you away. I couldn't understand why a woman like you would want to get mixed up with a man who might break her heart."

"I know. Oh, Ben, I understood. I really did."

He shook his head. "I feel reborn."

She closed her eyes and rested her cheek against his shoulder. "The first time we came here, I felt as if this place were magic. It's even better now."

They started walking again, and Elizabeth could hear the stream gurgling in the distance.

"I've brought marshmallows to toast," she murmured. "And apples to roast."

"Is that the kind of diet you've been on?"

"And steak."

"Steak sounds great!" In his enthusiasm, he wasn't watching where he was going and stepped off the edge of a rock, coming down heavily onto his right foot. He reached out to brace his hand against a tree, and she saw exasperation and fear flash across his face.

"Ben, it's not HD," she said softly. "You just missed your footing—that's all."

"My God, I'm so used to thinking—"

"I know. What did you say to me once? It must be wonderful to have the freedom to be clumsy. You've got it now."

He knit his fingers with hers, and they walked on more slowly.

"I have to tell you something. A kind of confession," she whispered.

"You mean about your calling Hopkins? Or about changing Ada's mind about Max being tested?"

"They told you about all that in Baltimore?"

"Yeah."

"Ben, I had to do something. I knew the waiting was tearing you apart."

"Don't apologize. I'm not complaining about the special treatment. Sometimes it's a big advantage being good friends with a prestigious doctor."

"Oh, go on."

The gurgling stream filled the silence.

"Actually, I wasn't going to confess about Hopkins and Ada," Elizabeth said in a low voice. Taking Ben's hand, she turned him toward her. "I was planning to tell you about what happened after my husband died."

"I already know, darlin'. I was going to give you as much time as you needed to tell me."

A tattered wisp of breath escaped from Elizabeth's lips. "Oh, Ben. How did you find out?"

"After I finished at Hopkins, I had a few hours before I needed to catch my plane. Instead of sitting around the airport stewing, I decided to take a cab across town to your parents' house."

"My parents' house?"

"Yeah. I introduced myself to your mother. Maria Salvatore is quite a woman."

Elizabeth stared at him. "Why did you go down there?"

"Partly to feel close to you. Partly because of all those stories you told me about your family. Meeting your mother, I see where you get your warmth—and your determination. I told her that we'd been dating and that I loved you, but I'd needed to clear up some medical questions at Hopkins. She gave me a cup of tea and a cannoli. After she satisfied herself that my intentions were honorable and that I was gainfully employed, she started talking about how devastated you'd been by losing Jim and then losing his baby."

"I guess you know why I couldn't tell you."

"Darlin', you've sure had it rough with me."

"Yes. Also very good with you. And it's going to get better."

"You're damn right. I'm going to spend the next hundred years showing you how much I love you." He folded her close, and they hugged again.

The feeling of magic stayed with them—and the wild emotional swings. By turns they laughed louder than they ever had, hugged, teased each other, cried and tried to come to terms with the broad new vistas that had opened up before them. After they ate the food Elizabeth had brought, Ben leaned back against a log.

"I'm exhausted."

"Yes. It's been quite a day."

"Can I tell you one more thing?"

"You can tell me anything."

He nodded. "I know. God, that feels good."

"Is that the topic of discussion?"

"Don't be smart. The topic of discussion is Ellen Jackson's article."

"You said it blew you away, if I remember the exact phrasing."

"Reading it was a strange experience for me," he admitted as he began to gather up the dishes. "Here was this sixteen-year-old girl thinking about all the things I was thinking about. Only I was healthy, and she'd been sick all her life. And she was handling things a hell of a lot better than I was."

"It isn't just illness or health that shapes a person's personality. It's heredity and family background. She comes from a warm, stable, loving family. She's always known that she could count on her parents. You didn't have that."

"Yeah. But still, she made me see things from another angle. She put some pretty scary ideas into my head, in fact. Stuff I'd never had the courage to face."

"I was afraid you might be getting ready to say goodbye."

"No. Ellen made me understand that you can only get as much out of life as you put into it." He reached for her hand. "For years I kept telling myself I was doing the right thing. The honorable thing. Then I realized I wasn't being fair to you by making all the decisions. Before I got the call from Hopkins, I was going to ask you if you'd consider taking a chance and marrying me."

"That's what I wanted. To make a commitment. To spend as much time as we could together. But I thought I couldn't get you to see it."

His eyes had misted again. "Dumb, wasn't I? I used to pray for God to make a miracle especially for me. I didn't know *you* were the miracle."

"Oh, Ben."

It took them each several minutes to get control over their emotions again.

Elizabeth watched Ben douse the fire.

"I used to think about fate when I was in the Marines," he said as he worked. "Back when I thought of it as luck. Good or bad. A couple of guys in my unit were killed in a training exercise. I got through boot camp with just a couple of bruises and some barbed-wire cuts. I asked myself, why me? Why was I the one who made it?"

She came over to massage the muscles of his shoulders. "I used to ask myself that, too. After Jim died."

He stood up and took her into his arms. "I feel so damn lucky. Having you. Not having the gene." His hand caressed her abdomen. "And this."

They held on to each other in the gathering darkness. "I wanted to be with you, but I couldn't make any plans," she finally said. "Nothing practical. Now I'm starting to think about my work schedule. On the other hand, I may be out of a job, now that Perry Weston knows I was dumb enough to fall in love with someone besides him."

"Weston won't be a problem. Not if he wants more grant money."

She tipped back her head and looked up at him. "You'd resort to bribery to keep your wife employed?"

"Sure." His grin was cocky. "Except that I don't need to. You're too good at what you do. And if you don't want to be the director of the new program at the hospital, maybe you can work as a counselor and just keep a few of your patients. Until our kids are in middle school.''

"Director of the program? Was that your crazy idea?"

"Cliff's. I guess I convinced him you could walk on water."

She laughed. "How many kids are we going to have in middle school?"

"At least two. As many as you want," he added expansively. "I have the feeling you're going to be up to your ears in babysitting help from Aunt Carrie and Uncle Cliff."

"Cliff and Carrie. I always want to include them in our lives."

"Of course."

"And Max and Ada. Do you think there's a chance we can get them to move down to the city, where she can get some help with him?"

"You want to be around Max?"

"Yes. If Ada will let us."

"You were so good with him."

"I wish I'd met him years ago. When there was still time to get to know him the way he was."

"Time. I used to feel it pushing me toward destruction."

She nodded. "It's not the enemy now."

Elizabeth reached for Ben, just as she had when she'd first seen him standing in the doorway. He came into her arms, and they embraced once more. Now they had all the time they needed to explore their love.

Harlequin Superromance®

**Experience the exotic world of
Hong Kong in Sharon Brondos's
latest Superromance novel
EAST OF THE MOON.**

Sarah Branson knew her trip to Hong Kong
would be fabulous and she was not disappointed.
What she didn't expect, however, was that she'd
become involved in a mystery over smuggled
diamonds with tall, dark and handsome James
Leigh, a man who literally swept her off her feet.

Coming in June.

EAST OF THE MOON (#505)

EM92